A Cut Above

Fiction by Ginny Aiken

The Shop-Til-U-Drop Collection
Priced to Move
A Steal of a Deal
A Cut Above

Silver Hills Trilogy
Light of My Heart
Song of My Soul
Spring of My Love

Deadly Décor Mysteries
Design on a Crime
Decorating Schemes
Interior Motives

A Cut Above

A Novel

Ginny Aiken

Revell
a division of Baker Publishing Group
Grand Rapids, Michigan

Published by Revell
a division of Baker Publishing Group
P.O. Box 6287, Grand Rapids, MI 49516-6287
www.revellbooks.com

Second printing, November 2008

Printed in the United States of America

Library of Congress Cataloging-in-Publication Data
Aiken, Ginny.
    A cut above ; a novel / Ginny Aiken.
        p.   cm. — (The shop-til-u-drop collection ; bk. 3)
    ISBN 978-0-8007-3229-5 (pbk.)
    1. Home shopping television programs—Fiction. 2. Television personalities—Fiction. 3. Gemologists—Fiction. I. Title.
PS3551.I339C88 2008
813′.54—dc22   2008029469

This book is a work of fiction. Names, characters, places, and incidents are the product of the author's imagination or are used fictitiously. Any resemblance to actual events, locales, or persons, living or dead, is coincidental.

Scripture is taken from the New King James Version. Copyright © 1982 by Thomas Nelson, Inc. Used by permission. All rights reserved.

Published in association with the literary agency of Alive Communications, Inc., 7680 Goddard St., Suite 200, Colorado Springs, CO 80920.

"There is gold . . . but the lips of knowledge are a precious jewel."

Proverbs 20:15

1 $\underline{00}$

Louisville, Kentucky

With both fists, I pummel my knight in gravel-encrusted summer-wear. The blows don't even begin to faze him. "Put me down, you great big jerk."

What does the great big jerk do? Put me down and help me inside? No. Not Max Matthews. He stuns the breath out of me. Again.

He laughs. And then he kisses me.

Long and hard.

On the lips.

Oh my . . .

Over the electric buzzing in my head, I hear the sweet, tender strains of "Stranger in Paradise." Again. As I've heard them a time or two since Max barreled into my life about a year ago.

"Dum-de-dummm . . . dum-de-dum-de-dum-dum-de-dummm . . ."

How can this be? These warm lips belong to *Max Mat-*

thews, the California surfer-boy gem-dunce . . . and he's kissing me! He showed up, ruined my TV shopping channel–hosting gig, and I couldn't stand him . . . but then he did save my life . . .

He eases me to the ground again. But only my feet touch down.

Max . . . I learned to tolerate him . . . he saved my life one more time, and now this . . . a kiss . . . an incredible, dizzying, Hollywood musical–worthy kiss . . .

Cue in the violins.

Oh yeah! This does tilt my world, all right. Swirls of light and color dance across my eyelids, and my heart seems to grow to the bursting point. I float through reality, clinging only to the warmth of Max's touch, the tenderness and sweet passion of his kiss. Max . . .

". . . *Take my hand, I'm a stranger in Paradise*—"

"Hallelujah! They're alive—"

"Hot diggity dog! Will ya look at that lip-lock?"

The two elderly female voices at my right ear pierce the Kismet-flavored illusion, and my eyes pop open wide. I find myself nose to nose with the best-looking male I've ever seen, our lips still grazing.

I jerk backward. A tiny squeak bursts from my mouth. My cheeks hit the scalding point.

"Um . . . ah . . . well . . . ." I let my voice drift off. Nothing I can say will change what my Aunt Weeby and her best friend, Miss Mona Latimer—my boss, no less—have seen.

Or what just happened between Max and me.

As I stumble and bumble, trying to catch up with my elusive composure, I watch Max—the rat!—approach the Daunting Duo, a mile-wide smile on his gorgeous face.

I press my hands to my hot face. What can I say? What should I do?

Aaaack! How am I supposed to work with the man now? It was bad enough when he was just a new hire, ignorant of anything related to our work, and I couldn't stand him. But he grew on me.

Sure, he did. Like fungus.

I sniff. *Mushrooms are fungi, and you do love mushrooms,* my too-honest and too-familiar-with-my-mental-convolutions conscience pipes in.

I'd done everything I could think of to avoid falling for Max, but now I suspect this is bigger than my will and my efforts. My stomach does a flip and a lurch. In the beginning, I'd thought Max a blight, but now . . . well, now he's gained some gemology basics, and as far as the not-liking-him business . . . *that's* changed, and has nothing to do with work. I sigh.

What is our work, you ask? We're in big-time bling-bling. On TV. We're the jewelry and gemstone cohosts on the Shop-Til-U-Drop Shopping Channel.

Oh. You want to know who I am? Well. I really should introduce myself, shouldn't I? I do it every single day in front of millions at the start of my show. But I am understandably flustered right now. I'm Andrea Autumn Adams, Master Gemologist and the *real* host of the S.T.U.D.'s show. At least, I was before the appearance of the heart-stealing, knee-melting, too-gorgeous latecomer.

So who's the latecomer on the other side of the killer kiss? This Max who turned my life upside down? He's Max Matthews, a former Ohio State Buckeye football player. You know, the kind who majors in football and minors in whatever.

9

This one, however, graduated *summa cum laude*, wouldn't you know? In Max's case, the whatever was meteorology, definitely *not* geology, or as he so . . . hmm . . . humorously put it once, rockology.

Okay, okay. I already told you he's acquired a basic grasp of gemological knowledge. And he's signed up, believe it or not, to work on his Gemological Institute of America Graduate Gemologist certificate. Who'd a thunk?

I shoot a glance at my erstwhile nemesis and spot Chief Clark heading toward me. Oh, joy. The man and I have a checkered past. And why not? He once tried to pin a murder on me—of course, I had nothing to do with the poor ruby vendor's demise, but the good chief took some persuading.

"Well, Miss Andie," he says as he approaches, "looks like you'll have to come on in to my office for a spell. I'll be having some questions for you, and I'll be needing a statement too."

I sigh—again. There's no getting around it. Doesn't matter whether I'm up to it or not. As if, after getting nearly run off the road, being threatened at gunpoint, and wrestling with a maniacal gem thief, I'm in any condition to try to string two coherent thoughts together. You know? If Chief Clark keeps Max in the room . . . well, then, I'm done for.

At least this time there's no possible question about my guilt or lack thereof. Chief Clark's buddies in blue have the culprit in shiny steel bracelets—not the kind I'm likely to feature on one of my shows anytime soon.

I square my shoulders. "Lead on, Macduff."

The chief arches a graying eyebrow. "I do believe, Miss Andie, that the Bard did write it as 'Lay on, Macduff.'"

Not looking good. Aw . . . come on. How many police chiefs do *you* know who know Shakespeare so well they can correct you when you misquote?

Yep. That's what I mean.

Sometime around midnight, our highly literate chief lets me head home—well, to Miss Mona's house. The gem thief the cops just arrested recently torched the Adams home, where I've been living with Aunt Weeby. After the fire, we moved in with Miss Mona, and that's where I head after the inquisition . . . er . . . interview.

I collapse onto the backseat of Miss Mona's new powder blue Jaguar, while Aunt Weeby slides into the front passenger seat. Miss Mona's behind the wheel—yikes! The woman's known for her lead foot.

"Never would've thought she had it in her," Miss Mona says, her voice full of regret. "If I hadn't hired her . . . the girl did seem so sweet." She shakes her silver-haired head. "Mm-mm-mm . . ."

My aunt murmurs a sympathetic sound. "Guess that there old cliché about the book and its cover works backwards and forwards."

I think about the beautiful camerawoman, who Miss Mona had hired about a year ago and who now finds herself behind bars, and her un-beautiful deeds. You never can tell about a person. And here I've been all bent out of shape with jealousy—yes, Andie. Face it. It *was* jealousy, and all because she'd spent most of our recent trip to Kashmir sucking up to Max.

Then it hits me. Did I miss a clue in her actions because

I spent the trip with my nose out of joint from the jealousy? Could I have brought her to justice sooner if I'd not been so caught up in Max's spell?

I drop my head against the supple leather seat back and close my eyes. The man's trouble—T.R.O.U.B.L.E.—for my poor, overworked head. And my heart.

Just like that, the sensation of falling through space, of warmth and passion and comfort and . . . and—

Max.

How can just the thought of him make me feel like I did when he kissed me? And what does it mean? How am I going to face him . . . or the piercing, revealing spotlight of the camera with him at my side?

I groan.

"You all right back there, sugarplum?" Aunt Weeby asks. "Mona, dear. Do you have any of that wonderful cod-liver oil Great-Grandma Willetta used to give us all at your place?"

I fight the urge to groan again. *Anything* but the infamous internal lubricant! "I'm fine, Aunt Weeby. Really. Just thinking it's too bad we didn't figure out what Miss Mona's newest hire was up to before she burned the house."

"Sure, sure, sure. But none of us have any of that there silly ESP stuff. We can't go reading nobody's mind." My aunt tsk-tsks, and does it better than anyone else I know, mind you. "You sure it's not that corroded gut a' yours kicking up a fuss again?"

I've known forever that I have to be über-careful around Aunt Weeby. Anything I say can and will be used against me. "Aunt Weeby, you've got to let go of that image. Good grief! I only said it once. I was overworked and overtired at the time, but you've latched on to it as if it had been your last slice of bread in a worldwide famine."

Silence.

Then, "Well! My goodness. That was some speech there, Andrea Autumn Adams." Miss Mona's voice doesn't hide the surprise or the hint of humor behind her words. "Something's sure worked itself—or maybe I should say someone's worked *him*self—under your skin. Looks like our boy's done a number on your wherewithal, and I say, good for him!"

Aunt Weeby titters.

Miss Mona laughs.

I groan—again.

We drive on. By the glow of a streetlight, I notice our driver's Cheshire cat grin. I love Miss Mona almost as much as I love Aunt Weeby, but the two of them and their antics can give anyone heartburn. And I'm a veteran of the ulcer wars; I need no help upsetting my internal equanimity.

"Oh dear," my aunt then says, her words devoid of any further humor. "You don't think this means they're gonna go all lovey-dovey on-screen, now, do you, Mona?"

The car bucks to an abrupt stop. Miss Mona's sleek, bobhaired head swivels. The darkness hides her eyes—for which I'm eternally thankful, since I'm sure she's glaring at me. "You wouldn't dare!"

I slink lower on my vertebrae. A quick glance out the window tells me we're nowhere near Miss Mona's house yet. At the rate I'm going, I'd better plan on calling my friendly neighborhood chiropractor in the morning.

Either that, or change the subject.

I inch up. "How soon did the contractor say his men could start on the house?" I ask my aunt.

Her hand flutters up in a dismissive wave. "Don't even think about that, sugarplum. Mickey's crews are on other jobs for about another two, maybe three weeks."

Miss Mona starts the Jag on its way back to her Mac-Mansion—have I mentioned how rich the Shop-Til-U-Drop Shopping Channel has made the already well-to-do widow? "Now, don't you go talking about moving out again, Livvy. You either, Andie, honey. We're going to have us the best, longest-running pajama party ever."

Me and the Daunting Duo. For weeks. What kind of nut-tiness will they cook up during that time? How am I going to keep them from dragging me along in their wake? Am I in trouble or what? "Maybe—"

"Mona, dear," my auntie says, ignoring my start. "I already told you we're hunting for a sweet little cottage for Andie. It's time she graduates from girl to woman, and nothing says grown-up more than your own home. A . . . what is it the kids say? Oh, yes! A pad, her own pad, is what she's needing."

And here I'd hoped she'd forgotten about that crazy idea.

"You do have a point," Miss Mona says before I can con-jure a diversion. "It'll be so much fun to go house hunting for Andie. Do you have a Realtor yet?"

"Of course. I'm working with that darling Evie Carson. Can you believe that child's gone and grown up like that? Why, I do remember when she was in my Sunday school class . . ."

The conversation continues without any input on my part, just as the hunt for a "pad" for me will also go, I'm sure. Not that I have any interest in moving out from the Adams home. I came back to Louisville to take care of Aunt Weeby.

She'd had an encounter with a bovine that ended with her leg in a sling at the hospital after surgery to repair multiple compound fractures. And even though her leg's now as fine as frog legs—her description, not mine—she has an astonishing talent for the unexpected. The woman needs a keeper. That's where I come in.

And while I don't want to have to drag her out of another of her escapades, I do like living with her. My parents are missionaries, and they'd decided years ago, during one of their assignments, I'd be better off with Aunt Weeby and her late husband. I spent much of my teenage years in the hundred-plus-year-old house, and to me it spells all that's wonderful about family. I may be an independent adult with a great career, but I had all the aloneness I could've wanted while I lived in New York. Besides, there's something very comforting in spending my evenings with my dearest relative and closest friend.

Don't! Don't even mention that kissing male to me right now, okay?

Sudden exhaustion drops over me. I don't have the energy to argue with Aunt Weeby. The wrestling match with the newly arrested gemstone thief nearly did me in, and my sore body is letting me know exactly what parts were most grievously assaulted.

I close my eyes and pray. I pray for a confession from the thief—I have no interest in testifying in another trial. Remember the dead vendor? Yeah. Once in a lifetime was more than enough for me.

I pray for Aunt Weeby and Miss Mona. They regularly court disaster, not to mention injury, and the thought of any harm coming to either of the zany seniors is more than I can stand.

But mostly, I pray for wisdom and guidance. I have a lousy track record when it comes to men. Men? Hah! Think college classmate—*one* college classmate, at that—who found what my brain could do for his cumulative grade-point average far more appealing than my company itself. I've been a coward ever since, and my cowardice made me treat Max like dirt. I'm ashamed of my actions.

I've since apologized and asked his forgiveness, but I really never expected God to stun me with these intense feelings toward my cohost.

My thoughts meander back to the kiss. Max's tenderness again moves me.

The Jaguar screeches to a stop. I bounce against my seat belt. My head snaps forward and back, and I blink at the sight of Miss Mona's well-spotlighted house. I blink again, and a random thought hits me like the proverbial ton of bricks.

Could Max feel the same way I do?

"Rise and shine, sunshine!"

I open one reluctant eye. "Wha . . . ?"

"Good!" Aunt Weeby chirps. "You're awake."

It'll never do me any good to tell her I'd still be asleep were it not for her. "What's up? How come you're impersonating an alarm clock so early?"

"Why, we have us an appointment with Evie Carson, sugarplum. She's got a couple of cute little places she says are just right for you." She marches over to the window on the east wall of the room Miss Mona has given me for the duration, and flings the two halves of the drapes wide open. Brilliant sunshine stings my bleary eyes.

16

"Hey!" I cover my face with my blanket, but Aunt Weeby drags it off me.

"Come on, Andie. Let's get to getting. We have us a house to find you. That's going to take some time, you know. Great houses don't grow on trees. And I just can't wait for the fun to start."

Fun. Yeah, right.

It won't do me any more good to object to the foray into the wilds of house hunting than it did to my rude awakening. And my lack of interest or desire for a new home has no bearing in this equation, you know. I drag myself upright, and mental images of last night's frightening events flash through my thoughts. The shock I felt when I realized who'd tried to run my car off the road was only slightly less than the revulsion I still feel knowing she's killed two men. And all for a pair of fabulous stones. A human life is so precious, so worth more than even the most valuable gem.

"Oh, Lord Jesus . . . thank you . . ."

I shudder, make my way to my dresser and wardrobe, pull out clean clothes, and then head for the shower. The spigots squeak as I adjust them so the water reaches the right steaming temperature, and then I let the hot water splatter against me.

As I shampoo my short-short hair—short, thanks to the fire—I let the image of Max replace the nerve-wracking thoughts of last night, danger, and murder. I have to be mature about this, about him. I have to face the reality that I'm going to have to make myself vulnerable, to let Max get close. I also have to face the possibility of heartbreak in the end.

What's most frightening is that this time, it won't be a matter of post-adolescent infatuation, as my college romance was. This time, I suspect, I'm going to have to give a hundred percent. I know Max. He won't expect anything less.

Neither will God.

"Lord?" I murmur, confident the shower will hide the sound of any confession I make from curious elderly ears. "I'm scared. This could be the real deal, and you know I don't know how to react when face-to-face with . . . well, the real deal. I know you'll be there to pick up the pieces afterward, but I don't want to wind up as a bunch of pieces for you to pick up."

I automatically reach for the squirt pump on the conditioner bottle, but then consider the minuscule scraps of red locks left on my head. There's not enough up there to benefit from the liberal application of emollients and bodifiers and who-knows-what-else they put into those bottles.

With a twist, I turn off the water, slide the shower curtain aside, and reach for the towel. The fluffy cotton is a comfort against my face.

"It's all about trust, isn't it?" As usual, God doesn't answer me, but I know the answer already. "Okay. I'm going to take your promises as seriously as I always promise to do. But it's up to you to help me hang in there." My stomach lurches. "Help me with my weak knees here. I want to remember all the time how you've told me you'll never leave me nor forsake me."

God never promised you an unbroken heart, my conscience says.

I roll my eyes. "Yeah, yeah, yeah. I know. What you really promise is to be there for me, no matter what comes. And all you ask is that I walk with you, no matter where I go. Just give me some smarts about this, okay?"

Not so sure about my romantic smarts but certain of God's

faithfulness, I dress and head down to the kitchen. Where I find Aunt Weeby impatiently checking her watch.

"Well, it's about time, sugarplum. We have us places to go, houses to see. Come on, come on. Let's go. Davina's outside waiting for us."

Davina is the S.T.U.D.'s limousine chauffeur, a quiet, intensely loyal, former racecar driver who tops the measuring tape at a lofty six foot one. I never know what she's thinking, but I hesitate to get on her bad side. She could take me down in a blink, should she so desire.

Truth be told, she strikes me as someone you'd see in a James Bond flick.

"Did you really have to rope her into this scavenger hunt of yours?" I ask my aunt as I snag a granola bar from the basket on Miss Mona's gleaming granite kitchen counter. I doubt I'll see food again until Aunt Weeby's inner Energizer Bunny winds down.

Aunt Weeby's blue eyes twinkle with mischief. Uh-oh.

"Davina's a smart girl," she says. "She knows we're going to have us some fun today."

I roll my eyes. "Sure, she'll have fun. At my expense. Davina's not dumb."

A chuckle comes from the far corner of the kitchen. I glance over my shoulder. There, on the ever-so-comfy, down-stuffed loveseat Miss Mona keeps by the walk-in–size hearth, I find the S.T.U.D.'s smirking chauffeur. Hmm . . . now I think of it, would the correct term, since she's female, be *chauffeuse*? Weird.

"Morning, Andie," the taller-than-tall driver says.

I know when I'm beat. "All right, all right. Let's get this over with. What time do we have to be at Evie's office?"

19

"Oh, no, no, no, sugarplum. We're not heading to Evie's office." Aunt Weeby slides her classic black leather handbag on her forearm and heads for the back door. "We're meeting the sweet girl at the first place she wants to show us. We don't want to waste any time, you know."

I know no such thing; I'd much rather dawdle than have to fabricate reasons why I don't like this or that splendiferous place. But who am I in this house-hunting deal? Just the schmuck who's being plunked into a house she doesn't want, is all.

"Lead on—er . . . *lay* on, Macduff," I say, remembering yesterday's English Lit lesson.

In the cushy limo, I stare out the window as we zip down streets lined with luxe mansions and out of the exclusive enclave. There are no "cute little cottages" in this part of town, and that's what Aunt Weeby is bound and determined to find for me.

"Oh, look!" Aunt Weeby trills as Davina guides the land yacht vehicle around a corner. "Isn't this a sweet street?"

I have to give her that much. On either side, 1930s and '40s bungalows line the street. Tall, leafy trees provide shade, and flower beds teem with fresh color. I get a sense of cozy comfort, pride of ownership, warmth, and permanence. "Nice . . ."

The canary-feathered smile on my aunt's face reminds me not to say a thing. The woman has laser-sharp hearing and an agenda in mind.

When Davina stops the car, I get out and study the house before me. It's a cute little story-and-a-half bungalow, slate blue with white trim and cranberry-red shutters and door. Both sides of the front walkway are lined with a riot of red and white geraniums, and lush green azalea bushes nestle up against the foundation. At the end of the driveway, I spot a matching one-car garage.

I'm in trouble, folks. I have just fallen in love.

Maybe the inside's a dump, all torn up and piled ceiling high with decades-old newspapers. Maybe it's painted in shrieking shades of purple and orange and slime lime-green.

Or not.

"Ooooh!" Aunt Weeby coos. "Isn't our Evie one smart girl?"

I face my wily relative. "And where is your smart girl? Wasn't she supposed to meet us here?"

Just then, a school-bus yellow SUV pulls up. From what I can remember of the Evie I once babysat, the vehicle is exactly what she would drive. The driver-side door pops open, and out jumps a livewire dressed in electric blue. Asymmetrically cut black hair frames a pixie face, a cell phone glued to the ear on the side with the shorter cut hair.

But, of course, Evie isn't alone. Nooooo.

And I'm sure you've figured this one out—well before me, no doubt. You see, out the passenger-side door comes a six-foot-something, blond male, a grin on his gorgeous face, his beautiful blue eyes hidden behind a pair of reflective aviator sunglasses. As he ambles toward us, I can't help but notice the way the light blue polo shirt enhances the gold of his tan. No one could miss the graceful energy in his step.

Max walks up to Aunt Weeby and kisses her waiting cheek. "Good morning."

My aunt smiles. "*Now* we're all here. Let's go find Andie a proper 'pad.'"

She sails up the walk with Evie, who hasn't quit jabbering into her phone, leaving me on the sidewalk standing next to Max.

"Ready?" he asks.

Seeing how my mind superimposes the picture of a slaughterhouse over the little house, I answer, in character, "Baa-aa-aaah!"

_2_<u>00</u>

Fast-forward four lightning-fast weeks. I have since signed more papers than I ever imagined a person might have reason to sign. And even though I refuse to admit it—it would give Aunt Weeby even more to crow about—I'm excited about my impending homeownership. I'm not so excited, however, about her living alone again.

Oh well. At least my new house is no more than four blocks away from hers, and I plan to spend a whole lot of my spare time visiting. In fact, she can count on it. Once Mickey and his guys get around to repairing the fire damage there, that is.

On the—ahem—male front, Max has been on his best behavior. Come to think of it, aside from some heavy-duty teasing here and there, he's really always been on his best behavior. True, he did horn in on our house hunting every chance he got, but I don't hold it against the guy. He gave me terrific input. I wouldn't have noticed some inconveniences in a couple of the houses on Evie's short list. Especially that one place with the crazy driveway. It resembled a banana, and early morning departures, since I'm hardly a chandelier-bright bulb (as Max put it) at that time of day, might have proven a mite dicey.

In the end, I put an offer on the blue house with the red shutters, the first one I saw. It's perfect for me. Now I can't wait to launch a shopping safari. I need tables and chairs and bookshelves and curtains and rugs . . . oh! A TV. I'll want a new one of those too. Wonder who's holding the best sale this weekend . . . ?

What's that? Oh, you're reminding me that I'm a reformed New York shopaholic.

Humph! I did reform. But a girl needs furniture, you know. The handful of items I brought back from the glorified closet they call an apartment in the Big Apple will hardly fill a three-bedroom cottage.

But that'll wait for another day. Today, Max and Josh Ross, my good friend Peggy's husband, are loading my belongings in one of Josh's pickup trucks, then moving me into my very own brand-new—to me—home. Josh owns a highly sought-after landscape design firm and its pickup-truck fleet. I'm saving my pennies to have him do something faboo to the front yard.

Ooooh! My very own yard. How cool is that?

Well, it's mine and the bank's. When it was all said and done, Aunt Weeby wouldn't take no for an answer on the subject of a down payment. She insisted it was a gift. She also said she could afford it now, thanks to me, since my shows have so increased the value of the nest egg she invested when Miss Mona started the S.T.U.D. Network.

But the mortgage? Ah . . . the mortgage is all mine. What's more, I can afford it. So the bank says. Actually, I *can* afford it—according to moi. I never would have thought I'd feel so good about that kind of commitment, but I do. I'm thrilled the Lord brought me back to Louisville, and the sweet little house crystallizes for me my determination to make a life here, in my hometown.

I scoot the kitchen chair away from the table just as the back door to Miss Mona's glam kitchen opens. "You ready?" Max asks.

"Readier than ready." I swig down the last drops of my too-cold coffee. "Is Josh with you?"

The door opens again. "Reporting for duty, ma'am, yes, ma'am." Josh gives me a jaunty, two-fingered salute. "You said you don't have a whole lot to move, so let's get it moved. The sooner we're done with that, the sooner we can get to that pizza-for-payment you promised."

I laugh. "Peggy warned me about you, you bottomless pit. How do you stay so skinny?"

"What?" Max asks, his voice full of overdone outrage. "Are you going to let her get away with that kind of insult?"

Josh shakes his head, a mournful expression on his craggy face. "What can I do? I'm just a poor old weakling."

That sets the tone for the rest of the day. By mid-afternoon, the three of us are sitting on the hardwood floor of my new kitchen, a giant pizza box in the middle, the cardboard decorated with grease stains, and only a handful of boxes left in Max's SUV.

"Are you guys done with that thing yet?" Peggy wails from the living room. "I'm sorry to be such a party pooper, but this baby doesn't like the smell of pizza. Pepperoni's the worst."

I scramble upright and head to her side. "I can't imagine foregoing pizza for nine months."

She rubs the mound in her middle. "It is a pain, but the end result's purely amazing."

A momentary pang of envy zings through my heart, but I squash it with the determination of an elephant on stampede. That's dangerous territory for a single woman. Especially when the man that makes her heart go pitter-patter is sitting cross-legged in the next room. A man who hasn't revealed his feelings for her yet. Maybe he never will reveal them.

Or maybe he has no feelings to reveal.

Other than those he revealed when he kissed the stuffing out of you one stressful night, whatever they may be.

Groan. One of these days I'm going to have to do something about the little voice my conscience uses on me at the most inconvenient moments.

"Umm . . . well, yeah. I admit your Andrew and Sophie are both pretty cute."

Peggy gives me a squirm-inducing stare. "Maybe you oughta do something about getting yourself a couple of pretty-cute little ones of your own."

I gulp. "Ah . . . I'm waiting on God. You know. He's in charge. He's driving this bus. I'm just the passenger doing the trust thing during the ride."

"You're protesting way too much, my friend." She grins. "And just so you know, I heard all about the mega-smooch in the PD's parking lot."

I cross my arms. "Just because I work in front of millions of curious eyes doesn't mean I want every part of my life to be put out on display, you know."

"I'm hardly one of those million viewers," she tried but failed to hold back a laugh. "You're just blushing and blushing and trying awful hard not to show what's written all over your face."

"Hmm . . . now that I think about it, that pizza *has* smelled up the house. Let me get rid of the box."

I spin on my heel, but get nowhere real fast. My escape is foiled by a football—not mine. Max never travels without more than his fair share of sports paraphernalia. Not even to the exotic locations we've visited for work.

Here I haven't fully moved in yet, but his junk has. And no. I'm *not* going to look at it as some kind of sign. I'm still on God's bus trip here.

"Hey, Max!" I yell. "No footballs, golf clubs, or tees allowed at my place. Come collect your stray toy."

My cohost saunters in, a wide grin on his face. He winks at Peggy. "She's cute when she's mad, isn't she?"

"Aaaaargh!" Enough with the goofiness. I have too much to do. "Have a lovely time chatting, folks. I'm more into moving into my new place. See ya when I'm done."

I march into the kitchen to the sound of their humor. But, seconds later, they join me. Before long, my pots and pans—the few I accumulated in New York—fill the first two shelves in the wall of cabinets, and I've set the glass and iron café table with my Pfaltzgraf dishes. Peggy and Josh have left to rescue their poor babysitter, and Max has gone out to his car to bring the last box of books inside.

"Andie!" he yells from the front stoop. "Get the door for me, please."

I let him into the tiny foyer, and he nods toward the living room. "Do you want them in there or in that extra room upstairs?"

"I don't know if I'll have enough room for this box of books in the shelves you and Josh took up there, but I don't think I want them in the living room, either. At least, not now."

"You're the boss."

And with those inspiring words—which suggest multitudinous future furniture-arranging episodes—we relocate the final boxes. After I drop off a load of linens in the dining room, the beautiful built-in corner cabinet catches my attention. It's that kind of detail that made me fall in love with the house. Then there's the delft blue tiled fireplace in the living room. It's wonderful. Oh, and I love the luscious natural woodwork throughout. You don't get that kind of workmanship in newer homes.

I can fill the china cabinet with the dainty teacups I started collecting back in my teens. Those two boxes remained packed the whole time I lived in New York. Not only did I not have the room in my postage-stamp-sized place, but I also felt . . . well, not exactly embarrassed, but their feminine nature and touch of antiquity seemed out of place there. Now, in this beautiful home, they'll fit right in. I can see myself pouring cups of tea for Peggy and me.

I will need a new table, though. The café set looks spindly in the middle of the room. I'd like something more substantial, with more staying power. I envision a gleaming wooden table and chairs—

"Congratulations," Max says at my side.

I blink and blush.

He lays an arm over my shoulders. "I'd be smiling too if I'd just bought this place. You made a great choice."

Oh my! That arm . . . and his warm, solid presence at my side, in my brand-new house . . .

Enough!

"Ah . . . er . . . well, you did give me some good advice during the house safari." Is that breathy, girly voice really mine? Whooo-boy! Am I in trouble, or what?

He gives me a little squeeze. "What? You didn't want to drive right off your driveway every morning? Let's face it. You're not at your best bright and early in the day."

I glance up and give him a wry grin. "You noticed, huh?"

"There's not much about you I haven't noticed, Andie."

My eyes widen at his deepening voice. Oh my! A girl could become a puddle of melted mush just from hearing Max talk. And me? I'm way too susceptible to those beautiful blue eyes looking at me as though I'm the only woman around.

Come to think of it, I *am* the only woman around. In my house.

Before I can get my act together enough to cobble a response, he goes on. "I mean that, you know. I'm always tuned in to you, no matter whether we're doing a show or you're bossing me around some foreign hole-in-the-dust dead gemstone mine."

I want to answer but find myself unable to break the spell of his gaze.

Hands on my shoulders, Max turns me to face him.

Dum-de-dummm . . .

As "Stranger in Paradise's" familiar notes echo from the farthest corner of my mind, Max presses a tender kiss on my forehead. "I've never felt like this before, Andie, and I don't know how to deal with it. I'm hoping you feel the same way too—"

BAM!

A pair of gasps follow the crash of the flung-open door.

29

"Oh, Mona, dear. Look! Don't they just make the cutest couple—"

"Didn't I tell you we should just leave 'em alone, Livvy—"

As if in slow motion, I slip out of Max's clasp. Don't ask me where my head is right now, because I really don't know. Half of me wants to cheer at their appearance—that's the chicken half. The other half, the one determined to stay on God's bus trip, is ready to toss the Troublesome Twosome back out.

I do neither. I step forward to hug them both. "Hello, ladies. Welcome to my home."

Either I'm having one of those out-of-body experiences or Max's effect on me is even more powerful than I know. Well, I know which one's which right about now, but . . . wow! I sound just like some sappy, chick-flick heroine. Max is dangerous. And I no longer feel like sniping him out of the picture of my life. Instead, I'm excited, scared, confused, and filled with anticipation.

Please, Lord! Don't let him rip my heart to shreds.

But no matter how hard that twinge of fear tries to take over, it can't smother the little hitch of excitement that hits my midsection every time I look at Max.

Especially when those blue eyes zero in on me as if I were too pretty and precious and priceless.

Oh, Father, I'm falling . . .

◆

"But I don't know what I'm doing!" I wail into the phone three hours later.

Peggy, the rat, laughs. "Who does? I didn't when Josh began to stick around. I was scared, yeah, but no way was I going to push him away. That might have sent him right into Lynnie Nash's arms. I wasn't going to be so dumb as that."

I remembered the jealousy I'd felt during that trip to Kashmir. Every time I'd seen Max's blond head near our gem thief's gleaming black one, I'd seen red. And not the red of my own locks, either. Oh, okay. So green's the color most associated with the jealousy monster, but I'd been *red*-hot angry mad. And scared.

"Why am I such a chicken?"

Peggy laughs—yet again. "You're only a selective chicken. Haven't heard you 'cluck' when it comes to taking trips to corners of the globe where I wouldn't dream of setting foot."

"Are you nuts? I'm scared stiff every time I have to leave."

"No, you're not. You may take a peek at the possible risks these trips might bring, but there's no stopping you once the lure of the exotic, not to mention the potential sparkle of a gem or two, wafts by."

"Yeah, but I don't go around looking for risky business."

"You don't back away either. And that's why I'm not going to let you get away with dodging the issue. It's not fair to you or to Max."

"What? Are you going to take the guy's side now? I thought you were my friend."

"I am your friend. That's why I won't let you do this. You're thirty years old, Andie. You can't dodge around adult feelings for your whole life. Face the facts, girl. You're crazy gaga over this guy."

Okay, fine. So I can't deny it. It's questions about the other side of the romance equation that have got me quaking in my shoes. Well, I don't have shoes on right now, since I'm

31

lying on my bed, in my new room, in my new house. "But what about him?"

Sure, I'm chicken. I can't even put my fear into words, audible words that another human being will hear.

"What about Max?" she asks, her voice ripe with disbelief. "Are you blind, deaf, dumb, and stupid, woman? The guy's so head-over-heels over you he can't see straight. Even Josh has noticed. And trust me, my husband's got many wonderful qualities, but emotional sensitivity ain't one of 'em, you get my drift?"

The nervous little giggle slips out before I can stop it. Josh is the classic guy's guy. He's a no-nonsense straight shooter whose down-to-earth sense of humor captured my buddy's heart. But subtle and perceptive in, as they say in those sappy-sweet chick flicks, matters of the heart? Not so much.

I try to think of something to say but give up, unable to scrape up a single thought I dare voice. See? Chicken. *Cluck-cluck-cluck.*

"Think about it, Andie," Peggy says, her voice serious. "Are you going to let fear and the memory of a wormy college jerk run your life? Are you willing to spend the rest of your days all alone because of that fear? And here I thought you came home because you'd had your fill of loneliness."

With those thoughts rumbling through my mind, I head out to the grocery store after we agree to meet for lunch next Saturday. I pick up a couple of bags of bare essentials, return to my cozy little cottage, grill a piece of chicken, toss a salad, nuke a spud. Then, when I'm done with the few dishes I've used to feed myself, I head for my still-empty living room, gather my Bible, and collapse onto a massive floor pillow Aunt Weeby has stored since those heartbroken college days of mine.

Why won't God just blare instructions out loud? It'd be so much easier to dump all these fears if he did.

Besides, I don't do patience too well.

⬥

After a splendiferous couple of days of homeownership and unrestrained catalog ogling, I return to work. Miss Mona had insisted I take time off to "feather my nest." She'll be mightily disappointed in me when she learns I'm on a slow track to savor the flavor of the experience, if you catch my drift. In my position, she'd have had a whirling dervish of an interior designer whip the place into shape by now, his nasal voice pointing out a "darling" this and a "darling" that.

Not gonna happen. Not here, at any rate.

Max and I are scheduled to host a diamond special show this afternoon, and in preparation for it, we have to choose the merchandise we intend to show our faithful viewers. Since I haven't seen him after that interrupted moment the day he helped me move in, I'm a bit uneasy.

Ah . . . no. I promised myself—and, more importantly, God—I wouldn't wishy-washy myself again. I'm not a bit uneasy. I'm rapid cycling between teenybopper giddy (and I've never been so beset before in my entire thirty years of life, I'll have you know) and sweaty-palmed, deer-in-the-headlights scared.

No way is anyone going to convince me this is good.

"Get a grip," I mutter as I walk into my dressing room.

But it's hard to get a grip when your heart won't quit flippity-flopping every time you think the object of your flusteration—is that a word? It works for me, so it is now—might walk in at any moment. And that's how I head off to hair and makeup. My cohost's lanky self is usually plunked in the makeup chair next to mine. And he's usually as punctual as I am.

But not today. I can't squash my disappointment.

As Allison Howard, our makeup genius, dabs on the last bit of beautifying potion on my right eye, the phone on the counter rings. Framed by the big, round Hollywood-starlet lights around the mirror behind her, Allie answers. "Yes, Miss Mona?"

That catches my attention. Miss Mona rarely calls any of us. She prefers to hustle on down and do one-on-ones. Allison listens, then waggles her eyebrows at me, a wicked grin on her lips. "She's right here."

"For me?"

She holds out the phone and jabs a makeup brush toward me. "Lucky you."

I laugh—briefly—then check in with our boss. "Hey, Miss Mona. What kind of trouble do I have to get you and Aunt Weeby out of this early?"

"Nuh-uh-uh-uh!"

Her singsong voice intrigues me. What is the woman up to?

"Why don't you come on up to my office, Andie, dear? I think you're going to like what I have to say."

"What's up?"

"Nuh-uh. Come on over. I have coffee and a tray of goodies all set up for us. Aa-aand, I can even see some chocolate from where I'm sitting—"

"O-kay. You got me with the chocolate. I'll be right there."

I hang up but catch Allison's arched eyebrow. "Chocolate?"

she says. "That's not the right shade for your lips, you know. If you go snacking with Miss Mona, I'll have to do some heavy-duty touch-up before you go on."

"Are you going to tell me you expect me to believe you'd turn down ooey-gooey chocolate for the sake of a smear of lipstick?"

Allison laughs. "No, but I'm not the one headed to a chair in front of a camera and the peepers of America's zillion bling-bling–hungry women."

From out in the hallway, I hear a familiar voice. I even recognize his footsteps. My heartbeat speeds up. I glance in the mirror, and smile at Allison's results. Better than the last time he saw me, all dirt-streaked and tired from moving.

Oh, good grief! Am I pathetic or what? The footsteps approach, and my middle does that flippety-flop thing again. I wonder if any other woman in history has tuned her hearing to a guy's footsteps? Okay, fine. I am a little weird. But Max does have that lean, panther-like walk, a perk I suspect he's gained from his sports mania.

I slide off the revolving chair. "Thanks, Allie. Gotta go see what the boss is up to. Gotta move, gotta groove."

As I step past Max, the appreciative smile he gives me slows me down. "Nice," he says, his voice low and intimate.

Be still, my heart! My eyes open wide with pleasure. I purse my lips, almost as if for a whistle, but only let out a happy puff of pent-up breath. Then I smile.

"Thanks," I say in the dopey voice of the shape-shifting alien who's moved into my body. "See you in the merchandise room when Allie's done her thing with you."

"I'll be there."

Wild horses won't keep me away.

But first I have to see what our fearless leader is up to. And, oh, do I ever mean fearless! Nothing fazes the woman.

I sail into Miss Mona's office, transported on that romance-scented cloud. "Good morning," I chirp.

Then I have to fight down a groan. Max is a menace. I, Andrea Autumn Adams, am *not* the chirping kind. Never have been. Refuse, absolutely refuse, to be the chirping kind again.

Note to self: deep-six the Max-inspired chirping.

"Help yourself," Miss Mona says, waving toward the cholesterol, sugar, and calorie-laden credenza next to the window at the back of the office.

But before I get there, I nearly trip over a stranger's mirror-polished, black leather wing-tip shoes. "Oh! Sorry. I didn't see you there."

I cast a questioning glance over my shoulder, and Miss Mona smiles, satisfaction in her gaze. "Go ahead, help yourself, then come sit here with us."

A few minutes later, armed with a steaming cup of primo Colombian and a to-die-for chocolate éclair, I head for the empty leather armchair across from Miss Mona's massive mahogany desk. I'm practically salivating over my totally unneeded extra-inch-for-the-hips, but you know what? Manners do count.

"What can I do to help you?" I ask my boss.

To my surprise, it seems I've hit a home run. Miss Mona beams.

"See?" she says to the dark-haired, older gentleman—of Miss Mona's vintage—in exquisite custom tailoring. During my years in the Big Apple, I learned to spot fine Italian workmanship, and this guy's slate gray wool suit is an outstanding sample of European haberdashery. Wonder who he is?

But instead of letting me in on the secret, Miss Mona keeps talking to him. "Our Andie has wonderful instincts. And that's what I'll be counting on, you hear?"

Although I'm dying to find out what's up, I decide it's time to taste my éclair. As I bite into bliss, I glom my eyes onto Miss Mona.

She stands. "I think you'll be happier'n a hog in a mud wallow, Andie, dear. This is Rodolfo Cruz. My vendor in town from Colombia."

I gulp down my mouthful of calories, then wash them down with a glug of scalding coffee. "Emeralds?" I manage to croak out.

"Emeralds."

"Green gold," Mr. Cruz says in richly spiced English.

"Green fire," I add.

"We're negotiating a new buy," Miss Mona says.

Mr. Cruz tips his head in a courtly manner. "I'm offering the lady the most beautiful stones at the most attractive price."

Forget the éclair. "Can I see them?"

Miss Mona's smile widens. "That's what you're here for, Andie. I need you to make the right choices for the network. Take it away, dear."

My eyes nearly fall out of their sockets. "Me? You want me to . . . to . . ."

I let my words dry up as Mr. Cruz starts to open up a leather pouch lined with what can only be real silk velvet. He sets it down on Miss Mona's desk and continues opening the folds. In the end, I gasp when he finishes revealing the treasures hidden within.

"Oh my . . ."

3.00

I set the loupe down on Miss Mona's desk, then meet Mr. Cruz's gaze. "They're lovely, all right. And you assure me they're untreated? Will you put it in writing?"

His jaw tightens visibly. "Yes, Miss Andie. Aside from the usual oiling to protect the gems from the emerald's natural dryness, they're untreated. It's my reputation I try to protect. Of course, if I say untreated, they're untreated. I'll put it in writing."

I give him a gracious nod. "So let's get to the bottom line. How much?"

"I use the AGL—American Gemological Laboratory—colored stone grading reports for pricing."

"I'm very familiar with the AGL."

He pulls out a small, black leather-bound notebook, riffles through it, and then studies the numbers on his chosen page. "For Miss Mona, I sell them at $11,000 per carat."

I nearly swallow my tongue. When I find it again, I explode. "You've got to be kidding!"

Miss Mona sputters. "Andie."

Mr. Cruz's cheeks redden under the tan. "I do not kid. Not about my emeralds. These are top, top gem quality."

I use my flattened palms against the desktop to push my chair away, and stand. "I'll grant you they're better than middle-of-the-road, but I wouldn't put them at the LI1—lightly included top level, where you could ask $11,000 for them, wholesale. True, they have the *jardin* type of accepted inclusions, not black carbon bits, but I can show you, and I'm sure you can see, that each stone has more than one or two slight inclusions."

He narrows his eyes. "Ah, but the color, Miss Andie. They're colored stones, and color is everything. These stones are at least 4 or 4.5 in color grade."

I glance at the beautiful green gems. They are outstanding, but Mr. Cruz is shooting for the moon, what with that kind of price. And these are stars, not moons. "They do have good color, but it's more blue than even a 4.5 deserves. You know as well as I do that a 4.5 or better, a 4 or a 3, has to be almost purely primary grass green."

He responds with an elegant shrug and a tight smile. "Primary grass green is—how do you Americans say? Oh yes. In the eye of the beholder. These are primary grass green to me."

"All right. It is subjective. But I would put the tone at no more than 50," I counter, absolutely certain of my assessment. "That's good, but not excellent. And we're not talking amethyst, citrine, or peridot here. I'd need at least a 65, above the mid-range, you understand, for that kind of price. $11,000 for these is retail, and high retail, at that. We can't sell for above-retail prices. You know that."

The vendor clamps his lips. He stands, meets my gaze

square on. "I know the cut is outstanding, and the brilliance is better than 50 percent. You must agree."

"Yes, the brilliance and the cut are fine. But that does *not* erase the other issues." I look the stones over again, pray for guidance, and then take a deep breath. "I think you know a fair price is closer to $3000 or $3600 per carat, and that's what I'm prepared to offer."

Mr. Cruz's right eye twitches and his nostrils flare. "If I'd wanted an insult, I would have gone to that other channel."

Miss Mona gasps.

"Mr. Cruz." I make my voice gentle and conciliatory, "I'm sorry you feel insulted, but in all good conscience, I can't advise Miss Mona to buy these stones at your original asking price."

"But my AGL assessment . . . you're discounting the quality. You want to take advantage—"

"No way!" He's the one doing the insulting here. "Ask around, sir. Other vendors will tell you I'm as fair as can be. I do know my gems *and* the rating systems, and I'm willing to pay what a piece is worth. These stones are only worth what I offered."

"You're trying to cheat—"

"Never." I shoot an S.O.S. skyward. "You see, sir, Miss Mona's not my real boss." I send her an apologetic smile. "I answer to God first, and my honesty matters very much. I couldn't face him every morning if I played that kind of game. And I won't take offense at your claim."

"Rodolfo," Miss Mona says, her voice stern, a tiny line between her elegant brows, "I've known Andrea since she was born. I can trust her with everything I own. She would never, ever stoop so low. I can't believe you'd think I'd try and deal with you in such a dishonorable way."

Mr. Cruz nods his concession. "Very well. But I see Miss Andie is not satisfied with these gems. Perhaps she should see our entire collection, and then choose."

His entire collection? Who travels with that much merchandise on him? Is this guy nuts?

"Why, Rodolfo . . ."

Miss Mona's delight sets off my alarm-o-meter. Before I can get in the way of whatever runaway train she intends to catch, she goes on.

"That's the best idea you've had so far."

I cringe. I know that tone of voice. It *always* means trouble. For me. I'm going to regret asking, but I have to have some idea where she's going with this. "What do you mean?"

The vendor folds a black velvet flap over the stones. "We can accommodate whatever you wish, Mona. You know that."

"Then it's settled," Aunt Weeby's cohort says, satisfaction in her voice.

No way. Nothing's settled. Not like this. Not until she puts out on the table whatever she's cooked up. "Whaddaya mean, it's settled?" I ask. "You haven't even told us what you're thinking. And, knowing you, it could be . . . it could be as insane as . . . as . . . well, as crazy as that trip to Kashmir—"

I stop. As soon as I mention the sky-high land we recently visited, I know what her wacky mind has settled. "Nope. No way. Nuh-uh. Not this girl. I'm not going."

Miss Mona waves. "But, of course, you're going to Colombia, Andie, dear. Who else is going to know whether Rodolfo's emeralds are . . . are 65s or 23s or Ms or Ls or As, Bs, Cs, or Zs. You, my dear, are headed for the Muzo mine country. And I won't hear another 'no' about it, you hear?"

Up until I took Miss Mona's offer of a job, I'd loved to travel. Who wouldn't?

But since then, I've known nothing but danger, fear, guns aimed my way, and the inside of grody foreign jails. Not my idea of jet setting, know what I mean? And there are guerillas and drug lords in Colombia. I do not want to step into that kind of trap again.

I glare at Miss Mona. "If you think it's such a great idea, then *you* go. I'll give you charts and photos to take with you, and before you leave, I'll teach you everything I ever learned about emeralds. But I'm not going. I've had it up to here with traveling to strange places where nobody knows we wouldn't hurt a fly."

My boss turns to Mr. Cruz. "Don't pay her no never-mind, Rodolfo. Of course, she's going. She won't be meeting with strangers when she's there, either. You'll take care of her, and she'll be fine, right?" She winks my way. "It's time for you to use your negotiating skills. And you'll be taking my credit card with you."

What negotiating skills?

Yikes! I'm sure you'll understand why I feel the waters on the deck of the *Titanic* licking my ankles.

I'm sunk.

◆

Okay. I must confess. Six hours and forty-five minutes after that crazy meeting this morning, including a two-hour show with Mr. Magnificent, who doesn't blooper once, but does do his charming best—be still, my heart!—when I gather my briefcase and purse and close my dressing room door, I'm not all that upset about the trip to Colombia any more. How could I be? After all, the Muzo mines there are just as legendary as those in Burma and Kashmir. Since I started my job at the S.T.U.D., I've visited both. Now I'm being given the chance to see the operations in Colombia, which is pretty cool.

What's not so cool is all the criminal activity that goes on in that country. Not only is the place notorious for its drug violence and anti-government guerilla warfare, but also the land of its emerald mines is bathed in the blood of murdered miners.

"Good night, Nellie," I tell the S.T.U.D.'s new receptionist on my way out of the building.

The rustle of magazine pages precedes her "See ya."

Nellie is unique. She's only been with the S.T.U.D. for three months, and in that time I've watched her voraciously consume every monthly issue of every health magazine known to mankind. And that's in between reading titles such as *Regularity Through Colonics in Sixteen Days*, *Iron Out Your Wrinkles*, and the inimitable *Halitosis Gone*.

I shake my head and push on the glass door. "A little knowledge's a dangerous thing, Nell."

She peers up at me through her bottle-bottom thick glasses. "Oh, I couldn't agree with you more. That's why I'm determined to educate myself." She waves a prodigious tome entitled *Digestive Disorders Digest*. "I'm telling you, girl, I know I've come down with . . . with—wait a sec while I look it up again."

I bang my forehead against the lobby door as she rustles through the book. I should've kept my mouth shut. I know

43

better than to get Nellie going. "Tell me tomorrow. I gotta go."

"Irritable bowel syndrome! That's it. You see, I . . ."

I let her go on for a few minutes, but when she starts in on the high cost of toilet tissue, I wave and sail out. I voice a prayer for her, that the Lord will bring her peace about her health, and head for my rental car. Our now-jailed gem thief bombed mine not so long ago.

Like a heat-seeking missile, the image of those lovely emeralds zips into my head as I pull out of the parking lot. They were beautiful stones, but at Mr. Cruz's $11,000 per carat, way overpriced. They weren't absolutely top-grade virtually perfect pieces. I'm not going to let anyone take Miss Mona to the cleaners like that. Not if I can help it. I'm going to have to be extra sharp when I face the vendor again.

Just pray the guy doesn't have something equally sharp aiming back at you when you get there, the overactive little voice in my head pipes up.

GULP. No doubt about it. There is a touch of danger involved in my upcoming trip.

And it's all about the money. Colombian emeralds are the most prized in the world. Their price tags do come with a lot of zeros on them. I rarely offer emeralds on the show for that reason. If we can't give our viewers a better price than they can get at their friendly neighborhood jewelry store, then I can't see why they'd be willing to buy anything sight unseen.

I've never thought of myself as a wheeler and dealer, but I held my own in Miss Mona's office, if I do say so myself. I suppose I'll find out how good I really am when I face off with Mr. Cruz on his turf. I'm looking forward to that.

That's kinda scary. Maybe Peggy is right about me. Maybe

I'm only an emotional chicken—*cluck-cluck*. Maybe I do like the adrenaline charge I get from teetering on the edge of danger.

Who'd a thunk a boring old rock hound would have a . . . a—oh, I can't believe I'm going to say this—a hidden-below-the-surface Indiana Jones streak to her? Maybe my former boss's crook of a wife got it right. She dubbed me Andi-ana Jones and made the dopey name public during her trial. I've fought that label like a bunch of politicians in DC fight over a handful of votes.

"Lord? Was Peggy right? Am I kidding myself here?" At the continued silence, I shake my head. "Okay, Father God. Show me those parts of me I haven't really met yet—or haven't gotten to know so well after the introduction."

At the red light, I drop my forehead to the steering wheel. Oh boy. I better brace myself. I know a dangerous prayer when I pray one, especially since God has been showing me a lot of unattractive flotsam inside me after I came home. But I really have to, as Peggy said, grow up. Thirty definitely makes me a grown-up.

I pull into my driveway, slip my garage door opener gizmo from the visor where I keep it clipped, click it, and then park my car inside the dim structure behind my house. I gather my purse and briefcase from the backseat where I'd dumped them, then head outside.

But I come to a complete and abrupt halt when I look up. I blink and blink, thinking my eyes have gone wonky because of the change from the dark garage to the sunny outdoors. There, however, on my driveway, sits a U-Haul truck that seems to have materialized since I parked. As I stare, the engine coughs itself to silence.

A second later, before I can nudge myself out of my frozen state of shock, Josh and Max jump from the two sides of the cab and slam the doors in their wake.

"Hey, you're home," Max says. "Miss Mona wasn't sure you would be when we got here."

"What are you guys doing here?" I wave at the truck. "And what's that thing for?"

The two guys swap conspiratorial looks.

You know that alarm-o-meter of mine? Well, it's *wee-uh-wee-uh-wee-uh*ing like crazy again. First, I have to deal with the Daunting Duo of Miss Mona and Aunt Weeby. Now . . . now it looks like these two are ganging up on me too. Not fair. "Spill it already."

Josh snickers.

Max saunters to the rear of the truck. "I think it'll be a better surprise, what Miss Mona wanted, if we just do our thing, and then Andie can find it all the way Miss Mona wants her to."

I cross my arms. "Are you telling me you have something in there that you plan to bring into my house without my knowing what it is? And what's worse, that Miss Mona put you two up to it?"

They swap another set of looks.

Max snickers. "You got it."

"Not on your life, Max Matthews. Back that Trojan horse out of my driveway unless you're willing to open it and let me look at what you stashed in there first."

He looks at Josh, then shrugs one shoulder. "Okay by me. But you're the one who's going to have to face the wrath of the ladies. Wouldn't want to be in your shoes for that."

"Bu—but, it's my house—"

"For which Aunt Weeby gave you the down payment."

My oomph wilts. He's right. I can't ruin their fun. Whatever those two kooks stashed in the truck will come into my house. And if I hate it as much as I suspect I will, well, then I'll have to deal with it later.

Much later.

After my trip to Colombia. Wonder if Mr. Magnificent—as I call Max, just not to his face—knows about the trip yet. I blow out a frustrated gust of breath.

"Okay. Go ahead with your joke. I'll just . . . ah . . . I'll run to the store for a quart of milk."

The two guys chuckle as I hightail it out of my place. After I toss them the keys. Maybe I do need to have my head examined.

But I don't dawdle on my milk run. Once I have the plastic container in my grubby paws, I rush back home, praying every step of the way. I've given them twenty minutes. I hope that's been enough for them to unload whatever.

I run up the front steps, pause to breathe a prayer, and then fling open the door. "Ready or not, here I—"

A gasp steals the rest of my words. Horror fills me. My eyes open so wide I feel my eyebrows meet my hairline.

My groan is heartfelt. "No way. Please tell me this is only a joke."

"No joke, pardner," the blond rat says between chuckles.

Josh holds his middle as he laughs without restraint.

I stumble in, beyond appalled. My lovely living room with its elegant natural wood-trimmed windows, carved natural-wood mantel over the delft-like tiles, and natural hardwood floors is now filled with Miss Mona's spindly frou-frou French provincial furniture. The fussy brocade upholstery and painted and gilded wood looks about as right as a rhino at a Buckingham Palace tea party would.

"What parallel universe did I just walk into?"

Josh wipes a tear off his cheek and laughs some more.

Max leans back against the far wall, his chuckles infectious—but I do resist. I wave my hand in the circular motion that translates into "Go on."

"Miss Mona . . ." His laughter breaks into his explanation. "Oh man . . . Miss Mona says she's . . . she's redecorating. You luck out with her . . . 'lightly used treasures.'"

"Why?" I drop onto one of the fragile chairs and it squeaks. I can't believe this. "Why me?"

Max gives me one of his rascally winks. "Because she loves you so much, and wants to do her part."

I press my palm against my forehead. "What am I going to do? I can't live with this . . . this stuff." I scan the room. "And there's so much of it too. But I can't hurt her feelings. Why couldn't she just have had a garage sale, like everyone else?"

"Miss Mona and a garage sale!" Josh wipes more tears after a new explosion of laughs. "Oh . . . I gotta go. I've laughed so much my stomach hurts. You'll figure it out, Andie. You always do."

I roll my eyes. "I'm so glad you have such confidence in me. I tell you, I don't."

He gives another chuckle, then opens the front door. "Don't bother, Max. I'll walk home. It's only a few blocks away. The walk'll help me work out the cramp in my gut from all this laughing."

After Josh leaves, the house goes right to too silent. I steal a look at Max, and find him studying me. A blush starts at the base of my neck and slowly spreads up my face.

"What?" I ask.

"It's not you." He waves. "This stuff of Miss Mona's doesn't work for you. And I'm glad. You're more . . . more fun, and what you need is furniture that's more laid back, more fun, more you."

"Thanks. That's a really nice thing to say."

"I do have my moments."

I flash him a nervous smile. "I know. You're not all bad."

"Wow! What a rousing endorsement."

I shrug one shoulder. "It's the best I can do on a day like today."

A puzzled look lines his forehead. "A bunch of old-fashioned furniture can bring you down like this? What's wrong?"

"Nothing's really wrong," I say, standing. "I just have a lot to do to get ready for the trip. The last thing I need is a houseful of Miss Mona's castoffs I don't want."

His eyes narrow. "The trip? What trip would that be?"

"Miss Mona didn't tell you?"

"Not a word."

I close my eyes. "Great." When I look at him again, I see he's not happy. Fine. There's not much I can do about it. "She's sending me to negotiate the price on an emerald lot. In Colombia."

"No."

I snort—lovely, huh? "That's what I said. But you know Miss Mona. It got me nowhere. She's going to sell emeralds, and I'm going to buy them for her."

Silence drops between us like a pot's worth of overcooked linguine. I twitch.

Max shuffles.

Where did the guy who kissed me that one night go?

"Fine," Max finally says. "When do we leave for Colombia?"

"What do you mean 'we'? There's no 'we' in the Colombia trip. I'm just going to meet with Mr. Cruz, the vendor who brought some samples to Miss Mona's office today. I'll pick out the stones we'll show, pay the man for them, and head back home. Piece of cake."

He crosses his arms. "I have just two words for you: Burma and Kashmir."

A shudder rips through me. I have more bad memories than good from those two trips. "That's not fair, Max. This time is different. I've already met Mr. Cruz. Miss Mona knows him too. I'm not heading out to meet crazed miners I don't know. I'm going to Mr. Cruz's office to do business, no different than if his office were in . . . oh, I don't know, Poughkeepsie, New York."

Max takes a step toward me, and if I were a betting woman—which I'm not—I'd wager those were angry flames in his eyes. "Might I mention that, unlike Poughkeepsie, New York, Colombia has hordes of gun-toting guerillas and a slight problem with the illegal drug trade?"

Why, Lord? Why are you letting him use my own thoughts against me?

"Believe me, Max. I want nothing to do with anything or anyone other than Mr. Cruz and his emeralds. He just didn't bring any stones worthy of the price he set on them." I start to pace. "Oh, they were good ones, all right. But not for $11,000 a carat. He told us he has better ones in Colombia, and Miss Mona insisted I go negotiate there."

"She insisted."

"Yes. She did. And you can ask her about it."

"Well, then, she'll just have to send me too. I won't let you risk your life like that."

Oooooh! "Excuse me?" I say in a voice dripping ice. "You won't . . . what?"

"I won't let you flirt with danger again."

That's what I thought he'd said. Not good. "You, Mr. Matthews, don't have the power or authority to say any such thing. It's not up to you to 'let' me do or not do anything at all. I would appreciate you taking your high-handed ways out of my living room before you say any more offensive things." Or I go back to my old defensive tactics.

He blows out what sounds like a gust of frustration. "Okay. So I didn't put it in a particularly diplomatic way. But I . . . I care about you. I don't want to see you hurt."

"Are you questioning my ability to look out for myself?"

"No. I just read the newspapers, and am aware of too many people taken hostage in Colombia. I don't want you to be the next one."

"Gee, thanks, Max. Now you're scaring the living daylights out of me. I'm going to spend my time in Colombia staring over my shoulder, seeing bogeymen in every shadow."

"No, you won't, because you're not going alone."

"I'm going. Alone."

"No, you're not."

"I am."

"What part of partnership equals more than one do you not get, Andie?"

"Me? What about you? Where's the part where you trust your partner's judgment? The part where you don't undermine your partner? The part where you don't go putting yourself on a high pedestal and tell your partner what to do?"

His eyes narrow again. "Still as stubborn as ever."

Am I? Am I being unreasonable, Lord? Or am I setting reasonable boundaries? "No, Max. Just an independent career woman who doesn't like caveman attitudes. I mean, I really thought, after the k—"

I clamp my lips shut as I realize what I'm about to say. I'm still that emotional chicken. I'm not ready to put the memory of that kiss into words. Max still scares me, even if I'm no longer letting myself hold him at arms' length with the sniping and fighting and sarcastic digs.

"Tell you what," I say. Reasonably, too. "Let's let this go for the moment. We can sleep on it, and then, in the morning, we can talk it over rationally."

He runs a hand through his blond hair. "I don't think there's much to talk about, Andie. It doesn't look like you want what I do."

Is that a hint of pain I see flash over his face? Could I have hurt his feelings? That's not what I intended.

Even though he scares me.

But no matter how bad I feel, I can't make myself say another word. After a few minutes, Max shakes his head.

"Have a good night," he says as he walks to the door. "I'll see you at the studio in the morning."

I follow; watch him climb into the U-Haul then drive away. A sense of failure overtakes me.

"What have I done?"

$4\underline{00}$

I collapse into my not-so-comfy window seat in business class and allow myself the luxury of a sigh of relief. The past few days have been a challenge, with all the verbal dueling I've had to do. Yeah, it's all about Max. He's no pushover, and he pulled out all the stops. Over and over again, he regaled me with gory details of past Colombian guerilla crimes. I knew what he was trying to do. He wanted to scare me.

Okay. So he succeeded. But I'm still going. Alone. See?

And he didn't scare just me. You got it. He filled Miss Mona's and Aunt Weeby's ears with the same sabotaging mumbo-jumbo.

Max has a way with women, and Miss Mona is a quintessential female, a true southern belle, no less. Have I mentioned how much Miss Mona and Aunt Weeby love Max?

Uh-huh. I had to take all three of them on.

Especially when they kept reminding me of his knight-in-shining-armor moments. And there were Aunt Weeby's and Miss Mona's matchmaking tendencies to battle too. I mean, in their romance-addled brains, nothing is better than to have

Max and his overprotective, hunky self at my side while I traverse the wilds of a romantic but dangerous land. Think Harrison Ford and Karen Allen, folks. Or maybe Michael Douglas and Kathleen Turner.

In their eyes, Max the Magnificent ranks right up there with the best of movie heroes, romantic and . . . well, studly heroic, sweeping in to save me just at the right moment.

Fine. So he did save my sorry hide a time or two. But he didn't *have* to do it. I'm sure I could've got myself out of those binds all on my own. Pretty sure. Besides, he has studying to do. That GIA Graduate Gemologist certificate isn't a piece of cake to get. I should know.

When faced by that reality, he concocted some lame line about needing to come with me because he needs my help studying. What's up with that? Mr. College Scholarship needs *my* help with schoolwork?

Humph!

In spite of all the pheromonal appeal Max put out, and all the grandmotherly oohing, aahing, and invoking of scary scenarios (which, of course, require Max's heroic intervention) the Daunting Duo deluged on me, I stand firm—I am woman, hear me bleat. In the end, I make it clear I'll only be gone for a measly three days, will meet Mr. Cruz, pick up faboo emeralds for our fans, and return refreshed and revived by virtue of time spent in proximity to the spectacular grass-green gems. What girl wouldn't perk up after handling bling-bling like that?

I'm glad I'm going alone. Max is way distracting.

So here I am on Avianca's flight 605 for the last leg of my multi-stop trip to Bogotá, buckled in and ready to indulge in some heavy-duty nail biting. Although I'd never confess it to another living, breathing being, takeoffs and landings tend to make me just a teensy-weensy bit anxious. All right, all right. So I'm petrified. Goes with the chicken part.

When the roar of the airliner's engines erupts, I clutch the armrests, close my eyes, and start to pray. By the time we reach cruising altitude, though, I'm calmer and manage to relax enough to drift off to sleep. After a while, the clatter of the service cart jars me awake.

A cranberry juice cocktail and a chicken-flavored sawdust something-or-other later, I draw out my laptop and figure it's as good a time as any to catch up on research I've downloaded over the last few super-busy months. An article on the ongoing controversy over finds of yellow labradorite—or is it simply bytownite?—and its kissing cousin andesine/labradorite—had caught my attention, but I hadn't had a chance to read it yet. Now that material's singing my song. Once I start reading, the article holds my attention as it goes into great detail about the recent discovery of a previously unknown treatment that seems to have turned lesser quality yellow stones into magnificent fiery scarlet or bluish green ones with intriguing color-shift tendencies in different light. The most interesting part of the article is the implication of a very large retail organization that invested heavily into the red and green material and sold it as untreated, natural-colored pieces . . .

Uh-oh.

You got it. This is a legal no-no.

I dive back in to read more. The FTC and the FCC have gotten into the mix now, and the dollars invested and then lost on the scam perpetrated by unscrupulous gemstone vendors have reached astronomical heights.

I drop the magazine onto my lap and sigh. Dishonesty runs rampant in my business.

But all that doesn't take anything away from the original stones. I still love the gorgeous yellow feldspar stones found in Mexico when mining for Mexican fire opal. I'd offered some for sale on a show a few weeks ago.

"I bought one of those yellow labradorites from you, and I love it," my elderly seatmate murmurs when I look away from the screen to glance out the window. She adds, "To be honest, I love everything I've bought from the S.T.U.D."

I'm still not ready for how chummy my viewers feel through just watching my shows. It catches me unaware at the most unexpected moments. Like now.

"Have you been a member of the S.T.U.D. family for a long time?" I ask.

"Oh, I'd bought a set of pans and an outfit here and there since the channel launched, but it wasn't until you and your boyfriend came on that I . . ."

Your boyfriend . . . your boyfriend . . . your boyfriend . . .

And here I'd hoped to gain some distance from Max during this trip. I need to put it all in perspective, something I'm not good at doing on a regular basis. Constant reminders of the man aren't going to give me the space I need to get myself off the emotional teeter-totter. And you know I can't go back and handle my feelings for him without dredging up some balance.

Especially after his possessive Neanderthal approach to my trip.

"Andie?" the woman at my side asks, concern in her voice. "Are you okay?"

"Oh! I'm so sorry. Your comment made me think of something, and then my thoughts just stole away with me."

She chuckles. "My darling Howard is a lot like your Max, if I do say. I used to have trouble keeping track of my thoughts, once upon a time too. I don't mind changing seats with him so you two can sit together for the rest of the flight."

I fight the wince with everything I've got. "Max isn't mine. He's not my boyfriend." And how *do* I feel about that? Hmm . . . "He didn't come on this trip. You don't have to change seats."

"I'm surprised. Don't you two work together?"

Do we? Together? Really? Or do we just butt heads? "We do cohost the shows, but we're not joined at the hip."

"He has gone with you to Burma and . . . was that Tibet?"

"Close. Kashmir."

"That's right! The old sapphire mines." She holds out her right hand to admire a stunning and substantial ruby ring. "I wouldn't have minded a Kashmir sapphire, but I do love this ruby I bought after your trip to the Mogok Valley."

I check out the piece. She's not hurting for funds; the stone's one of the finest ones we brought back from that ill-fated trip. I remember its price tag for its slew of zeros. "Congratulations. That was one of my favorite pieces."

"You know the individual stones?"

"I picked out the rubies myself at the vendor's office."

"And you remember each stone? I'm impressed."

"Many gemstones have thumbprint-like characteristics. Rubies fall in that group. Since I handpicked the stones, I spent a good chunk of time studying each one. It's not hard to remember the best ones, and yours is one of the best we bought."

"Oh my. I loved it the minute I saw it, but now I know I have something really special." She gave me a sly look. "Like you and Max do."

"No, really. We're not . . . not—" What are we? I can't even say what we're not, since I have no idea what we are to each other. "Look, he's not my boyfriend or anything like that. The squabbling you see onscreen? Well, it's for real. He came to our network knowing nothing about gems. He made me nuts with his ignorance—the arguments were really real."

She patted my arm with the hand sporting the spectacular Burmese ruby. "That might have been the case on the surface, but take it from someone who's been married for fifty-two years. That kind of . . . oh, I guess you young folks call it 'chemistry' these days, is rare. Don't cheat yourself out of a great partnership *and* a spectacular romance. The boy's crazy about you, you know."

No, I don't know. And that's why I don't get to dump my flapping chicken wings and clucking. But I don't need to share that. I shake my head. "Ah . . . it's for the camera's sake—"

Her laughter cuts off my protestation. "Keep telling yourself that, Miss Andi-ana Jones. Just remember this: if you let Max Matthews slip through your hands, you'll spend the rest of your life kicking yourself."

Oh, what a pretty picture of foot to butt—*not*.

Since she doesn't get the hint from my drawn-out silence and stare fixed on the screen but instead continues to study me, I shut down my laptop and scrabble around my Max-invaded head for a new topic.

In my role as super-saleswoman for the S.T.U.D., I remember I'm on a business trip. And this woman is a loyal customer. "How do you feel about emeralds?"

She shrugs. "I can take them or leave them."

Just what I'd hoped for. "Oh nonononono! That'll never do. Let me tell you about emeralds. Carat for carat, and quality being equal, an emerald will bring in almost twice as much as a ruby every time . . ."

As I rattle off facts and details of emerald legend and lore, my excitement bubbles up. I, Andrea Autumn Adams, am going to the Muzo mines. I'm going to get to handle the emeralds most other gemologists settle for dreaming about from a distance. You know. They drool over pictures of them. I get to ditch the picture, since I'm going to touch them and check them out one on one.

Gladys Bergen and I spend the rest of the flight talking about jewelry, the S.T.U.D.'s many other quality offerings, interior design, and the similarities between air travel these days and root canals—there are more than you'd think. Trust me.

Once I land, I turn on my cell phone, then head out into the terminal, where I quickly find the immigration booths. One of the natives who are supposed to speak fluent English greets me with a spew of Spanish. See? Only minutes after landing I experience one of those dental trauma similarities.

A Spanish-speaking government wonk shouldn't be a problem, since back in the Dark Ages of my youth—translation: high school—I took years of Spanish. But today, my Spanish decides to go A.W.O.L.

Figures.

"Sorry." I cast frantic looks around, hoping to spot someone with the label BILINGUAL stamped on the forehead. No such luck. *No hablo español.*

The guy behind the glass wall glares. *"Necesito ver su pasaporte, señorita."*

Among those words he's machine-gunned at me, I think I catch something about a passport. I hand mine over, and before long, I have earned another foreign stamp on the little blue booklet. I smile. Neat.

"*Qué tiene para declarar usted hoy?*"

"I don't know what you want." Am I in trouble here or what? Memories of foreign jails dance in my head. "*No hablo español.*"

A warm hand drops on my shoulder. "Allow me, *señorita.*"

I glance at the man, and nearly swoon—I'm no Victorian, either, get my drift? Wow! How can anyone be so stunning and not look anything at all like Max the Magnificent?

"Ah . . . er . . . umm . . ." How sophisticated.

As my eyes have themselves a feast, the hunk rambles on in melodious Romance language—now I get why those languages are called that. Whoo-ee!

Anybody have a fan?

"Excuse me," he says, his liquid-ink eyes gentle and interested. "He wants to know if you have anything to declare. He has to do the usual customs questionnaire."

The stranger's English is flawless, if spiced with a hint of his native tongue. And it seems to have scrambled my brain. "Do you have anything with you that could be seen as an import?" he says, then winks. "Contraband?"

Contraband? "No!" I squeal, jolted back to the moment by the thought of another confrontation with foreign authorities. "I have clothes, shoes, my laptop, and that's it. Well, I do have a new bottle of shampoo. He can have that if it's a problem."

He laughs. "You can keep your shampoo, I'm sure." Turning to the guy in the booth, he resumes in Spanish, and I just stare some more.

Less than a minute later, he places a hand at the small of my back and guides me forward. "You're clear now. I'd like to escort you to the luggage pickup area, if you don't mind."

Mind? What girl wouldn't give up a pair of Manolos to have this guy at her side? The question's going to be, can I keep it together enough to put foot in front of foot without tripping in his intriguing presence?

I'm glad to report that I can. And do. Once we reach the carousel—still empty—he faces me and holds out his hand. "Marcos Rivera, miss . . . ?"

In my hyperventilative—hey! I think I just made up another new word—condition, an image of the feisty American TV personality by the same last name flashes through my head. Good grief.

Gotta get it together here. "Ah . . . I'm Andie . . . er . . . Andrea Adams."

"Welcome to Colombia, Andrea."

Be still, my heart! The way he rolls the *r* in my name makes it sound like poetry . . . a symphony . . . something far more exotic than a common, everyday name.

Then I realize I have to corral my bucket of mush for a brain again. "Thank you, Mr. Rivera. I'm looking forward to my time here."

"Marcos. Please call me Marcos." When I nod, he goes on. "Are you on vacation in our country?"

"No. Not this time."

He arches a jet-black brow. "What kind of business brings you here?"

"I'm a gemologist. I'm on a buying trip for my employer."

"Ah . . . our emeralds."

"Exactly." I figure the fewer words I utter, the less stupid my fascination with the old Hollywood-handsome one-man welcoming committee will make me sound.

My cell phone rings.

Marcos glances at my handbag, then steps toward the luggage carousel.

I nearly swoon at his polite sensitivity, but get a grip and burrow in my purse to open the chirping gadget. "Hello?"

"Andie?" Max says. "Is everything okay?"

What's up with him? "Of course, everything's okay. Why would you think it isn't?"

"Remember? I've traveled with you before."

"That is so not fair! Your lack of faith in me is the reason I insisted on coming alone. And it's the reason it's going to stay that way. I don't need a babysitter."

As I go to close the phone, I hear him squawk something about what I think. I know where he's going, and I'm not joining him. I can so take care of myself. I even find people willing to help me along the way. Mr. Rivera is a case in point. Too bad Max isn't a little more like the Colombian.

Men!

Then the oddity of my current situation dawns on me. Since when do I, Andie Adams, have men like Max and Mr. Rivera flocking to my side? I'm still using the same vanilla-scented body lotion and spray, not some exotic come-hither elixir. So what's the deal here?

I ponder the conundrum—but not for long. The luggage carousel coughs to life, and suitcases and duffels belch out of a black maw onto the rubber surface. Round and round other people's bags go, and that dreaded lurching starts in my gut. Will I have more than the clean pair of underwear I always stash in my briefcase?

"There it is!" I yell in ecstasy when the glaring orange suitcase bounces out. *Thank you, Jesus.* Damp, hand-washed underwear in a foreign land does not a happy me make.

"I'm happy for you," my companion says, humor in his eyes. "Can I take you somewhere?"

CRASH-BAM-BOOM!

Reality clunks me down from that flattery-flavored cloud I've been floating on. Am I nuts? I don't know this guy from a rat in a New York alley. And here he's offering to take me "somewhere." I'll bet.

In spite of his killer looks he could be a . . . well, a serial killer. "No, thank you. Everything's been arranged for me."

Oh, he's good. There's that touch of disappointment in his expression . . . I almost fall for it. Almost.

"Well, Andrea. I suppose I shouldn't be keeping you any longer. Here." He holds out a business card. "If you should need anything during your stay, please call. I'll be honored to help you."

Is he laying it on too thick now? Or is paranoia my new middle name? In either case, my alarms have gone off, and I refuse to put myself in danger. I don't even agree to call for help, should I need it. That's what boring but safe embassies are for.

I sigh. And take the card.

"Thank you for your help back there," I dip my head toward the customs and immigration booths. "And *adiós.*"

As Mr. Rivera strolls away, I wonder what he'd been doing in the airport. No normal being hangs out in an airport for the sake of hanging out in an airport. I glance at his card, and my eyes nearly drop out of their sockets. If I can believe what

I'm seeing, the hunk in a white silk shirt and finely tailored black linen pants is a Colombian lawmaker. A *senator*.

Maybe I should have trusted him.

Then again, word has it the government of Colombia has a small problem with internal corruption. Small. Yeah. And I'm a flying squirrel.

I slip the card into my jacket pocket, yank out the telescoping handle of my garish suitcase—easy to spot, so there is a method to my madness—and head . . . where *is* that information center Mr. Cruz told me about on our last phone conversation? That's where my ride is supposed to meet me.

Should've asked the senator before I sent him away.

Bottom lip between my teeth, I scour the crowd. A woman with three kids, the youngest bawling at the top of his lungs . . . three men with golf bags over their shoulders . . . an elderly couple holding each other upright . . . a couple billing and cooing and kissing as they bump into innocent bystanders . . . teens . . . and more. Then I spot what I'd hoped to find. "All right!"

I make my way toward the uniformed gentleman by the door. My pathetic Spanish at least manages a decisive *"Información, por favor."*

The policeman tips his head, and in fractured English, directs me to a kiosk in the center of the luggage area. Hopefully, whoever's manning that location can fish up enough English so that we can communicate. And she can—hallelujah!

"I have a *mensaje* for you, Miss Adams." She hands me an envelope, my name front and center.

Not good.

An envelope is not a car.

And I don't even ask for air-conditioning. Just a means

by which to get to my hotel, whichever and wherever that might be, since Mr. Cruz handled all the arrangements for my stay in Colombia's capital, Bogotá.

My fingernail tears open the heavy paper, and I scan the typed words. "Lovely. A 'scheduling complication.' At least he's arranged a cab for me."

From her perch behind the counter, the pretty girl with the olive complexion waves, and a thin, balding man trots up to us. The two of them fire Spanish at each other, and then the girl smiles at me. "Pedro will take you to the Hotel de la Opera. I'm sure you will like it. It's a beautiful old building made into a hotel. *Muy elegante.* I think it's our nicest."

Since we'd found some—ahem—undesirable aspects at our lodgings in both Burma and Kashmir, I hope the info desk clerk is right. Believe me, I want to like the Hotel de la Opera. And I'm looking forward to a peaceful, relaxing evening. Can't wait, actually.

"Is it far from here?"

"Not really. Maybe twenty minutes, in the historical colonial part of Bogotá. Follow Pedro to his cab. I'm sure he'll get you there soon."

Ready for something to go especially well, I follow Pedro out of the terminal. That's where I hit the heat face-first. Wow! This place really is equatorial. I start to "dew" immediately. By the time we get to Pedro's yellow taxicab, the "dew" has become a downpour. Ladylike or not, I'm sweating.

Then I slip into the cab's backseat—vinyl. You know I'm gonna "dew" a whole lot more and maybe even stick. Oh joy.

My enthusiasm for the trip begins to wilt—like me.

Pedro starts the car, and we pull away from the curb at the El Dorado International Airport. Easy, right? Well, let me tell you. Leaving the area is something else. The street is cram-packed with vehicles dropping off travelers, and picking up arrivals, dozens of taxicabs, vans, a handful of buses, and masses of people who see nothing wrong with jumping out in front of our cab.

Pedro maneuvers through all this, one arm out the window, gesturing wildly, bellowing what I'm sure are insults to those who don't cooperate with his wishes, other hand on the steering wheel, and one foot down on the gas pedal—*hard*.

That should've been my first warning. You see, when Pedro gets out on real roads, he only pushes harder on the gas. He zips in and out of traffic at warp speed, ignores universal red STOP signs, dashes under amber-to-red traffic lights, and gets me so turned around, I have no idea whether we're coming or going.

Not that I know anything about the El Dorado International Airport and its surroundings. But I usually can tell from which direction I've come. Not this time. Not with Pedro at the wheel.

One thing I do know: Colombian traffic laws are nothing like ours up in the States. Actually, they don't seem to have any traffic laws. At the next corner, Pedro uses his turn signal.

Turn signal? What turn signal?

The maniac sticks his left arm out the window again, waves, then shoots across all the lanes, the whole time letting out belligerent bursts of Spanish at his fellow drivers.

Foolish me. Thanks to Marcos Rivera, I'd thought the language inherently romantic. Hah! Behind us, a cacophony of honks and yells lets us know what other drivers think of Pedro's expertise—in driving and insults. I shudder. Glad I don't speak the lingo. Don't wanna know what they're saying.

I pray.

Good thing the nerve-wracking ordeal should only last about fifteen more minutes. At the speed Pedro's going, he might even shave more time off our drive than that. I hang on to the armrest on the door for dear life.

SCREECH!

For some unfathomable reason, since he hasn't once done it since we left the airport, Pedro hits the brakes. With all his might. I jolt back and forth. The seatbelt engraves its imprint on my chest. My head bangs against the seat. Then, before I can catch my breath, he speeds away again, careens around yet another corner, our car on only two of its tires.

Ever take a drive on two of a car's four tires?

Me neither. Not until today.

Where's a good, mean, ticket-happy traffic cop when you need one? Obviously, not in Bogotá.

By now, I'm sure more than two hours have gone by since I sat in this thwarted racecar driver's vehicle. Maybe more like two days. Will you buy decades? And there's no lovely, old hotel in sight.

"Lord?" I whisper. "Help!"

For some reason, the theme song to *The Twilight Zone* wafts through my head. Pedro speeds up. The structures outside become an indistinct blur. My stomach spasms. My head pounds.

Did I remember to tell Miss Mona and Aunt Weeby how much I love them before I took off?

You know, don't you, I'm not just in trouble here.

I'm a dead duck.

$5\underline{00}$

A few hair-raising minutes later, we hurtle to a stop in front of a stunningly beautiful old building. Shaking, I look around, and notice the lack of traffic. We're at the curb beside a narrow, cobbled street that seems to be used only by pedestrians these days. The building itself, a two-story, soft coral stucco structure, with arched windows and wrought iron grilles on balconies, looks like something right out of old Zorro movies. All I need is for that masked man to swing down from the rooftops.

Colombia's yellow, blue, and red flag waves from a second-story balcony, and everything shines with the gracious beauty of a bygone era.

As I soak it all in, praying for my heart to stop pounding, trying to calm down after that berserk ride, the cab's door is yanked open. Pedro jabbers at me so fast that he would've left my high school Spanish eating dust even at the zenith of its fluency. I assume, since he's holding my radioactive orange suitcase, that he wants his money in his hand and my body out of his cab.

I rummage in my purse, pull out a wad of Colombian *pesos* I swapped dollars for before leaving home, and step out of the cab. That's when my quaking legs betray me, and I nearly wind up doing a face-plant in the ancient cobbles. I'm still under the influence of the rush of fight-or-flight hormones that tried to rescue me during that demented ride. Too bad they didn't succeed.

With a glare for Pedro, I shove the money at him, only to have him shake his head and push my cash and hand away. Horror on his face, he argues, objects, shakes his head, and in the middle of millions of Spanish syllables, I catch one I understand: Cruz. Evidently, the emerald vendor has paid for my transportation ahead of time.

I work to send some starch to the cooked spaghetti impersonating my legs, and shove the money into my jacket pocket. With a quick *"Adiós"* Speedy Gonzalez's way, I wobble into the hotel's shaded doorway, my suitcase clattering in my wake.

And then, almost as if I'm walking onto a movie set, I enter a different world, a most genteel one about, oh, two hundred years old. Walls more than a foot thick lend the building a coolness I've previously only equated with well-adjusted air-conditioning. Under my feet, red brick terracotta tiles form a beautiful herringbone pattern, one I suspect has been there for more than a century, if not two. Hand-plastered walls, with the kind of texture that only comes from age and coats upon coats of paint, now glow with a warm yellow color. Scattered throughout the vast lobby's mile-high coffered ceilings are six-armed chandeliers hung well above even the tallest guest's head. And everywhere I look, I see antiques worthy of the Louvre or other European museums.

So tasteful is the lobby that it welcomes you like the living room of a country estate. I follow the lure of the large fireplace and plop down on one of the Williamsburg-blue-with-soft-coral-stripe overstuffed armchairs at either side of the hearth. The refined atmosphere begins to soothe my battered nerves.

Ah . . . I could get used to this luxury.

But not on my paycheck.

That reminds me I'm here on business. I stand, head to the front desk, where I'm thrilled to find a clerk who speaks excellent English.

"Welcome to Bogotá, Miss Adams," the man says. "We hope you enjoy your stay with us. Please let us know if there's anything we can do to make your stay more pleasant."

Yep. A girl could get used to this, all right.

Then, when minutes later the porter in the handsome, gold-trimmed uniform throws open the door to my room, I moan my bliss. Now I know how the other half lives—I like it, I like it.

The brick tile floor on the balconied hall gives way to mellow wood once inside my room—

"Room?" I murmur. "What room?"

This is one honest-to-goodness suite they've put me in. Immediately on the other side of the door there's a lovely sitting area with a pair of very European wood-backed and upholstered seat-cushion chairs, a small table in between. Then comes the arch . . .

Oh my, oh my, oh my! Looking up, I feel as though I've walked into a fairy-tale castle. Four round columns attached to the walls give the appearance of holding up a luscious, flower-bedecked, wedding-cake-frosting white arch that soars high, higher than any ceiling I've seen outside of mammoth office buildings.

This ain't no office building, know what I mean?

An "ahem" catches my attention.

I glance at the porter, trying to look nonchalant, then snag some bills from my wallet and hand him his tip.

He smiles, nods, and leaves, closing the door without making the slightest sound.

I step into my new digs.

Luxury all the way, is the name of this game. I step across to the other side of the amazing arch and there I find a very modern king-size bed, covered in what sure looks like silk from where I'm standing . . . and touching.

But no amount of luxury could have prepared me for the windows. I'm not sure you can call them something so boring as windows. Ten-foot-tall glass and wood doors open inward to reveal one of the beautiful, waist-high wrought-iron grilles I'd admired from the street below. Warm tropical air wafts in to caress my face. If this isn't exotic and foreign, I don't know what is. I feel like Elena in *The Mask of Zorro*.

A totally open door to the world outside . . . how romantic!

I'm in love. If I could find some way to afford it, then this is where I would live out the rest of my life.

But I can't afford it. I've a job and a mortgage and a dead car and all of that back in Louisville. I'm a regular girl, not some movie heroine in a fantasy world.

All of a sudden, the strain of the day hits me. I'm swamped with exhaustion, and the bed sings my name. I toe off my tan pumps, drop my jacket on one of the two nightstands, and set my cell phone's alarm to blare in time for dinner.

Soon, I'm asleep. "Stranger in Paradise" creeps into my dream . . .

Mr. Magnificent sweeps the lovely young woman with the red hair up into his arms. Her froth of wedding gown train trails down, kisses the red brick tile floor like something out of an early Hollywood film.

"Aren't you supposed to carry me over the threshold and into the room, Mr. Magnificent?" the bride with the red hair asks as they whirl away. "You know, not out of the honeymoon suite."

Mr. Magnificent runs down a vintage staircase, his feet barely touching the treads, her gown fluttering behind them, her veil like a wind-tossed cloud. "Don't fret your little old head with such thoughts, my lovely young damsel in red-headed distress," he says. "I know what I'm doing. Me Tarzan, you Jane."

"But Mr. Magnificent, I am woman, hear me roar!"

Mr. Magnificent smiles, his footsteps echoing in the hacienda's *wide halls. "I know best . . . I know best . . . I know best . . ."*

Then, sinister Pedro twists the end of his new mustache, greets them with an evil smile, and opens his yellow cab's door. Mr. Magnificent crumples the lovely young woman and her fluffy gown into the modest confines of the backseat. The car door slams shut and Pedro speeds away.

On two wheels, the cab spins circles 'round the fountain in the hotel courtyard, drowning out the last strains of "Stranger in Paradise." The lovely young lady with the red hair feels sick, queasy, ready to barf into the air-sickness bag in the rear pocket of the seat in front. Pedro laughs, a madman's peal, then cries out in glee. "Whee-eee-whee-eee-whee-eee—"

I bolt upright, gasping, disoriented.

"Where am I . . . ?" I look around, trying to catch my breath. Then the details of my Mad Hatter day slam back into my thoughts. That's when the piercing squeal gets through to me. I reach over to the nightstand and turn off my cell phone alarm.

A quick shower and a clean cream skirt and top later, I head for the hotel's rooftop restaurant. I'm led to a small, yellow-linen-covered table, and the maître d' pulls out one of the two wrought iron chairs for me. He shakes out my napkin, then hands me a tall menu and murmurs something about his hopes for my enjoyment of my meal.

With the open menu before me, I reach back a bunch of years to my vacationing high school Spanish in hope of deciphering the hotel kitchen's offerings. I get nowhere.

"Is that you, Andie? What a surprise!"

I turn at the sound of the familiar voice, and blink at the sight of Gladys Bergen in a gorgeous sage green silk summer dress. "Are you staying here?"

"Nowhere better to stay when visiting Bogotá." She gives the restaurant an appreciative and approving gaze. "Ever since Howard and I discovered this treasure ten years ago on his first business trip to Colombia, we've returned time and time again. We've never regretted it."

"That's good to know. Especially since I'm at the mercy of my business contact here. He made all the arrangements."

Gladys frowns. "Is that wise, dear? The hotel choice is impeccable, but can you trust him with your safety?"

And there you have it. That's the monster dancing in the ballroom of my head ever since Mr. Cruz insisted on treating me, as he put it, to a worry-free time in his native land.

73

I didn't like the lack of control back when I first heard of it; I hate it even more now. How am I supposed to get myself out of any potential jam, since I know nothing about anything Colombian?

But I can't share these fears with a virtual stranger—are we seeing a trend? I'm not feeling the love here. So much for telling Max I wouldn't be surrounded by strangers like I'd been in Burma and Kashmir.

I'll have to give that some more thought—just not when my stomach's gurgling its emptiness for all to hear. "I'm sure everything will be fine, Gladys. My boss, Miss Latimer, knows the vendor, and she's a pretty smart cookie. I doubt she'd put me in any danger."

"I hope you're right." Gladys then glances around the large crowded room again. "Oh dear. It looks as though I came up for dinner at the wrong time. It's very busy tonight."

I gesture to the chair across from mine. "I'm alone. Why don't you join me?"

"Oh, I wouldn't want to intrude."

"Intrude?" I give a snort of laughter. "On what? Me, myself, and I? I have nothing on my schedule for tonight other than a pleasant, quiet dinner. Your company would be wonderful."

She still looks reluctant. "Well . . . I would prefer company to eating alone too, but I didn't stop by to shoehorn myself on you."

"I would've stopped by your table had I seen you in a restaurant. And I don't want to eat alone, either. Besides, I invited you, so please. Join me." I glance at my menu, then back at Gladys. "You're probably the perfect dinner companion for me. I have no idea what any of this might be."

Fortunately for me, Gladys has visited Colombia enough times, and loves the country and its culture so much, that she gives me a detailed description of every item on the long menu.

Once I narrow down my choices, I close my menu. "I get why all these fancy cosmopolitan restaurants try to cater to American tastes, like this one does, but it's way boooooring to order a T-bone, baked potato, and green salad when I go out of the neighboring forty-eight, if you know what I mean."

Gladys takes a sip of ice water, then draws a deep breath. "Smell the spicy scents. Why waste the opportunity? I love Colombian cuisine."

"I think that *ajiaco* soup dish you described sounds wonderful. You say it comes with rice on the side? I'm pretty hungry—that stuff we got on the plane wasn't much to speak of."

Gladys laughs. "Trust me. I suspect a serving of *ajiaco* will be more than you can manage. It's a soup, but one with about a quarter chicken per serving, an ear of corn, delicious tiny potatoes native to Colombia, and other vegetables thrown in according to the chef's inspiration. They'll also bring you a dish of white rice and a couple of *arepas*. You'll have more than enough to eat."

"Well, then. When in Colombia, do as the Colombians do." I close my menu and smile up at the waiter who'd materialized at my side. "I'll have the *ajiaco*."

Hey! I can't be making a mistake. Gladys orders the same thing. Then she focuses all her attention on me, and I realize how much she reminds me of Miss Mona—minus the wacky quotient, that is.

"Tell me all about your trip, Andie. I'm just here to meet

my husband. He's on a buying trip too, but he buys boring stuff like ores and minerals. Even though I'm not crazy about emeralds, wheeling and dealing for gemstones has to beat ores any day."

I don't know about wheeling and dealing, but I do tell Gladys about Mr. Cruz's visit to the S.T.U.D., and while I have no idea how my negotiations will go in the morning, I can share details of my last two disastrous trips. I do skip over those scary parts I can't turn into Calamity Jane comedy bits.

As I finish the last bite of *arepa*, a soft cornmeal flat bread, delicious when dripping with sweet butter, the maître d' approaches and tells Gladys someone's waiting for her at the front desk.

"Oh my," she says. "I can't imagine who'd come to see me here. It can't be Howard. He's not due back from the interior until tomorrow afternoon. I wonder if he finished early. That'd be nice. We can start our little holiday sooner."

She stands, takes a bill from her chic brown handbag, slips it under her empty plate, and then, on her way out, lays a hand on my left shoulder. "I'm sorry about this, Andie. I had a lovely dinner, and I certainly hope I have the opportunity to introduce you to Howard before you go back home. We're planning to spend a week visiting the city once he's back. Have a good night and a very successful day tomorrow."

When Gladys hurries off, I lean back in my chair, take another sip of the finest Colombian coffee I've ever tasted, and again admire the view from the wall of windows at my right. Red-tiled roofs, many over a century old, spread in a carpet of age-softened red for many blocks. In between the tiles, a handful of church domes rise, their crosses reaching for the sky. As the sun drops farther down on the horizon, more lights flicker on.

Another sip . . . this is the life.

Briiiing!

I pull out my cell phone. "Hello?"

"Andie, dear!" Miss Mona says. "How was your flight? Did Rodolfo find you at the airport? How's the hotel?"

Shocked, I drop the coffee cup onto its saucer. "Is everything okay at home? This call's costing a fortune. Why are you calling? What's wrong?"

"Now, Andie. Why would you think I'd only call if something's wrong? I just wanted to see how you got there."

Hmm . . . "I'm fine. The plane didn't crash. The hotel's wonderful, and local food rocks. How're you, Aunt Weeby, the S.T.U.D., and everyone else *really* doing?"

Silence. Then, "No need to get smart, young lady. I'm just thinking about your well-being."

"Uh-huh." Something tells me there's more behind her call. Chalk it up to knowing the woman all my life. But I give her the time and silence to hang herself.

"Are you and Rodolfo heading out to the mine in the morning?"

"It's me by my lonesome, Miss Mona. Mr. Cruz left a message for me at the airport's information counter. He had some kind of scheduling conflict, so he arranged for a cab to bring me to the hotel. And the hotel's the most amazing place I've ever seen. Think museum crossed with palace."

"He stood you up? What's wrong with that man? We don't send our number one host to do business with him, only to have him stand you up."

My thoughts exactly, but it's not good to give Miss Mona

any fuel. "I'm fine. And his arrangements have been wonderful. I'm going to go back to my room as soon as I finish this super cup of coffee. I'll go meet Mr. Cruz in the morning."

"Coffee? At night? And you with that hole in your gut? Now, Andrea, dear . . . how wise is that?"

I sputter.

Miss Mona ignores me. "Now you be careful, you hear? You're all on your own, and maybe I shouldn't have pushed you to go in the first place. Or maybe I should send Max, like he's wanted all along—"

"Whoa! No need to rehash old stuff. We settled that before I left. Okay?"

"I don't know how okay I am on all this, but I'd sure feel better if we prayed."

"Now there's the best idea you've had in a long time." I'm not about to confess how weird I feel about Mr. Cruz's absence at the airport; if I did, she'd have Max at my side faster'n I can spit. "I'd like to pray too."

We do, in spite of the distance between us, and as soon as we bring God into the picture, I feel better, far more confident than I'd felt before. "Thanks, Miss Mona. And please, don't worry about me. I'll be back before you know it. In one piece—you know?"

"Well, honey, I have no doubt God loves you and will do everything he can to protect you, but there's all that free will he gave some pretty rotten characters . . . well, before they chose to become such rotten characters." She falls silent. Then, "And there's those crazy choices you've been known to make too."

Me? *She's* calling *my* choices crazy? Who insisted I had to come to Colombia? Good grief. "I'll be careful, okay?"

"Of course you will." There's a distinct lack of certainty in her voice. "And have fun, you hear?"

Fun. On a business trip. Yeah, right. "Okay. Love you. And bye."

I reach for my purse to stash my phone away, and grab air. Uh-oh. I look at the chair back, where I'd hooked the purse strap, and feel every last chance for fun on this trip disappear.

Nothing. Nada. Zip. Zilch. No purse.

I push away, look under the table, check the floor close by. I could probably crawl to check under other diners' chairs, but you know they'd object, and the dread in my gut tells me I wouldn't find anything there even if I did. Then I spot a young man darting out of the restaurant. As he whips down the hallway, I see a blur of familiar black leather.

"Hey!" I point. "Stop him! He stole my purse."

The maître d' glares. "I'm sure there must be some mistake—"

"No mistake." I bust out of the restaurant after the wretched thief. In the hall, I spot the top of his curly-haired head descending the stairs. I follow, at a clear disadvantage in my high heels and skirt.

I pray for ankle strength, for my skirt to stick to my thighs, and hit the lobby running. I keep my eyes on the little creep as I dart between clusters of other guests, all of whom stare as though I've escaped the nearest loony bin. And who can blame them?

You know they can see the plume of steam spewing out of my red head. I'm mad, and, if nothing else, my anger's sure to show on my face. They, on the other hand, are enjoying a beaucoup-star hotel like normal humans have a habit of doing. Me? I'm charging after a crook, rudely shoving them all out of my way, yanking my creeping skirt down from my butt, yelling for help—you get the picture.

"Sorry," I yell and give another yank.

Then the scrawny kid whips out the front door. I follow.

At the entrance, the doorman steps into my path. "*Señorita. No puede—*"

I shift to his left.

He follows.

I dip to the right.

So does he, concern on his kindly face.

"Please! That guy . . ." I point. "Has my purse. My bag." Where's my skimpy Spanish when I really need it? "*Bolsa!* That's it. That kid stole my *bolsa*! I have to catch him."

The doorman steps aside. "*Policía!*"

"Thanks!" I give chase. But in the precious few seconds I lost dancing with the doorman, my quarry seems to have vanished into the shadows. A handful of pedestrians, none with my bag, continue to meander down the cobblestoned street.

But then I spot a whisper of movement in a shadowed doorway about thirty yards away. I give chase.

He takes off again, darting, casting looks over his shoulder.

"Give me back my purse!"

My cry acts like gas on flames. He's fast. And now runs faster.

I'm out of shape. I'm wearing heels. And I just finished downing a huge meal; let's not mention the instant case of indigestion I've developed. But I'm not going to let him get away with my bag. Not if I can help it.

The twerp turns a corner.

I do the same, and soon realize we're in a dark alley behind the glamorous hotel. Let me tell you, alleys are short on glamour these days. This one's lined with aluminum trashcans and scented with dead dog. At least Eau de Alley's what I figure dead dog must smell like. Not that I've smelled a dead dog, but I'm sure this is close.

Gag.

I fight back the urge to barf, and keep after my quarry. He's got to get tired sooner or later, right?

Eyes glued to his scrawny back, I spot a welcome sight right in front of him. "Aha!"

A wall. The alley ends no more than twenty feet ahead. He's got nowhere to go. And then I realize that, even though he's skinny, he's young and male. Probably a whole lot stronger than me. Even with hands tied behind his back any day of the week, maybe even in his sleep. Who am I kidding?

I can't fight him for my purse.

And what am I doing in a back alley, anyway?

Out of a normal sense of self-preservation, I slow my pace. But, since things rarely ever go my way, my shoe catches on one of those oh-so-historically accurate cobbles, and I wrench my ankle. But instead of crying, I grin.

Guess what? I have two weapons.

In seconds, I have one of my stilettos in hand, rage in my belly, determination in every inch of my being. That's when the thief skids to a stop right smack up against the wall.

I come up behind him; raise my shoe; give him my fiercest glare. In a flash, the surreal nature of the moment flits through my mind. Andrea Adams, Wonder Woman? Not likely.

My stomach twists. I tremble.

But, hey. The kid still has my bag. "Give me my purse, you little brat!"

Fear darts across his face. I approach.

He snarls.

I wince. He sounds serious. Am I nuts? Do I really think I'm going to get my purse back? *I'm* going to wrestle him for it? What alternative universe did I just barge into?

But my adrenaline is pumping, my heart is beating faster, and my determination hasn't quit.

Then everything goes downhill. The creep lowers his head and runs straight at me. Before I can jump out of his way, he smashes into my very *ajiaco*-and-*arepa*-full gut. "Oooof."

I stumble backward. My bare foot lands on something wet and squishy. As ooze works through my toes, the other high heel skids out from under me, and I go flying through the air backward, my arms windmilling, my legs trying to regain footing.

CRASH!

Of course. You know it. I smash into the aluminum trash-cans, which happen to be full to the brim. With an earsplitting clatter, they fall over, dumping their contents everywhere.

Yeah. On me.

I did say everywhere.

The stench of dead dog seeps way down to my marrow.

I gag.

Tears pour down my face.

I gag again.

Why do these crazy, miserable, awful, and now disgusting things keep happening to me?

I look up at the black sky, but its winking stars have no

answers. I don't need to check for the thief. While sprawled out on my odoriferous bed, my dinner about to make its abrupt and unceremonious exit, I know the wiry teen has disappeared. My purse, passport, money, and Miss Mona's bottomless American Express card with him.

"Fun, Miss Mona?" I wail. "Is this what you call fun? 'Cause it sure isn't in my book."

The *ajiaco* erupts.

6$\underline{^{00}}$

How did I wind up here? Flat on my back in a dark alley.

Sick, slopped, and stinky.

Out of the country.

Minus passport.

And license.

But with a glob of shredded lettuce that's more than half-way to the state of brown slime impersonating a brooch on the front of my formerly nice cream-colored top.

Oh joy.

Up a creek without a paddle sounds just dandy about now.

"Why me, Lord?"

I go up on one elbow, and realize I'm still clutching my cell phone in the stiletto-free hand. Too bad I don't know if 9-1-1 works in Colombia. But what I do know works is to alert Miss Mona of incoming charges on that American Express card.

"Andrea?" my boss asks, her voice rising. "Why are you

calling so soon after we talked? Are you all right? What's wrong? I'm going to have Rodolfo's hide. What did he do to you?"

The love and concern in Miss Mona's voice breaks open the floodgates, and I start to sob. I tell her Mr. Cruz had nothing to do with my misadventures, and then, in spurts broken by sobs and sniffles, I relate the events of the past few minutes.

I hate blubbering. But I can't help myself. Even though it gives Miss Mona more reason to insist on my return.

"Now you just pay no never-mind to those emeralds, Andie, dear. You come on home where we'll take care of you. My goodness. Who'd be thinking emeralds at a time like this? I tell you. A body never can tell what's what when one's not under Uncle Sam's beady ole eyes. Come right on home tomorrow, you hear?"

"But I can't!" Fresh tears flood my face, and in the midst of the burgeoning hysteria, it occurs to me the salty tsunami could do some good and wash the trash muck off my cheeks.

It's a good thing the Daunting Duo can't see me now.

Miss Mona makes sympathetic noises. "Of course you can. I don't even want those emeralds anymore—"

"It's not the emeralds, Miss Mona. It's my passport. That stupid kid got away with it. I *can't* go home."

And that reality brings on yet another briny flood.

Dead silence.

Until footsteps run into the alley. Fear, gut wrenching and icy, claws through me.

"Gotta go." I clap my phone shut and scramble up to a sitting position. I can't just splay on antique cobblestones like a beached whale. That'd make it too easy for the approaching runner to plug me.

Okay. So I watch too many black-and-white B movies. They give me ideas. Like this one: *move*. Question is, can I?

As disgusting as the goo around me is, I have to stand if I'm going to have any hope of getting away. So I plant my hands on the grimed-up ground and stand on wobbly legs. And come face to face with a uniformed stranger.

He recoils.

Can you blame him?

Eau de Dead Dog is bad.

My hope tries to rally, but considering my circumstances, it droops again. "You didn't come to tell me you found the kid who stole my purse, did you?"

The officer shakes his head.

"Or my purse, right?"

"Sorry, *señorita*. I don't have your handbag." He takes a couple of steps away. "The hotel called to report the situation. I'm here to ask some questions."

Looks like cops everywhere operate out of the same rulebook. "I suppose you need to take me to the police station for a statement, right?"

"Your *cooperación* is needed, miss."

That's when the brainstorm hits—or prior experience, bad, of course, instructs. "I can ask for embassy help, can't I?"

He nods. "Of course. And we can certainly escort you there. We'll ask you questions with an embassy person present. We see no problem with that."

And before I can ask for a chance to clean up, something I desperately need, but after he does give me a second to put my weapon—er, shoe—back on, he bundles me into a cop car and we zip down the narrow streets of the colonial neighborhoods to a more modern area. In a daze, I follow my escort to a plain room at the embassy building, and there, with a Mr. Sloan at my side, the police ask me the same kind of questions Chief Clark would have asked had this happened back in Louisville. Between questions, I pick off carrot peelings, soggy paper, and some questionable yellow-brown stuff that reeks. But then again, everything about me stinks right now.

By the time I've recounted my evening's events at least three times, the gloppy garbage bedecking me has begun to dry into hard crusts, making them easier to remove. Unfortunately, the stench hasn't decreased one smidgen. Then my foot begins to itch. Yeah, the one that landed in the ooze from the trash.

I kick off the shoe I'd wielded and try to scratch with the chic, pointy toe of the goo-free shoe. No go.

As I grow twitchier, I dart glances at Mr. Sloan. He gets the picture by my fourth glare. He stands.

"I believe," the middle-aged embassy operative says, "we've gone over this information enough times. You would agree with me that any more questions you might have for Miss Adams can be asked at a later time. I'm sure you understand her desire for a bath and clean clothes."

At that, the officer can't apologize enough. Once he's gone, I thank Mr. Sloan. "I thought I was going to lose what's left of my mind."

He chuckles. "They're trying to be thorough. The current president is known for his anti-crime stance."

I sigh. "If that's the case, I sure hope his police can find my purse. I'll be needing that missing passport in a couple of days."

"Your best option is to start the process to get you an emergency passport. We can expedite things, but it will still take a few days."

"Great." I run a hand through my short hair but encounter a crusted bunch glommed flat against the left side of my head. Grossed out, I wipe my hand against my ruined skirt. "What do I have to do to speed things up?"

We arrange to get together again before I leave to meet Mr. Cruz in the morning. "Can you help me call a cab? I need a shower in the worst way."

Mr. Sloan's brown eyes twinkle. "You'll forgive me if I don't deny that last part."

I laugh. "And you're not even the one carrying the stink of Eau de Dead Dog around with her."

The middle-aged man laughs, then shakes his head. "Couldn't have put it better myself." Then he grows serious. "As far as getting you back to the hotel, I'll see about getting one of our military police officers to drive you there. A beautiful young woman shouldn't be getting into a cab alone in Colombia. Certainly not at night. Let's go check with the duty officer out front."

And here it turns out that when I jumped into Pedro's cab I'd taken my life in my hands in more ways than one. Who'd a thunk?

We start down the long, silent hallway. My gross shoes' high heels echo eerily in the cavernous space. As we reach the entrance, another set of footsteps rings out. When I turn out of curiosity, I can't swallow my gasp.

"Marcos!" I cry before I realize what I'm doing.

I mean, what girl wants to draw the attention of a gorgeous man like Senator Rivera when she's wearing produce well

88

on its way to reverting to primordial ooze? But the deed is done.

He peers at me, then his eyes widen with shock. Do you blame him?

"Andrea? Is that you?"

"In all my stinky glory." Best to make as much of a joke as I can out of the outrageous situation. "For your nose's sake, you won't want to come too close."

His nostrils flare as he approaches the effluvium. One does, though, have to give the man credit for impeccable manners. He waves my concern away. "Is there anything I can do to help? What happened?"

I dish up the digest version of my dining experience as Mr. Sloan ducks through the metal detector setup to speak with the uniformed man at the desk.

As I reach the end of my tale of woe, he comes back to our side. "I've arranged to have one of our guys drive you back to the hotel."

"You don't need to bother anyone," Marcos says. "I'll be happy to take Miss Adams. It's not far out of my way home."

"Oh, you don't really want this"—I wave down the length of my clothes—"in any car you'll drive again. I'm sure an embassy vehicle will be easy to clean."

"I have leather seats. What can be easier?"

For a moment, I dither. Do I really want to head out to the hotel at the side of one of those strangers that have recently thronged around me? But then I remember his business card. And the guy had just walked out of an office in the U.S. embassy. Plus, Mr. Sloan knows I'm with him. I don't think he's dumb enough to do away with me tonight.

Here goes nothing. "Only if we keep the windows down, okay?"

He laughs, and we both leave the safety of the embassy. The trip back to the Hotel de la Opera is uneventful, and Marcos and I discuss the theft. He bemoans the high level of crime in his country. Since I'm not heavily into politics, I turn the conversation toward the beautiful old hotel.

"The older one of the two buildings," he tells me, "was once Simón Bolívar's headquarters."

My eyes nearly pop. "Are you telling me I've been walking on the same tiles the famous liberator of practically half of South America walked on?"

"Of course."

"Wow!"

"I'm sure you can visit George Washington's Mount Vernon. It would be no different there."

"I suppose you're right. But this is so . . . so *foreign*."

He laughs. "It's foreign only to foreigners."

"You have a point." I begin to relax. "How come you speak such excellent English? It seems all my years of high school Spanish decided to stay back in high school. It sure isn't helping me here."

"I attended an American school here in Bogotá, and then college in Washington, DC. Afterward, I returned to study law at the university here."

"How'd you get from law school to the Senate?"

Marcos spends the rest of the drive to the hotel telling me stories of his time as a new attorney, and then of his political start. I have to keep from pinching myself. This kind of thing only happens in movies, not to me.

Not the super gross or the super cool.

If it weren't for the pervasive miasma of rot, I would think I've been plunked into a romantic movie. Then again, the stench belongs in a horror flick.

Before I know it, we're at the hotel. I thank Marcos for his kindness, we say goodbye, and I head for the front desk. There, I get a new room key, and then hurry through the thankfully empty lobby. Up the stairs, and I'm outside my room. I slip the key into the lock, but then hesitate.

The windows. Those huge openings I liked so much when I first saw them. Only now does it occur to me to wonder about their safety. True, there was that grille on the little balcony, but really. What self-respecting creep would be deterred by something so surmountable? Besides, a simple door lock was all that latched the windows shut.

And I can't remember whether I latched them before dinner.

"Aw . . . come on! Don't be such a sissy." I open the door, flick on the light, and hold my breath. "Hello?"

I figure if someone's out to get me, they'll probably rush me right now and get it over with. But nothing happens. I don't even get a breeze from the windows. When I look that way, I breathe a sigh of relief. I did lock them before I headed down to dinner.

But there's still the bathroom and its matching door to check out.

My pulse kicks up, and I fight down the rising fear. I have to make sure no one's hiding in the enormous claw-foot tub. Or inside the linen closet. In the corner behind the door.

I catch sight of myself in the room's mirror and cringe. I look more like Marcos should have dropped me off at the nearest homeless shelter than here at a super-luxurious hotel. The fear burns in my eyes.

"What are you doing?" I ask my reflection. "Here you're looking for a burglar, and you're scaring yourself with one crummy scenario after the other. What sane woman would do that to herself?"

No answer.

So I give the answer business a whirl. "Then again, who ever said I was sane?"

Yep, folks. I've really gone off the deep end. Now I'm asking myself questions. And I'm even answering.

I turn on the bathroom light and sigh in relief. Although there are potential hiding places here, the room's empty. So, unwilling to spend another moment in my grody garments, I strip, turn on the hot water, and spend the next half hour scrubbing. I soap up. Twice. Three times.

By the time I've shampooed yet another time, I feel ready to consider sleep. My skin tingles from all the friction, but at least I know I no longer stink. A thick slick of body lotion plus clean pajamas later, and I'm ready to crash.

What a day. It's time to call it a night.

I crawl under the blankets, Bible in hand. But I can't concentrate on reading, not even God's Word. So I close the leather cover and call out to the Lord.

After my "amen," I turn off the light and hunker down to sleep. The minute I close my eyes, a thought strikes. Did I lock the door when I came into the room? Not the automatically latching lock, but the bolt and even the little chain thingies.

Probably. It's not something I'd be likely to forget.

And I'm so tired.

Of course I locked the door.

But the more I try to tell myself I locked up, the more uncertain I become. Finally, with a groan, I jump out of bed and hurry to the door. Sure enough, the latch is bolted and the chain's in place.

I can sleep in peace.

Back in bed, I snuggle under the crisp, clean sheets. Ah . . .

The windows. I know they're not wide open, but did I ever throw that lock? Before dinner. I didn't even check when I got back. I saw them closed and left it at that.

"Come on, Andie. Of course you locked up before you went to dinner. You don't ever forget to do something like that."

Again, I grow more anxious the more I try to tell myself to go to sleep. "Aaaargh!"

I drag myself out of bed again, then head to the windows. This time, my heart leaps to my throat. I hadn't locked the doors. I take the time to make sure both of the ones in the bedroom are latched, and then I head to the bathroom. That door is locked.

The lecture I give myself goes a ways toward calming me. Maybe now I'll go to sleep. So I try again.

Riiing, riiing!

The cell phone. Who would be calling at this hour?

I sigh and fumble in the dark. "Hello?"

"Are you ready to admit I was right?" Max says, barely leashed anger in his tight voice.

Lord? Do I really need this? Now? "Hi, Max. How's your evening going? Lovely, I hope. Mine was interesting, but I chalk it up as part of the experience of foreign travel. At least I've gotten my fair share of crime while abroad out of the way. Everything is hunky-dory now."

"Your fair share!" The leash on his anger has just loosened. "Murders in Asia and purse-snatching in South America? That's enough for a whole continent's worth of travelers. Of course, you need a babysitter. So don't you argue with me. I'm coming."

The memory of my encounter with the petty thief in that back alley rushes at me with the oomph of a runaway rhino. Maybe I do need help. Just not from a heavy-handed, over-bearing, testosterone-poisoned babysitter.

"Don't you dare, Max Matthews. You stay where you are, and I'll stay where I am. With God's help, I'll handle anything that comes my way."

"Faith is one thing, Andie. Bullheaded stubbornness is another."

"I'm not bullheaded."

"Yes, you are."

"Am not."

"Quit the grade-school routine. I care about you and don't want to get a body bag back at the end of your trip."

His graphic comment gives me a moment's pause. I pray. Then, "Max, I appreciate your concern, but I've already set things in motion to get my passport replaced. I contacted Miss Mona about the network's credit card right away—as you too obviously know, and I'm going to negotiate the emerald buy tomorrow. By the time you make arrangements to get down here, I'll be back in Louisville."

"Just keep your room door locked. I'll be there before you know it."

"Are you deaf—"

Before I can finish my question, he's hung up. Fine. He can visit Colombia. By the time he gets here, since you can hardly book a transcontinental flight for the next morning, I'll be home.

It'll serve him right. Arrogant male . . .

And I've been entertaining the thought of a relationship with *him*? How can I be so . . . so . . . I don't know. But I know I'm going to have to think long and hard about it. I mean, can I live long term with that kind of pressure? Not being able to go anywhere without having my competence questioned?

I don't think so.

My heart sinks.

Then, as I consider the ramifications, another, totally un-connected thought hits. Did I make sure I locked the doors *after* I checked them? I opened them all to see if they were locked or unlocked, but did I make sure I locked up again? I'm so discombobulated, I *can't* be sure. How'm I going to sleep if I don't make sure?

"Oh, help me, Lord!" At the rate I'm going, I'm going to need treatment for obsessive-compulsive disorder. I can certainly understand what those poor sufferers go through on a regular basis.

I punch my pillow into a more comfortable shape, pray for all the folks afflicted with OCD issues, and finally find it possible to relax. Amazing how this faith thing works. You throw your problems to the Lord, focus on those less for-tunate than you, pray for them, and your own troubles fade in comparison.

"Thank you, Father," I murmur, and then, trusting, I close my eyes.

At ten the next morning, a couple of hours later than I'd initially planned, and after I've bought a new purse, posed for a passport photo, checked in with the police, and fielded three calls from Aunt Weeby and two from Miss Mona, Mr. Cruz comes by in a beefy-looking SUV. Before we take off, however, he has me pose in front of the vehicle, and I smile, thinking his a nice gesture for a tourist.

When I thank him, he blushes under his dark tan. "So sorry, Miss Andrea. The photo is for identification purposes. Our guerilla problems are better than they've been at times, but kidnapping is still a very real occurrence in Colombia."

Great. He had to go and tell me. I try to put the whole scary possibility out of my mind as we head out toward Mr. Cruz's camp in the Muzo emerald-producing region.

When we reach the outskirts of the capital, the vendor-turned-travel guide warns me we might be stopped at various checkpoints, the government's effort to cut down on criminal activity on the roads in and out of the mining regions.

I snort. "I'm an expert at checkpoints." He looks surprised. I go on. "Colombian ones can't be any worse than Burmese or Kashmiri ones."

Before long, I doze off—I didn't sleep well even after all the checking and rechecking of doors I did. When I wake up again, I notice the drizzle that's started up as we've climbed higher into the Andes Mountains.

"How far is the Muzo region from Bogotá?" I ask.

"Oh, about seven or eight hours' drive."

My groan escapes me before I can shut it off.

Mr. Cruz laughs.

We climb up from the capital to the Andean range. According to Mr. Cruz, we'll go up to about twelve thousand feet above sea level. We've now reached a barren landscape, covered by a blanket of clouds that shrouds the more luxuriant, green valleys below us. The damp cold penetrates the car, and I fight constant shivers.

The stillness around us feels quietly mysterious.

Neither the long drive nor the silence outside inspires conversation, so we bump along the rough road in a deep silence. Finally, as dusk approaches, we begin to descend into the jungle-covered Muzo region. On the peaks, the clouds had surrounded us with a whitish paleness. Now, I get a sense of sinking into the depths of darkness, the unknown. When I realize what a dangerous trip my imagination is taking, I give myself a mental shake.

Get a grip. You're about to see emeralds like few ever see.

But, hey. It's really weird out here in the wilds of Colombia. The last five or six miles of our approach to the mining camp at Muzo prove impossibly steep, and our SUV creeps along through thick mist, the leftovers of the earlier drizzle.

Then I see ahead of us three buildings of rough, cement block construction with Tin-Man hat roofs. Since Mr. Cruz aims right for them, I can safely assume they're his camp. As he slows down the SUV, a handful of camp workers come out from different directions to greet us. They chatter with Mr. Cruz, then lead us to the medium-sized structure, which turns out to be the kitchen. As soon as I step inside, I'm offered a cup of amazing, fragrant coffee and a pair of *arepas* with butter.

Yum!

I take my snack to a table next to a dingy window, and as I sip, I study the landscape outside.

97

Perched on a steep slope, the rest of the camp seems carved right out of the hillside. Underlining the buildings, a road disappears up toward the peak and into more clouds. From where I'm sitting, the whole mountain appears cobbled out of little more than jagged rock covered with ragged patches of vegetation, deep, rich green decorations for the stark, black outcroppings. According to what Mr. Cruz told me on the road, because of the misty cloud-and-steam cover, I won't be able to see down to the actual mines until the fog clears, hopefully when the sun burns it all away in the morning.

Sitting here, sipping hot coffee, less than a frog's hop away from the legendary Muzo mines, the source of the world's most amazing emeralds, the horrors of the night before pale in importance. A riff of excitement plays through me. Just to think of how close I am to the emeralds makes me wonder if I might be just a night's dream away from finding a treasure.

In spite of how tired I am, I begin to relax. "Thank you, Father."

7⁄00

In the morning, I dress quickly and leave the relative privacy of my quarters in the bunkhouse-like dorm building. Fortunately for me, I was escorted to a small room with a narrow single bed and small chest of drawers when I arrived. I didn't have to sleep in the large room with multiple beds. From everything I saw last night, I'm the only woman at the camp.

The scent of fresh-brewed coffee greets me when I open the door to the kitchen building. Rich, potent, heady, and oh so welcome. But by the time I reach the large pot, I get a whiff of a different undercurrent. There's chocolate in one of them thar pots!

As I stand, sniff, and scout for food, the cook—a short, wiry man in a greasy apron—comes out, chatters in fiery Spanish, shoves a plate and mug at me, then smiles and returns to his fragrant domain.

In the center of my plate is a mound of fluffy golden scrambled eggs. To a side is a big, steamy *arepa*, butter dripping from between its sliced halves, a small mound of rice, and two oval, golden-brown potatoes. On the other side, forming a luscious food triangle, are slices of—I think, I hope—ripe, juicy mango. In my other hand, I clutch a massive mug of creamy hot cocoa.

I hurry over to the same table where I sat last night and glance out the window. A dark Jeep pulls to a stop fifty yards from the kitchen building. The same miners who greeted us when we got here hurry out from a multitude of directions to check on the newest arrivals at the camp. The misty *neblina*, as the men call the ever-present blanket of fog, is negligible already, and I hope what's left will disappear as the sun heats up.

Right now my breakfast is calling my name. I sit, pray, and dig into the eggs. "Mmm . . ."

"I see you managed to stay out of trouble since last night," Max says as I take a sip of cocoa.

Shock makes me spray it back out. I choke. Cough. Sputter.

The rat slaps my back in a—fake, I think—helpful gesture.

"Wha . . . what are you doing here?" I stammer once I can breathe again.

Max leans a hip against the corner of the table, then sticks his hands in his pants pockets. "I told you I was coming."

"But you couldn't have bought a ticket, flown into Bogotá, then driven here after you talked to me."

He shrugs. "Nobody says I did. I called you when I landed at the El Dorado airport."

He'd stunned me by just showing up. Now? Well, now he's just made me plain old mad. "So you'd already made up your mind. No matter what, you were going to discount everything I'd said to you and come do your Neanderthal thing."

100

He crosses his arms. "No Neanderthal here. Just someone concerned for someone else's well-being."

"If I hear you say the word 'concerned' again, I'm going to . . . going to . . . oh, I don't know what I'll do, but I'll do something. And you won't like it. I promise."

Mr. Magnificent has the gall to laugh. "I think you need your coffee. No matter how delicious that cocoa might be, it's not your fuel of choice."

You can be sure Marcos Rivera would never treat me like a slightly stupid child. "Oh, go eat."

Max strides off laughing, and I return to my now cold breakfast. As I watch him, I work overtime to convince myself I'm really and truly mad at him. But I fail.

Okay, sure. His lack of trust in me burns. But somewhere deep in my heart I'm glad Max is here. Not only does he have that hyper-awareness effect on me, but he also brings a sense of familiarity along with him. I find that bit of comfort dangerously welcome.

I plunk an elbow on the table, then drop my chin into the palm of my hand. I don't want to come to depend on him. If I do, and things don't work out between us, then when he takes off, I'll be left with a gaping hole, not just in my heart, but also in my life, and worse yet, my confidence.

Max comes back, a heaping plate in hand, and pulls out a chair across from me. In spite of my irritation, my heart gives a little leap at his nearness.

Oh boy. Do I have it bad or what?

But I don't want him to figure it out. Not how much his appeal affects me. So I decide to ignore him. As far as he's concerned, you understand. There's no way I can ignore Max Matthews. No way. No matter what.

"Got something going with your breakfast?" he asks after he puts a mountainous plate across from me, and two cups of coffee between us. I grab one and gulp down a scalding shot of the deep, dark stuff.

He goes on. "You were staring at those eggs as though they might give you the answers to the universe's mysteries."

I shovel in a bite of cold eggs to avoid answering. Out of the corner of my eye, I see his smile and arched brow. What's a girl to do when a guy like Max knows her too well?

This girl finishes her now less-than-appetizing breakfast, grateful for the oomph provided by the excellent Colombian coffee bean. I sip and stare out the window. Anything to keep from looking at the blond hunk with me.

After a while, he sets down his coffee mug and pushes back his chair, but instead of standing, he stares at me, questions in his blue eyes. Finally, when he does talk, he goes the unexpected route.

"What's the plan for today?"

I'd fully thought he'd get into my irritation or my short-sightedness in coming to Colombia alone. But I gotta give the guy credit for his understanding. I'd rather talk about emeralds any day. Especially today.

"Mr. Cruz is going to show me the stones he's willing to offer us. And, if it's possible, he's going to get me to the mine site. I suppose I have to tell him you'll be tagging along. He'll have to take you into account."

Max tips his head to the side. "He knows I'm here."

They'd all conspired against me. Max, Miss Mona, and Aunt Weeby. None of them had trusted me. They'd gone behind my back and manipulated my situation as though I were an incompetent boob. And now I'm stuck with the

California surfer-boy gem-dunce for as long as I stay in Colombia.

Hah! Who am I kidding? I'm stuck with Mr. Magnificent even after I go home. He's everywhere, he's everywhere. I roll my eyes.

So how am I going to handle this? Lord?

I sigh. I'm not the one who's going to handle this. I'm going to have to trust God and simply obey. Not just in the "biggies," like the ten whopper-sized ones, but also in the little things, the so-called gray areas that aren't so gray to God, but hide deep inside us. The first one is to set aside my pride.

Which, in my case, I guess isn't so little after all.

I have to accept that Max is here, overprotective as can be. "Well, since Mr. Cruz knows, then I guess he's expecting you this morning. We're going to the negotiating table—but I do warn you, Max. Don't stick your nose into the haggling. You don't have your GIA certificate, and you sure haven't seen anywhere near enough emeralds to know what you're doing."

He looks as though he's about to argue, but then he makes a grimace that I read as acceptance. "Fine. I don't question your competence, not when it comes to gemstones. Just think of me as the brawn to your beauty and brains."

"Don't even go there. No amount of buttering up is going to make up for your lack of trust. And your sneaky arrogance."

"Are Miss Mona and Aunt Weeby sneaky and arrogant?"

"They're just plain sneaky."

He slaps his hands on the table. "Tell you what. I'm not going to go over this anymore. It's moot. I'm here, and I'm going to make the best of it. I suggest you do the same."

"I thought I just did when I told you we were going to the mine. It's not as if I tried to sneak away, and I'm not going to try and ditch you before I take off." I glance at my watch. "Be ready in forty-five minutes. That's when Mr. Cruz arranged to meet me."

"Where?"

"Out front here. In the parking lot."

"I'll be there."

And he is. As am I. Moments after Max and I meet, Mr. Cruz arrives.

"*Buenos diás*," our host says. "I hope you slept well, Miss Andrea."

"I was exhausted. And the silence out here is incredible. Very peaceful. It was the best night's sleep I've had in a long time."

He smiles. "My country has worked very hard to eliminate the war that raged years ago. It allows us to explore new veins in relative peace."

I know more than I ever wanted to know about run-of-the-mill bandits. "Any new strikes here?"

Mr. Cruz gestures us into his SUV. "We're working some white calcite veins in the shale rock, but we haven't hit a new strike yet. The old veins are still producing, even though not as much as two years ago."

"Any albite in the new veins?" Albite is usually a strong indicator of emerald material.

He looks at me with a touch of admiration. "Not yet. But we're sure we'll find emerald."

The SUV roars to life, but before we pull out of the parking area, the cook runs toward us, three lunch pails in his hand. He and Mr. Cruz chat for a moment, Mr. Cruz passes the pails to me, I place them in the large, ice-filled cooler in the rear, and we leave the camp.

"We won't have to return for lunch this way," our host says. "The road down is long and very steep, and it would take more time than I think you want to spend in a car. The food is not fancy, but it should be good."

"I don't need fancy," I say. "I'm thrilled about the opportunity to see the mining operation, as well as the stones you mentioned."

"As you will." He handles the SUV with the ease of a man used to doing this on a regular basis, even though the terrain is fast getting scary.

"Thank you, Jesus, for his expertise," I whisper.

We eventually approach a chewed-up looking part of the mountain, where the black carbonaceous shale has been removed in the fervent search for green gold. As we come closer, I hear the rumble of heavy machinery. Soon, I see a bulldozer take another bite of rocky mountainside. By now, the sun has done its thing, and the *neblina* has burned away.

Mr. Cruz parks. Two miners come out from yet another cinder block and tin building. The men speak, and I wish I'd retained a whole lot more of that vanished Spanish.

I walk to their side. "Could you ask them if they've found any more indicators in that new vein?"

Our host turns to the miners, asks, and then listens to their responses. He wears a broad smile when he faces me again. "Emilio says the best indicator of emerald is emerald. And the new vein hasn't yielded yet. But we do have excellent product. You'll see."

I chuckle. Emilio is totally right on, and probably knows

better than the best geologist what's what in the mountain of rock. "I can't wait to see the stones."

"Before we go," Mr. Cruz says, "do you mind getting a bit dirty? He suggested I show you a few interesting spots."

At my side, Max laughs. "She doesn't mind any amount of dirt if she can look at rocks."

"Excellent!" Mr. Cruz gives me an admiring look. "Smart woman, Miss Andrea. Very smart."

I slant a glance at Max, and realize he's grinning from ear to ear. Is he making fun of me or is he agreeing with the Colombian?

But as Mr. Cruz heads toward the far end of the cleared slope, I realize this isn't the time to worry about Max's reaction. Not if I want to see whatever the gemstone vendor wants me to see. I hurry after our host.

Ten minutes later, after we've scaled a nearly perpendicular path up the wall of rock, Mr. Cruz points toward a shale ledge on the mountain. A few hardy, stray vines have clung to their spot, and we use them to help us approach the ledge. When I'm close enough to see anything more than the rocky shape, I notice it's been worked in the past.

"Are you digging here?" I ask Mr. Cruz, surprised by how inaccessible it still is.

"No, not really. Most likely, a local *campesino*—a farmer—has probably brought his pick and done a bit of looking on his own. We can run the best mine operation in the world, but sometimes these folks are the ones who are most successful at finding new emerald veins."

"That makes sense." I glance back down the way we came. Getting down's going to mean I can't look—the flat starting point is farther down than I thought. I squirm as a drop of sweat works its way down the middle of my back. Since we left the camp, the bright sun has warmed up the air, and by now, the jungle is becoming steamy.

Oh yeah. It's hot. By the time we get down from our mountain goat impersonation, I'm back to extreme "dewing." I swipe the worst of the sweat from my forehead with the back of my hand and give a longing thought to that marvelous invention, central air-conditioning.

Our lunches are cold, though, thanks to the cooler in the back of Mr. Cruz's SUV, and my can of icy-cold Coke tastes better than any I've had before. Once I'm done with my rice, meat, potatoes, and *arepa*, I dart a look at the single structure here at the mine site. The promise of emeralds is proving a powerful lure.

Not so much for the males. They're discussing, of all things, the PGA. Golf? Out in the Colombian jungle? Only Max. And another man. Show me gems.

Finally, Mr. Cruz gestures toward the building. "We should go to my office now. I'm sure you want to see the emeralds."

"Finally!" The word is out before I can stifle it, and both Max and Mr. Cruz laugh as we head inside. Unfortunately, the heat goes with us. On the upside, I notice the large fan in the office window the moment I walk in.

I also spot the four-foot-square iron safe behind the desk. My heart speeds up at the thought of beautiful green bling. I catch my bottom lip between my teeth and watch our host twirl the safe's lock.

First, Mr. Cruz withdraws a small plastic bag. "Miss Mona told me the network has recently contracted with a jewelry manufacturer," he says. "You're now making the pieces you offer in the shows. She said you'll be wanting small stones for cluster settings."

He opens the bag, and then turns out its contents onto a white velvet square. The small stones tumble out, ranging from one millimeter to three millimeters in size. I draw in a deep breath at the sheer beauty of their color and clarity.

Once I've chosen a sizable lot of stones for future rings and pendants, we move on to the large loose pieces. And that's when a girl wonders if diamonds really are her best friends. The spectacular near perfection of Mr. Cruz's inventory has my head reeling in no time. I start to pick out the best stones, buying pieces that range in price from $100 per carat to one magnificent, crown jewel–worthy emerald on which Miss Mona authorizes me to spend, get this, $30,000 per carat. I feel faint.

At my side, Max sucks in a sharp breath when he hears Miss Mona's okay. But, true to his word, he stays otherwise out of my negotiations. By the time I've racked up a solid, seven-figure buy, I hear the even rhythm of a heavy jungle rain start up against the tin roof.

"Oh no!" I cry. "And we're still here."

The road out of the jungle didn't strike me as the kind that might be the least forgiving of a vehicle's wheels in the rain. I'm not looking forward to skidding down an Andean foothill, my pockets stuffed with a king's ransom in green gems.

"Ah . . ." Mr. Cruz says, a twinkle in his eyes. "But the rain is as good as it is bad for us."

The man might sell the world's most amazing emeralds, but I think he's got a loose screw. "Oh, really? How's that?"

"You know the Itoco River's close to us, don't you?"

I nod.

"Well, Miss Andrea, rain runs into the river and takes with it emeralds that wash from the matrix that's thrown away at the official mines. Our *guaqueros*, the men we call 'diggers for treasure,' pick up these stones."

"Hmm . . . wouldn't that be stealing? I thought the government controls who can mine. Does the government give permits to these *gua . . . guaqueros*?"

"*Ciertamente*, the government controls mining. When we entered the Muzo region yesterday, I'm sure you saw the fences and the checkpoint."

"Trust me. I could never miss an armed guard."

Max coughs—I don't buy. He's hiding a chuckle.

Mr. Cruz flat out laughs. "Of course, we're a licensed operation, with paid miners. The *guaqueros* carry on what we call 'unofficial' mining. Those of us who pay a fee to run a legitimate mine have made an agreement with the government to permit the local *guaqueros* to work the mine tailings in the river."

"They're gleaners then."

"Gleaners?" Mr. Cruz asks.

"Yes. Poor people who gather whatever's left on a farm field after the main harvest is over."

"Oh, I like that word. Our *guaqueros* are just that, gleaners. Letting them do this helps keep our region of the country at peace." He gives a small shrug. "Whatever they find, they can sell at the river, in the town of Muzo or in Chiquinquirá—another town some hours away. Some even travel to the market in Bogotá."

"That does make a strange kind of sense," I say. "But the government really has no problem with the lack of control over those stones? I can't imagine they can charge a tax on that money."

"It's a trade. Less tax for some peace. And it gets confusing to try and follow them. Some stones sell over and over, at least once in each one of all those places, so following the money is almost impossible."

When the deluge slows, we get in the SUV and start back to the main camp. I pray all the way up the narrow, slippery road—if you really want to call the glorified path chopped out of the mountain rock a road.

After brief goodbyes to the men, I head to my room. I need a shower before I can think of eating. Forty-five minutes later, I'm in clean clothes, with my scraps of hair dripping random drops onto my forehead and neck. After the success of the day's buy, I'm pretty pleased, and head for the kitchen building. There, I find Max, who'd obviously been waiting for me.

"Did I abide by your rules, Madame Wheeler-Dealer?"

"Can't object."

"So can we return to our truce?"

"I suppose."

"Will you allow me to break bread with you?"

"I just said we can redo the truce. I don't imagine you're going to sit with the miners who don't speak a word of English. That is, unless you speak Spanish too."

"I do speak some Spanish, but not enough to carry on a conversation with the locals. Besides, I'd much rather share a meal with you than with a pack of grubby males."

I squash the chuckle that threatens, then head to the open window of the kitchen proper. There, the cook hands me what I'd call a platter, but when I look around, I realize this is what they use around here as individual dinner plates.

And what a dinner it is! My stomach rumbles, and I murmur my delight as Mr. Cruz joins us.

"This is amazing," Max says, holding a matching platter.

"It's what we call a *bandeja paisa*," Mr. Cruz says as he reaches for his own meal. "A traditional Colombian dinner. Very good, but not good for dieters."

A quick study tells me the cook likes to fry. Besides the rice, beans, and *arepa*, there's a fried egg, fried plantain slices, what looks like fried pork crackling with a good-sized chunk of meat still attached, and while it's not fried, a glistening sausage of some native kind.

"It smells wonderful," I say, refusing to think where exactly on my hips each individual item of food will lodge.

We have a pleasant meal, and before long, it's time to head to bed. The generator only runs until nine at night. After I check on the gems I've squirreled away, I pray, and crawl into my narrow bed. I fall asleep to the song of the rain on the metal roof.

◆

In the morning, after another breakfast of eggs, potatoes, rice, *arepa*, and excellent coffee, we load up our belongings into the SUV and start back to the capital. This time, we'll be going by another route, one Mr. Cruz says his mine manager insists will cut an hour off our total travel time. The vendor is staying behind, since he's expecting another buyer's visit, so one of his men takes the wheel.

Loaded with our lunch pails, we start out, this time on a road as narrow and scary as the one we took down to the mine workings. For hours, we climb straight up into the Andes peaks, and my ears feel awful from the pressure. When we

111

reach the *páramo*, a highland region at the top of the Andean altitudes, we see the clouds around us again, and on the side of the road, a truly unique span of vegetation.

I point. "Oh, Max! Look at those golden grasses. They're so tall and wild and exotic. I guess it's what writers mean when they use the word 'desolate.'"

"It is different out here, isn't it? I find the shrubs and the twisted trees even more interesting than the grasses. Grab your camera. I don't think you're going to be hitting the Andes again anytime soon."

"Do you blame those poor trees?" I snap a couple of photos. "I can't imagine trying to grow out of rock in the middle of clouds. How much sun can they get? That's probably why they twist and turn."

"I'm no botanist, but I figure that's about the size of it. No matter what, it's not very welcoming."

I shudder. "We won't get to Bogotá soon enough for me."

Just as I say those words, we go around a tight curve. I hold my breath, sure we're about to plunge into the cloud-shrouded valley below, but we don't. As I let out my breath, however, I spot trouble up ahead.

Yeah, it's me here. Calamity Jane in Colombia.

You didn't really think I was going to get out of the country that easy, did you?

Up ahead, a clunker-junker of a truck, with three different colors of paint smeared across three different areas and enough dents to give it a well-chewed appearance, sits diagonally across the road, blocking all access. Facing us are three men; each one cradles a machine gun.

"I can't believe this," I whisper.

Max reaches out and takes my hand. "Just pray."

8:00

You know Murphy of the famous law? He's got nothing on me.

The bandits with the hokey handkerchiefs over their mugs swarm the SUV. They proceed to dump the driver into a patch of tall grasses, waving their guns all over the place. When the man doesn't stand back up, I pray he's only unconscious.

My heart pounds and my stomach churns. Max hangs on to my hand the whole time. And I pray—keep on praying, actually. Non-stop.

Then, as Max and I continue to shake in the backseat of the vehicle, the bandits yank open both our doors. I feel like I'm going to throw up. But I don't have the luxury. The brutes drag Max and me out of the questionable safety of the SUV, and we stand at the roadside, wondering what will happen next.

We don't have to wonder long.

As we watch the creeps ransack my new purse—*with* the cell phone in it, which, by the way, they don't give back—I hear an engine approach. I let my tension ease, happy for the possibility of help, or at the very least, a distraction. Not that I'm crazy enough to think we can overpower three thugs with machine guns.

A navy blue SUV comes around the curve we'd just conquered, and I catch sight of a face that tickles my memory, but I can't quite place. Strange, since I don't know anyone here in Colombia.

I try to catch Max's attention. "Pssst!"

"This is no time for a chat."

"I don't want to chat. I want to survive."

Then I hear voices raised in argument, a real one, not like Max's and my minor spat, in the vicinity of the blue SUV. When I look in that direction, I see the kerchiefed goon drag that driver out too. The guy seems to have only one technique; everyone gets treated like trash. And then I recognize the man in the goon's clutches. It's the uniformed guard I'd met at the embassy the night my first purse was taken.

Hmm. . . coincidence? Don't think so.

Out the side of my mouth, I whisper, "Looks like the cavalry has arrived."

"Huh?"

"The guy who just got here. He's a guard at the embassy. I saw him there the other night. Maybe they sent him to help us—"

I stop. He wasn't on his way to help. My anger grows into rage. "They put a nanny on my tail! The embassy had him follow me. How else would he know to be here?"

"Easy, Andie. You were the victim of a crime. You went to them to report it and get a new passport. What did you want them to do?"

"Get me the new passport. Not shadow me around the country."

Two of the gunmen dive into Mr. Cruz's SUV, then emerge with Max's and my suitcases. Swell. First the purse, now this. Don't you just love international travel?

"Come on, Andie. You really think the embassy's likely to let a high-profile American TV personality roam alone around one of the most violent countries in the hemisphere *after* she's mugged?"

"High-profile? I'm not Simon Cowell or Barney the Dinosaur under my makeup, for goodness' sake."

He snorts.

The embassy guard lets out an agonized grunt and collapses to the ground. The creep who obviously knocked him out kicks the motionless man's shoulder.

"No!" I cry before I can stop myself.

Max slaps his palm over my mouth.

A goon takes aim at my head.

I collapse back against Max, thankful for his warm, solid support. "This wasn't a gig I wanted. I knew better than to come to Colombia. I told Miss Mona this was a lousy idea. I'm tearing up my passport when I get back home."

A glance up at his face reveals anger and frustration in his blue gaze, lips clamped tight, jaw squared and iron-hard. His stare hasn't left the bandit, even at my dopey attempt to ease the terrible tension. His arms slowly wrap around me, draw me close, and then slowly begin to ease me behind his bulk.

The thought of what he's contemplating sends a chill right through my veins. That I can read him like this is something I'll have to think about later. Right now? Now, I'm scared. For him.

"No, Max. Don't. Please don't put yourself in any more danger. I should never have been here in the first place, and right now, I wish more than ever that you hadn't come. I—I couldn't stand it if anything happened to you because of me."

"*Ey!*" one of the bandits bellows. He then rattles off a truckload of words, and I do catch "*silencio*"—silence—within the flow. Then he jabs the machine gun in the direction of the truck blocking the road.

"*Vamos! Al camión.*"

Max nudges me gently from behind. "Looks like he wants us to head on over there."

"But that poor guard . . ." I look at the man lying in a patch of golden grasses on the shoulder. The sense of helplessness is almost more than I can bear.

"There's nothing you can do for him right now. Let's go before they help us to the same fate as our driver and the embassy guard."

I shudder on my way to the truck. When we reach the vehicle, one of our captors points to the open tailgate—with his gun, of course. I look at Max.

He shrugs, then holds out his hand.

"Are you kidding?" I take another look inside the truck's open cargo bed and quit counting after I get to twelve huge black bags. I don't need super-duper-X-ray-vision powers. Get this: from the scent of it all, they're full of trash. "It stinks up there."

"It stinks up there, but there's a machine gun down here. Which would you prefer? The choice is pretty clear to me."

"Put that way . . ." I roll my eyes, brace myself, grab his hand, and clamber up into the putrid truck.

He follows.

116

Another whiff, and I turn my eyes skyward. *What's up with another dose of Colombian trash, Lord?*

The minute Max is seated next to me, our backs—you got it—against squishy trash bags, the goon with the gun slams the tailgate shut, yells to his pals, and one of them cranks up the noisy engine. The contingent of crooks piles into the cab, one jabs the barrel of his gun out the open rear cab window—aimed right at us—and the vehicle starts to roll.

I look at Max. "Do you really think they're going to get this great big honking piece of ugly junk—"

A yell breaks over the rattletrap's ruckus. When I crane my neck to peer over the side, I see the embassy guard rise to his feet, rocky, teetering, but with a determined look on his face. He takes a step toward the truck, then another.

A shot rings out.

The guard falls to the ground, hands clutching his leg where blood blooms across his thigh.

"Stop!" I yell.

Max again slaps a hand over my mouth.

The rank rattletrap rolls away. Sobs rip through me. Every inch of me wants to jump out, run over, and see to the man who came and tried to help me, but the gun aimed at us holds me back. My frustration and misery grow with every roll of the tires beneath us.

As our new chariot rattles on down the twisty, fog-frosted road, I lean on Max's shoulder and pray. What else can I do? I trust the Lord.

❖

Several hours later, the crummy vehicle slows down. I blink awake, and notice we're far from the Andean highlands

117

where our captors ambushed us. The sky burns a bright blue, the sun overhead beats down, and the trash exuds the pure essence of putrefaction.

I gag.

"How can you stand it?" I ask Max when I think I can talk without humiliating myself.

"Who says I can?"

"I don't see any green around your gills. I'm sure if you look, you'll notice that verdant hue all over me."

He shrugs. "You get used to it."

"How? I've been here just as long as you, and I'm about to lose it—literally."

Alarm widens his blue eyes. "Please don't. I think we've arrived wherever they've been taking us."

I again peer over the side. This time, from my vantage point, all I see is a patchwork of green and gold flatlands and the dusty road we've traveled. "Who knows where it is they've zipped us to. All I know is I'm ready to ditch this odoriferous form of transportation—too much luxe and glam. Know what I mean?"

"Too well," he says, his voice, in comparison to mine, tight and serious.

The truck coughs to a stop. Against the wishes of my stiff joints and cramped muscles, I scramble up. A sweeping look around tells me we're far from Bogotá, far from the Muzo mining region, far from everything but a sprawling *hacienda*. The ranch house, a white stucco structure, wears an age-softened red-tile roof. Wide windows set at even intervals are covered with graceful, wrought iron grilles whose beautiful floral patterns do nothing to diminish their true protective purpose. The wide wraparound porch is shaded, and wood-

and-rattan rockers are arranged in comfy groups around a couple of small wooden tables. A knock-your-socks-off pair of carved mahogany doors sweep open as I stare.

A woman in a pink uniform and white apron runs out, chattering in rapid-fire Spanish. But when she gets within fifteen feet of the truck, she slams on the brakes. Her nose twitches, wrinkles. She turns her face to a side.

"Pee-yuuu!"

"My thoughts exactly," I murmur.

The driver and his pals spill out of the truck's cab, their response to her chatter defensive and loud. It's good to see she's not buying any of it. A kindred spirit on the subject of refuse might be an ally. And we need all the allies we can get.

She resumes her tirade, and then, to my surprise, smacks the driver on the shoulder, points at the truck, and yells some more.

One of the goons trots over to our high-class hot-wheels, then drops the tailgate. He waves at us, and we hop down. I'm only too glad to get away from the stench.

From the way the uniformed woman bellows at the men, I begin to hope our ordeal might be coming to an end. But then, when she comes to our side and points toward the house, one of the goons closes in on Max's side, his machine gun at the ready. I sigh. Not over yet.

Inside the house, I again experience the welcome change in temperature, thanks to the eighteen-inch-thick walls. And while I'd love to take the time to check out the too-cool antique colonial furniture and the fortune's worth of art pieces, our escorts make it plain we have places to go, people to see. They hustle us down a corridor flanking a magnificent

119

red-tile-floored courtyard filled with a handful of trees in huge clay tubs, masses of red geraniums in painted pots, and black-painted iron furniture cushioned in hibiscus-patterned fabric. The air of old-money gentility crashes head-on against the reality of the gun aimed at us.

It's more than obvious that the goons, and now the woman I suspect is the housekeeper, are doing a take-me-to-your-leader. I'm not sure I want to go there. On the one hand, I want the ordeal to be over; I want to know what these people want with us. On the other hand, I'm afraid once I do know what they want, they'll be ready to dispose of us. If you know what I mean.

I'm into recycling, not disposables. I'm not ready to wind up in a dump, next to diapers and empty food containers.

At the end of the corridor, we reach another of those amazing carved mahogany doors. The woman opens it and gestures us inside. The machine gun–toting goon does not follow.

Once my eyes adjust to the dimmer light, I see an elegant office, its walls lined with bookshelves up to the ceiling. At the matching pair of windows on the far wall hang lush velvet draperies, unexpected in this remote country location. Underfoot, a large oriental rug cushions my steps in red, blue, cream, and black luxury. A broad wooden desk dominates the center of the room.

I blink. Then I blink again.

Am I seeing things?

There, in the tall executive-style leather armchair behind the desk, sits an older *woman* of stunning beauty. Her sleek silver hair is woven into a braided coronet high on the crown of her head. Creamy skin is unmarked by wrinkles and enhanced by the lightest touch of expertly applied makeup. Large brown eyes are focused on us, while red-glossed lips remain neutral.

A welcoming smile would be nice. Especially since I'd expected a slimy weasel at the end of our not-so-excellent adventure.

But she makes it way clear this isn't time to play nice, *capisce*?

"So you are Andrea," our hostess says in a Spanish-accented alto voice. She stands, staring at me as though through a microscope.

Her height surprises me; most Colombians I've seen so far tend toward the shorter end of the spectrum. She looks me eye to eye, and I stand at five foot ten.

"You've gone to a whole lot of trouble to meet me," I say. "Would you mind telling me why all this drama was necessary?"

"I expected something different," she says, ignoring my question, her gaze still glued to moi. "I don't know why, but I thought you'd be smaller, more girlish."

Huh? I've just been insulted. I think.

Max snickers.

I glare.

Before I can say anything else, the woman steps out from behind the desk, and I get a load of her glamorous duds. The coffee-colored silk blouse is tailored to perfection. It follows her Sophia Loren curves as though it were the country's signature beverage poured over her. Straight brown trousers are smooth and unwrinkled, even though she'd been sitting. During the years I lived in the Big Apple, I came to know that's the mark of perfect construction in exquisite fabric.

Somewhere I'm sure there's a matching jacket to those pants, and the whole ensemble has to have set her back a good thousand bucks or more.

Never mind the to-die-for brown-leather-with-stacked-wooden-heel Christian Louboutin pumps, perfect down to their trademark red soles.

As I stare, she hikes a hip on the corner of her desk and crosses her arms. No one with eyes can miss the massive emerald ring on her right hand. From where I'm standing, I figure it's got to clock in at around thirty-five to forty carats. And unless I'm much mistaken, the diamond-dusted setting is platinum.

Her chuckle hits me the wrong way.

"I don't carry a weapon," she says.

"That hadn't crossed my mind," I answer, which says a lot about me, none of it good. Plant me in front of glitz and glamour and my common sense jumps ship. It's best to keep her guessing.

She arches a brow. "And your partner is as handsome as the camera presents him."

Max mutters something under his breath.

I notice the blush on his cheeks. My chuckle slips out. "So you've seen our show."

Never taking her gaze from my face, she picks up a television remote control gizmo and clicks on the flat-screen set on a console next to the door.

To my amazement, a video recording of Max and me pops up. Figures. We're arguing, this time over the merits or lack thereof in heat-treating quartz to obtain the delicate prasiolites better known as green amethyst.

"I visit the United States on a regular basis," she says.

As if that clears everything up. Hah! Nothing makes sense. "And you bothered to tape us?"

Off goes the video—thankfully.

"I make it my business to know everything about the gem trade."

At my side, Max gives a heartfelt groan. "Not again."

I shoot him a warning glare. I hope his little comment was low enough for our hostess not to have heard.

When I turn back to her, she's again wearing a blank expression.

What's up with all this? Why, why, why? Why would she want to drag us here? What's it all about?

"I'm sure you're not interested in interviewing us," I say, "so how about you tell us why you hauled us out here? Especially since an old-fashioned invite to lunch would have worked. You could have spared us the machine guns and the skanky truck, you know."

An elegant eyebrow arches. "You would like me to believe you'd come to a stranger's home just because of an invitation?"

"Maybe—"

"You wouldn't have to be a stranger," Max lays a hand on my shoulder, then squeezes. "You could have made arrangements to meet Andie in Bogotá if you'd only wanted to meet her. It seems to me you knew this would be the only way, because you knew she'd refuse if she knew whatever it is you're up to."

I slant him a look—an admiring one. "Okay. So what *are* you up to?"

"You won't accept a fan's interest in meeting an American TV star?"

I snort. "I doubt you're wowed by my on-screen charisma, much less giddy at meeting me." I gesture toward her. "I don't see the giddy just yet."

Max whispers, "Easy."

I bite my tongue. And wait—not something I'm good at.

Finally, our bewildering hostess gives us a brief nod. "Well, Andrea. It seems you have something that's mine. And I want it back."

A snarky feeling starts rumbling around in my gut. "How can I have something of yours if I've never met you before?"

Had I not been staring at her I would have missed the tightening of her lips and the slight narrowing of her brown eyes. "There are those who think they know everything, but actually know nothing at all."

"Amen, sister," Max mutters.

I shoot visual daggers his way. "Don't you dare." I face our hostess again. "Look. Consider me as stupid as you want, just tell me what you want, and I'll give it to you—not that I have much of anything anymore."

Her forehead lines with a slight frown. "What do you mean?"

Arms extended out to my sides, I turn a circle. "I have nothing. My suitcase is in the SUV at the side of that sorry excuse for a road where your goons stopped us."

She waves her dismissal of my comment. "Your luggage is here. My men brought it along."

"Thank goodness for small favors—oof!" Max's jabbing elbow tells me to keep my mouth in control. He does have a point.

I give it another whirl, more copacetically this time. "Since you have my luggage, I suppose your . . . *men* . . . have already searched it, and taken whatever you want. How soon can you have us back to the capital? I can't wait to catch the earliest flight home."

"You haven't fallen under Colombia's charm?"

Her sarcasm doesn't escape me. "What charm? The guy at customs didn't speak a word of the English he was supposed to be fluent in. A petty thief takes off with my purse when I'm minding my business, sitting in a restaurant, eating my dinner. I'm forced to go up and down and around the worst roads on earth just to get my business done. And then, when I'm heading back out of here, you have us accosted by machine-gun-topped jerks. You tell me where the charm might be hiding, 'cause I sure haven't seen it so far."

She smiles.

Great. I amused her. Not exactly what I wanted to do.

With a leopard's sleekness, she steps away from the desk and strolls to one of the bookshelves. There, she runs a finger across a series of tall, slim, leather-bound books with gold writing I can't make out on the spines. The tomes look like a set of those some people buy to make them look more educated than not, like something you've seen on the set of a TV show or movie, familiar and yet not.

The emerald catches the light and winks at me.

Our hostess sighs. "Let's take care of, as you say, business, shall we? Then I'll be happy to show you the charms of my country."

I cross my arms and tap my foot. "I'm waiting. What is it you want from me?"

"Why . . . the emeralds, of course."

9<u>00</u>

Remember that snarky feeling I mentioned? Well, I shoulda paid more attention to it. Way more attention.

I don't need to fake shock. Mine's real, all right. "What emeralds?"

Now it's her turn to cross her arms. "I'll do you the favor not to consider you stupid if you do the same for me. You know what emeralds I'm talking about."

I have a sneaking suspicion, but do I *know*? For sure? Nuh-uh. "I really don't. You'll have to enlighten me."

My answer achieves a crack in her demeanor. She tightens her lips and taps the elegant open toe of her Louboutin pump. "You came to Colombia to buy emeralds, Andrea, not for a vacation. Rodolfo has emeralds—good ones too. I want the stones."

I blink and give a small shake of the head. Nothing. It's still pea-soup clear. She seems to know Mr. Cruz. Why doesn't she hit him up for whatever emeralds she wants?

I take a step closer to our hostess—whose secret identity

is beginning to bug me. Why doesn't she tell us who she is? A plain ol' name would help.

But noooooo.

She couldn't really have meant what I'm afraid she did, could she? "Let me get this straight—"

"What is there to, as you put it, 'get straight'?" She turns both hands palms up. "I want the emeralds."

My next step brings me within sniffing distance. I catch the familiar scent of Joy and recoil. That's Aunt Weeby's signature fragrance. A woman who'd pull a stunt like this . . . well, she shouldn't smell like my sweet auntie. Illogical, I know.

She wrinkles her nose—Tang of Trash Truck isn't much better than Eau de Dead Dog.

I smirk and come closer. "I told you you should've skipped the stinky truck."

She steps back but holds her hand out. "The emeralds."

"Okay. Back to the emeralds. You're telling me the deal is, Miss Mona buys emeralds, but *you* get them? What part of 'the customer's always right' do you not get? Miss Mona's the customer, she writes the check, she gets the emeralds. She's right. Again: *she* gets the stones, not you."

Two red blotches mar the beautiful olive skin over her high cheekbones. "Those stones belong to me. They weren't for sale."

"Tell Mr. Cruz that. Not me."

"Ahem." Max says. "I have to agree with Andie. This would seem a problem between you and Mr. Cruz. Why don't you let us get back to the capital, and then you can take it up with the man himself?"

Her eyes blaze. "I want the emeralds, not another argument with Rodolfo."

127

My frustration grows; she has a one-track mind. And a history with the vendor. So . . . "If you wanted them in the first place, why didn't you just buy them?"

"Sometimes things aren't as simple as they would seem." She heads back behind her desk. "Give me the emeralds, and I'll send you on your way."

Somehow, I don't think she means that send-you-on-your-way part. I mean, get real. What self-respecting world-class gem thief is going to face her victim, take the loot, then send said victim off *to tell the cops who did the stealing*?

I stare at the outstretched hand, the one with the honker emerald. I point. "You've got that one. Why would anyone want another stone with that one on her hand?"

She turns her hand so she can better admire her ring. "Yes, it is the finest stone Colombia's produced in many years." She looks me in the eye, and I see the ghosts of flames in her searing gaze again. "But this one's *mine*."

Call me Dumbo here, but I'm not getting what *she's* getting at. "And the others aren't."

"Yes."

"Right. But you want them, even though they're not yours."

"Of course."

"Let me repeat that: you admit they're not yours."

"Yes." A thread of impatience runs through the brief word.

I shake my head again. "But you have no right to them."

"That's an arguable point."

"Nope. Miss Mona paid, so they're hers. You're fast outta luck."

The eyebrow arches again, but this time it's accompanied

128

by an ugly smile. "That's why you're here. To persuade you as to the rightness of my point of view before the emeralds travel to the U.S."

Max laughs. "Andie's a tough nut to crack."

I shrug. "So far, the lady's batting zero with me."

"See?" he says.

Her eyes narrow. "Well, then. I suppose I'm going to have to use less pleasant methods to persuade you. It's your choice."

"No, ma'am." I try for a last stab at politeness. "The choice is yours. You can choose to do what's right and let us go, or you can choose to break the law. You know what they say. Crime doesn't pay."

"Ah . . . but you're in Colombia now."

I get her drift. It's not hard. I gulp.

"I see we understand each other. So, Andrea. What will it be? Will you give me the emeralds or will I have to take them from you?"

A momentary zing of panic shoots from the depths of my soles right through the pit of my gut, to the middle of my heart, and straight to my head. I can't believe this is happening.

But I do believe God's still in control. Even now. And I can't just cave in to this madwoman's demands. So I'm going to have to go for it.

Lord, I'm about to fib—a big one too, but you know my heart's in the right place on this, don't you?

I take a deep breath. "You took a gamble, and you just lost. I don't have the stones."

Max sucks in a rough lungful of air.

The woman in brown goes pale. "What did you say?"

"You heard me. I don't have the stones."

Her nostrils flare and her eyes blaze again, but the tight line of her lips develops a white rim. She comes right up to me, toe-to-toe. "Of course you have the stones. You bought them from Rodolfo. Don't waste any more of my time. Give them to me."

The "or else" doesn't have to be said out loud. My heart whomps harder'n a drummer in a thundering marching band.

But as chicken as I am, that's how stubborn I also am. "Read my lips: I don't have them. And Rodolfo has plenty more where those came from. Go get 'em, lady!"

She scoffs. "I don't care for *anyone's* leftovers. I only want the best of the best." She shrugs. "This is so disappointing, Andrea. I truly had hoped to avoid such unpleasantness, but you've made the choice." She whirls around and goes back behind her desk, pushes a button, speaks when she gets a response, then faces me again. "As I said, I didn't want to have to do this. You've left me no alternative. I'm going to have to search you for the gems."

Now I'm the one I'm sure has turned whiter than the polar caps. "You don't mean . . . ?"

Steely determination freezes the older woman's face into a hideous distortion of her natural beauty. "That's precisely what I mean."

At my side, I can feel Max practically quiver with rage.

My stomach dives. *Lord, I'm trusting you, even in this.*

◈

A strip search is no picnic.

Even if Doña Rosario, as the housekeeper called our host-

130

ess, refrained from touching me. Especially since she'd had the outraged Max taken away before he could intervene.

Still, being forced to bare my body to the hateful stare of such an evil person was more than I could stand. I broke down. Tears rolled down my face.

But I clenched my fists and refused to let a sob escape. I might not have been able to stop my tear ducts from going hyper on me, but I could sure stuff down any sob that even tried to give Creepella the satisfaction.

I roll over on my side into a tighter ball in the middle of the bed.

After she'd demeaned me to her satisfaction, and ripped out every hem in my pants, blouse, and jacket, Doña Rosario had the housekeeper, Milagros, lead me to a room. To her credit, Milagros had seemed as horrified by what had taken place as I was—still am.

The quiet servant had been gentle, and she'd plumped up the pillows on the large, hand-carved mahogany bed, clearly giving me a moment to regain some composure. Then she'd walked into the attached bathroom, drawn a hot tub, handed me a towel, and then left. The only sound she'd made was the tumbling of the lock on the door as she closed it from the other side.

I'd torn off my trashed clothes and soaked until my skin pruned. Then I'd scrubbed until I'd turned fuchsia all over. Still, even now, after all that, I feel filthy. Humiliation does that to a person.

The tears flow again. "Lord? This really hurt. Please pour your healing love, the balm of your mercy, all over me. I need it. I need *you*."

As I struggle with my ravaged emotions, I miss my Bible

most of all. Right now, when I could really use a mega measure of his Word, I have to remember the Scriptures I've learned over the years. As distraught as I am, I find they come more easily than I expected.

"Thank you, Father. Even in this mess I can give you thanks."

❖

BANG, BANG, BANG!

I leap upright, my heart racing, my head spinning. Hard to believe, I'd fallen asleep. God had been merciful, for sure. I couldn't have stood to lie there and remember the search— No! I'm not going to go back there. Not while someone's pounding on my door.

"Who's there?"

"Señorita Andrea. La cena está lista."

The housekeeper! What's she saying? Come on, Spanish 1. Don't desert me now. *La . . . la . . .* the. Okay, the what? *Cena.* What's *cena*? *Está*—that one I remember. The something-or-other is . . . Oh! Okay. Got it.

As if on cue, my stomach gurgles. I'm hungry. Dinner's ready. "I'm coming."

I look down at myself with a grimace. I'm still wearing the filthy, ragged clothes Doña Rosario searched to the max. And speaking of Max, I hope I see him at the table. Last I'd seen of him, he was being dragged out of Doña Rosario's office by two of her goons.

I grab the century-old door latch, and go to open the door, but find it still locked. "Sure," I mutter. "Come tease a girl with the promise of food, and then leave her behind locked doors."

Hysteria gooses the edges of my consciousness, but I fight it off. I have to keep it together if I'm to have any hope of getting out of the madwoman's clutches. And poor Max. Ever since he came to work for the S.T.U.D. he's been chased by Burmese . . . was it soldiers or just crooks? Then he was arrested in Kashmir. With me. Oh, and there was that time the maybe-maybe-not Taliban guys followed us down the side of a Himalayan peak. Not to mention, the times he's been suspected of heinous crimes.

Yeah, yeah, yeah. Even by me. Mostly by me.

Now he's in the clutches of a Colombian nutcase in jetsetter's clothing. Oh, and that faboo emerald of hers . . . Can't forget that bauble.

The key clicks in the lock, and I don't waste a second. I open up, and nearly crash into Milagros, the housekeeper. "Oooops!"

She gives me a tentative smile, then gestures for me to head down the corridor to the left side of the beautiful courtyard, now shaded in the muted light of dusk. If my situation weren't so . . . so insane, I'd be loving every second of my time in this gorgeous place.

Too bad.

A handful of seconds later, we enter a huge room dominated by an equally vast table. A pristine white tablecloth lays over its top, and fine china, cut crystal, candelabra, and silver are unexpected niceties. Again, I feel disoriented. I mean, Doña Rosario is a criminal—she's a wannabe thief and successful hijacker-slash-kidnapper. But she's also living this deluded life of luxury. In the State of Denial, I'd say.

Tall white tapers rise from the candelabra in the middle

of the table, and the scent of Latin spiced food sends my empty stomach off into a set of cartwheels.

A large, warm hand covers my shoulder. "Are you okay?"

I place my own hand over Max's. "Slightly worse for the wear, but by the grace of God, I'll be fine—I'm trusting *he'll* make it fine."

He squeezes. "Amen."

When I lean back against him, needing and welcoming the reassurance, he slips his other arm around my waist. "Andie—"

"I see you're both here," Doña Rosario says as she sweeps in. She's taken the time while I slept to dress for dinner. Her russet silk dress fits her like a caress, and her high heels tap against the aged and gleaming brick floor tiles. Her hair, while still upswept, is no longer in the coronet but rather in a loose knot. She looks about a decade younger than I suspect she must be.

How someone as outwardly lovely as she is, with all the advantages of wealth—inherited from a noble family, from the looks of this place—could possibly be so hideous inside, I'll never know. Other than it's the result of rejecting the Lord and his will for her life. I wonder if she's ever met the Savior?

But she doesn't give me long to ponder much of anything.

"Please take a seat," she says with a grand gesture. "I hope you'll enjoy your meal."

By now, my curiosity is about to kill me—*meow*. "Have you lived here long?" I take my seat.

"My whole life." She rings a small silver bell beside her place setting.

Milagros hurries in.

They speak in fiery Spanish, of which I catch little. Actually, I don't catch any of it. Before long, though, I figure out what they'd discussed. Milagros returns with a carafe full of dark, red wine.

She pours a tall goblet of the rich-hued liquid for her boss and turns to me, the decanter lifted in silent query.

I shake my head. "I don't drink—but thanks."

Max covers his glass.

Doña Rosario studies first Max, then me. After a moment, she shrugs and takes a long drink. "Excellent. Chilean wines are actually better than those from France or Italy, but you know how it is. The European ones have the long history and fame."

Dandy. She's acting as though she's at some high-powered soirée here, not playing cat to our mouse—mice. I take a sip from my water glass. Max shifts in his chair.

Doña Rosario sighs. She puts her wineglass back on the table, picks up her bell, and rings for Milagros. The housekeeper enters the room, holds the door open with her body, and eases a serving cart over the threshold. Silver domes cover a number of platters. The fragrance makes my mouth water.

In no time, I have a slab of roast pork, a mound of golden browned potatoes, crisp salad, a roll, marinated tomatoes and cucumbers, an ear of corn, and a tiny dish of butter in front of me. I catch Max's gaze; we swap smiles.

He knows I enjoy eating. And he also knows my concern for the size of my hips.

"What hips?" he asks, a mischievous twinkle in his blue eyes.

I pause. First I knew what he'd been thinking a bit earlier; now he's just read my mind. *Lord, is this for real?*

Oh, Andie, Andie, Andie. This isn't the time to think about Max, his blue eyes, or how he's begun to do some kind of mind-meld on you.

I bow my head, breathe a quick prayer, pick up my fork. As I bring bright green salad to my mouth, it occurs to me to wonder why this woman, so intent in robbing us, would go to so much trouble to entertain us with such a lavish meal. A kidnapper's hardly the queen of hospitality or anything.

Does the meal hide an ulterior motive?

Has she poisoned our food?

I shoot her a look, and watch her slice a piece of pork from her generous serving. She slips it in her mouth without pause, her eyes narrowed in pleasure, her shoulders at ease. I look down at the plate before me, fear suddenly stealing my appetite.

Across from me, Max is about to dig in. I clear my throat.

He meets my gaze. I mouth the word, "Poison."

His fork clatters back down to his plate.

I wince.

Doña Rosario looks from one to the other of us, then stuns me by bursting into heavy-duty laughter. "Oh my!" she says. "You are something, aren't you? Go ahead. Eat. Your food is fine. What earthly good would you be to me dead?"

Okay. So maybe Max isn't doing any kind of romantic mind-meld with me. Maybe I'm just one of those people who blare their last puny little secret on their faces.

I look back at our maniacal hostess, at Max, and finally at my food again. It's time for the rubber to hit the road. Am I going to trust God? Really trust him?

Fine, fine. If it's his will for me to zip on upstairs to get face-to-face with him for eternity, then I'm going to have to be ready. I *am* ready. I guess. I do love him—that I know for sure.

The salad is cool and the dressing tangy. The pork is seasoned with herbs, a whisper of garlic. The potatoes were cooked in super-rich olive oil; the roll is cloud light; the butter creamy and very lightly salted. I'm in foodie heaven.

The cheesecake . . . well, what can I say about cheesecake? It rocks.

During the entire meal, you could hear the proverbial pin drop. None of us says a word—other than the woman at the head of the table, but it's only to give instructions to her housekeeper. I have the awful feeling of treading water. Nothing happens. At least nothing bad happens. But then again, nothing good happens either.

When we're all done, I deliberately wipe my mouth on the linen napkin, fold it and place it next to my dessert plate, then turn to study my hostess. But, in keeping with the silent treatment she's given us so far, I say nothing right back.

She arches a brow. "Have you decided to give me the emeralds?"

It figures I'd stumble across a highly discerning thief with impeccable taste in rocks. I hadn't been willing to settle for Rodolfo's second-best either. I sigh. "I don't have them."

Then what to my horrified eyes should appear but my snazzy pink cell phone and replacement purse too. I scrape up all my bravado, stand, and say, "I'll take that back now."

Our hostess laughs. "I don't think so."

While my frustration reaches stratospheric heights, she pops open the phone and starts fiddling with the buttons.

Her eyes grow wide after a few clicks. A pure de-malevolent look spreads on her face.

"You would be wise not to speak." Her wicked smile says volumes. "Listen."

Moments later, I hear Miss Mona answer. She calls my name, twice, three times, each one more frantic than the last. "Are you all right, Andie girl?"

"Miss Mona—"

Doña Rosario's threatening glare shuts me up. She stands, looming larger than life with that aura of menace.

I bite my tongue, but everything in me wishes I could've reassured Miss Mona. As my boss continues to call my name, more frantic by the minute, our hostess makes a production of closing the phone. She then sits back down and slips the phone under the lip of her large dinner dish.

"How could you?" I ask, ready to . . . ready to—oh, I don't know what I want to or worse, can do.

She shrugs. "The emeralds?"

I dig in my heels. "I don't have them."

She flips open my phone again. Clicks a couple of buttons. Aunt Weeby answers.

"How's your trip going, sugarplum?"

The much-loved voice touches something deep in my heart. I glare at our jailor. "You didn't have to involve my aunt. She has nothing to do with the studio's business."

"Speak up, girl," my aunt calls out. "I can't hardly hear you!"

When I don't dare say another word, her voice rises with anxiety.

"Tell me you haven't gone chasing some good-for-nothing

138

kid down a back alley again. Oh, no! Surely y'ain't been rolling around in dirty trash heaps again . . . Andie? Andie!"

My heart aches, and tears burn my eyes.

Our hostess looks bewildered.

Max laughs. "Only your aunt, Andie."

"It's not funny. She's going to be so worried. How can you laugh at a time like this?"

"What else do you want me to do?"

"Exactly," Creepella says, snapping my phone shut again. "There's nothing for you to do but give me the emeralds."

"Repetitious, aren't you?" I'm now fed up, worried, anxious to leave and reassure Miss Mona and Aunt Weeby. There's more than a little frustration buzzing around in me too.

She shrugs. "Well, then. I suppose you must be ready for bed. I had Milagros send one of her girls to fetch your suitcase earlier. It should be waiting for you in your room." She turns to Max. "Yours too."

She rises, drops her napkin on the table. "Good night."

When she's gone, I turn to Max. "Ready to make a break for it?"

He snorts. "Last time I saw Larry, Curly, and Moe, they were still hugging their guns. I don't want to find myself at the business end of the barrel again."

"You don't think she's just going to keep us around here like a pair of pet monkeys, do you?"

"Speak for yourself, Chimp—er . . . Champ."

"You're in fine form."

"What else am I going to do? I can't see you forking over the—"

"Oh my!" I say in a louder voice than necessary, my eyes wide, telegraphing—I hope—the need to keep his trap shut.

139

"I'm sooooo tired, Max. What a day, huh? I think I'm ready to hit the sack. G'night."

He gives me a crooked grin, shrugs, takes my elbow, and leads me to the door. "Good night, Andie."

"Good night, Max."

We find Larry (or is this one Curly?) on the other side, his gun cradled in his arms. Without a word, the unmasked bandit leads us down the corridor. As we go past the courtyard, I look up at the stars in the inky sky.

Will I ever see any more than this small square of sky?
Are you going to get us back home, Lord?

I remember my promise to trust him. The rubber's hit the road. Either I do or I don't. I sigh.

With a last longing look at the twinkling stars, I open my bedroom door. The minute I'm safely on the inside of the room, our jailer locks me in.

Fear sends fingers through me again.

The light on the nightstand gives off a golden glow. That's when I notice my nightgown draped across the foot of the bed. The thought of how many people have pawed through my things makes me cringe. I'd rather sleep in my clothes.

I've never felt so vulnerable, not even when I sat for the better part of a night in a filthy jail in Srinagar or when a crazed murderer held me at gunpoint. A tear rolls down my face.

"Never again, Lord. Once you get me back there, I'm not leaving Louisville again."

10.00

As easy as it was to fall asleep earlier in the afternoon, no matter how I try, I can't get my eyelids to stick shut now. I fluff my bedding, punch my pillows, wiggle, toss, turn. Do it all again.

Nothing.

And praying? Well, even that's become tough. My mind has discovered a heretofore unknown case of ADD or something like that. I can't focus on anything, not even my love for the Lord. Too many stray rags of thought keep popping into my head.

I can't help worrying about Aunt Weeby. That phone call . . . it frightened her. And my aunt is known for her . . . umm . . . insane reactions to fright. The last thing I want is for her to hop the next flight to Colombia and come look for me—us. I wouldn't be able to stand it if anything were to happen to her. Especially if it happened because she was trying to help me.

"Lord . . . ? Help us, please, so she doesn't think she has to."

I flop over onto my other side. I still can't believe I'm locked up in a room at a *hacienda* somewhere in Colombia. I mean, these things only happen in movies or in books. Not to plain, old gemologists from Louisville, Kentucky. Like me.

Right?

Ah . . . well, I guess I'd better change that idea. These things didn't used to happen to me. Not before I came to work for Miss Mona, that is. Oh, don't get me wrong. I don't blame Miss Mona for any of the wacky things that have happened this last year. Not really. True, she does get these ideas . . . but it's not as if she goes out of her way to come up with stuff that leads to danger or disaster.

That's just what happens while I carry out her plans.

Trust me. I'm not the one with the ideas.

And when I get home? Neither will she *idea-ize* (yep, new word!) again.

I'll make sure of it.

From now on, vendors will come to the S.T.U.D. to vend.

I roll over onto my back. Stare up at the ceiling. Count the seconds oozing by.

Aaack! I quit.

In a single, dramatic move, I toss off the lightweight sheet, totally frustrated with my inability to zonk out, and with a half twist, swing my feet over the bed and vault upright on to the floor. What good is it to be jailed in a luxe cell like this one, if you can't even veg out for real? I mean, sawing logs and z's and doing like Rip Van Winkle isn't that tough, is it? It should happen just because it's nighttime, I'm drained from what's happened, and I *want* to sleep.

It's understandable for my nerves to be on edge. There's the memory of those machine guns prancing in the back of my head. And I'm being held against my will. But understanding isn't accepting.

I start to pace the room, and come face to face with the shuttered window. It's über-quaint, with its wooden shutters that open inward. While I hold no illusions of freedom, I'd rather look at the amazing endless night sky, with all the twinkling stars I remember from when I walked down the corridor by the courtyard, than at the quaint but uninteresting shutters. When I open them, a balmy breeze wafts in between the curving iron bars. If they weren't jailing me, I would think them gorgeous, mysterious, exotic. Since they are, I don't.

Propping my elbows on the deep windowsill, I plop my chin on the heels of my hands and stare out over the vast expanse of empty land. All that emptiness is unsettling.

Once again, the hysteria begins to work its way back up, and a hint of desperation joins it.

What am I going to do? I want out of this place. I can't just sit here and watch the banana moon crawl across the black sky all night. *But what, Lord? What can I do? How can I get out of here?*

And Max . . . poor guy. He came to try and help. Here he is now, locked up just like me. Even if I could figure out a way to make a run for it, I can't leave the guy behind.

Scritch . . . scritch . . . scri-scritch—scritch!

I spin around, heart thudding, throat tight. Someone's at my bedroom door.

Oh, help!

Determined not to just wimp out and let the inevitable happen, I dig deep for some bravado. "Stop! Don't even try it."

To my horror, the door swings open. So much for my

bravado. I back up against the window wall. That hysteria? Well, it's hit full blast.

My goose is cooked, as we say in the South.

A large black shadow slithers into the room. My head spins and I fight to draw a breath. And here I thought Doña Rosario had meant it when she'd said I wasn't any good to her dead. Or maybe she sent her goon to torture the emeralds from me . . .

Instead of charging me, the shadow waves me over. "Come on, already!"

"Huh?"

"Stop with the 'huh,' Andie," Max mutters. "Let's get out of here before that crazy woman or one of her lackeys comes and finds us."

Am I actually sleeping—dreaming? "Max?"

"Of course it's me. Who'd you expect? Santa Claus?"

"Bu—but how? How'd you get a key to my room? Or to yours?"

A big hand claps around my wrist. "I didn't. I palmed a fork during dinner, then picked the locks. Anything in your suitcase you can't live without? If there is, then you'd better get it now. We're out of here."

So the guy's got hidden talents. Picking locks, eh? I'll have to think about that—later, of course. I glance out the open window again and take another gander at the rough landscape. "My sneakers."

I slip my feet into the comfortable, beat-up running shoes I always take with me, no matter where in the world I travel. Then, without bothering to tie the laces, I head for the door.

"Whoa!" Max says. "What about the—"

"Don't even think it. This isn't the time or place, okay?"

The weak light from the moon outside illuminates his face. I see the questions in his eyes. But then he shakes his head and only holds out his hand. I place mine in his, and we slip out of the room. Without making a sound, we hurry down the dark, empty corridor.

At the magnificent double mahogany front doors of the house, Max presses a finger to his lips, then pulls something— probably the purloined fork—out of his pants pocket. He crouches, fiddles with it and the old-fashioned lock; I hear again the *scritch, scritch, scritch* I'd heard from inside my room. A handful of seconds later, the click of the opened lock echoes in the silent night.

Who would'a thunk? Max the Midnight Man. Hmm . . .

"Shh!"

He grabs my hand to drag me out behind him . . . and right into the waiting arms of Doña Rosario's goons. Well, two of them have empty, waiting arms. The other one has, of course, the ever-present machine gun at the ready.

In the resulting scuffle, I get dinged, danged, and bruised, but not nearly as much, I'm sure, as Max. Those hard thuds can only be the sounds of a fistfight. And while I know Max is tall, strong, and in great shape, he can't be any match for two against one. In the end, we get hauled away like ornery mules, digging in our heels, fighting every inch of the way.

That's when I start praying again. I hope Max is doing the same. You know, that "two or more gathered in his name" Scripture. We need the Lord's presence in this mess if we're ever going to have any hope of getting out of it. Oh yeah. Something close to a miracle's what's going to have to happen. And I've never seen anything in the Bible about the Lord getting out of the miracle business.

On our way to wherever, I look at the sky, to both sides, out to the black horizon. I even throw a look back at the house. Most of all, I keep darting glances toward poor Max. One goon has his right arm twisted up his back in a visibly painful angle, while the other holds the machine gun's barrel maybe an inch, no more than two, away from his temple.

Please, Lord, don't let him try to be a hero. These monsters mean business. And I don't want him hurt. I want . . . I haven't even told him—

Right then, in the most ridiculous, dangerous situation imaginable, I realize how deeply I do care for Max. I don't want him hurt, no matter what. More important, however, is my deeper reason why. I don't want him hurt because I haven't been able to tell him how much I do care. Here, in the clutches of a trio of emerald thieves, I find myself at the point where I'm willing to bare my heart and let things land where they may.

Am I weird or what? What other woman realizes she's honest-to-goodness falling in love with a man—*the* single, solitary, most impossible man possible—at the time when they're both about to be snuffed out?

Because my epiphany leaves me so discombobulated, I don't see the the steel door of some outbuilding until I'm smack up against the stupid thing. Panic bubbles up in me, as does a scream, but I realize that if I were to make so much noise, it would only enrage our captors. Not something I really want to do. Even if a scream would let me release some of the tension stuffed to bursting inside me.

The door clangs open. I'm thrust into the thick, tarry

blackness within, then shoved farther along. The sound of something heavy being dragged fills the room. Seconds later, I'm pushed forward again. This time, the bottom falls out. I drop . . . down, down, down . . .

THUMP!

I don't land gracefully, but painfully. Seconds later, another *THUMP* strikes inches away. Max, I'm sure, even though I can't see a thing. It's lightless, thick, black, and impenetrable in here.

I check all my limbs and find them, while sore, still functional. I register no movement from Max. With every bit of my body screaming against the effort, I drag myself to his side.

"Max! Are you okay?"

"I'm . . . alive."

"Barely, from the sound of it." I reach out to him. "Do you think you broke anything?"

A rough sound I think he means as a laugh grates in the smothering silence. "Maybe it's more like . . . if there's anything . . . they didn't break."

"Oh, Max . . ." I reach out, come up against warm, cotton-covered human, an arm. "I couldn't see what they were doing to you, but it sounded awful. They must have been brutal in those few minutes."

"They were . . . but I wasn't going . . . easy, either."

As I flounder for something to say, I sense a rustle, movement. And not so far away. Nor from above. Only a few feet away.

I gasp. "Max . . . we're not alone."

"Hello?" a young female voice calls out, weak and reedy. I scoot closer to Max. I don't know if it's to protect him

147

or to suck up some comfort from his nearness. I do know I appreciate the warmth of his bulk at my side. "Wh–who are you?"

"Laura . . . Laura Cruz."

Cruz! A bad feeling lands in my gut. "Are you related to Rodolfo Cruz, the emerald vendor?"

"My father . . ."

Oh, Lord Jesus . . . that woman is beyond insane. She's evil, pure evil. Help us, Father—help me help these two. It's obvious they're both hurt.

"What did they do to you, Laura?"

"I was out shopping," she murmurs in perfect English. "Two men were waiting at the door . . . they pushed me into a car . . ."

Her voice grows fainter with every word.

"They didn't—" I catch myself; I can't even voice some of the horrors that occur to me. "I mean, how did they hurt you?"

"They didn't. I fell down on my leg. I think it's broken."

I crawl toward through the darkness toward Laura, guided by her voice. Is there anything I can do to ease her obvious pain? *Oh, Father! How am I going to get a girl with a broken leg and poor, beat-up Max out of here? There's just one of me.*

"Hey!" Max's voice cuts into my prayer. "I'm okay. Just give me a little while to shake off the soreness."

"But, Max—"

"But nothing. I'll be fine. And you don't have to worry. We're going to be okay. We're getting out of here."

"Oh, really, now. And you know this because . . . ?"

"Because I trust God."

That zips me up. I do trust God. I just don't trust an emerald-hungry madwoman who surrounds herself with brutes and their ugly machine guns. "Okay. Yeah. You're right. We're going to get out of here. But for us to be able to do that, we need to be in as good a shape as possible. We should all try to sleep."

Did I just say that? Am I able to be that rational? Is all this nightmare experience becoming less . . . oh, I don't know, less daunting? Less intimidating? Less terrorizing?

I hope not. I don't want this to become my normal. Should there ever be an Andie "normal" again, if you get my drift.

"Good night," I whisper. Then I pat around under me, only to realize we're in some kind of dirt-floored basement. I'm about to sleep on that dirt floor. Yuck.

Keep your eye on the goalpost, Andie.

As I wriggle around to try and get comfortable—comfortable? Hah!—Max reaches out, curves his arm around my shoulders, and pulls me close. "Let's pray."

My heart swells big enough to burst. Is this—is Max— really real?

As hard to believe as it is, I do sleep. I realize this when a sliver of dim light pierces the thick darkness of our cell. The trapdoor above us is lifted, and we see a large basket at the end of a thick rope. Inch by inch, it's lowered down to us.

"*El desayuno,*" a gruff male calls out. "*A comer!*"

I scramble to my feet. I don't want our breakfast to spill out over the dirt floor. "It's nice to know they don't plan to starve us."

"Wait." Max says. "Move slowly."

He comes to my side, nods, and I reach out for the food. Before I can grab the basket, though, he takes hold of the rope and yanks hard.

The man above yells, then tumbles down. What happens next is a blur, but by the time Max is done, our jailor is tied with Max's belt, his mouth stuffed with one of Max's shirt-sleeves.

"Here's the deal," Max says after we've all scarfed down enough to keep us going. "I'm going to hold you on my shoulders. I need you to get up there and find something strong and fixed to tie the rope to."

"Me!" I'm embarrassed to admit the word comes out in a scared squeal. "But what if—"

"Forget the what-ifs. This is the only chance we're going to get. I'm not about to let it pass us by."

I realize the truth to his words and gulp my fears away. "Okay. I'll go up there, but I don't know how we're going to get you out of here. And I'm not going anywhere without you."

"Me neither. Just go tie the rope to . . . oh, I don't know, a beam or something structural. We'll figure it out as we go."

I get the picture. "You're going to climb up, aren't you? But what about Laura? She can't stand or walk or climb or much of anything."

Max gives me a gentle nudge toward the edge of the opening overhead. "Once I'm up there with you, Laura can tie the rope around her waist, and you and I will pull her up. Think you can do that, Laura?"

"I can do that," the teen says, hope palpable in her voice.

"Sounds good to me," I add. "I just hope it works as well as it sounds."

"It will. Your job's to pray we don't bump into one of his pals."

"Is the rope long enough?"

"It's got to be long enough, Andie. It's all we have. Let's go."

Max wraps the rope around my waist, and I tie it in a loose enough knot. I don't want to have to fiddle around with a tight knot once I'm above ground. Then I send up a silent prayer, take hold of Max's hand, and slowly—oh, so slowly—climb onto his broad shoulders. He sways a time or two under my weight. Panic threatens.

Wonder what he thinks about my hips now?

After a precarious moment, though, Max stands firm. I find I can curl my fingers as far down as the first or second knuckle over the edge of the opening above if I stretch full out.

"Ready?" he asks. "I'm going to grab your ankles and push up. I hope I can hold you long enough for you to get a good hold, and then you can pull yourself out."

"You know I haven't joined a gym since I came home to Louisville, don't you?"

"This isn't the time to kid around."

"I'm not kidding. Not at all. I really don't know how much strength I have in my arms."

"Trust God to make you able. And remember. If this doesn't work, we're stuck. Who knows for how long? In this hole. With what's-his-face over there."

The thought of spending more time in the subterranean jail gives my determination a healthy dose of starch. I square my shoulders, tip up my chin, and reach. Inch by inch, Max lifts me up into the opening. I feel the strain in his muscles

151

as he quivers from the effort. Knowing how hard he's trying wipes out my last bit of fear. I have to do as much.

With a burst of energy, Max pushes upward. My head breaches the opening. I reach out, plant both palms on the wood floor, and push . . . push . . . push. Muscles screaming against the unaccustomed effort, I get high enough to fold myself at the waist, half in the hole, half on the floor.

"One last push!" I ask Max.

Somehow, don't ask me how, he comes up with a final burst, and gives me the momentum to slide forward. Once my hips clear the edge, I drag myself all the way out, with my hands and elbows, until I can haul my legs up too. Then I collapse where I wind up. I pant from the exertion. And promise myself to sign up at the nearest gym the minute I get home.

Because I *am* going home.

"Hey!" Max calls out. "You okay?"

"Yep, muscle man. I am. Give me a minute to find somewhere to tie the rope, okay?"

Dark as the room still is, I realize it's some kind of large shed or small barn. The main doors are to the right of the trap door. And it's those doors that provide me with an anchor. A tall, inch-thick rod runs floor-to-ceiling, holding one of the metal doors fixed while the other can swing open. The bar sits deep in a hole in the cement threshold.

"Found it!" I call out. "I have something to tie the rope to."

"Just do it—and fast. I don't know how long we'll have before they send one of this one's pals to find out what happened to him."

I unwrap the rope from my waist, slip one end of it around

the rod, and tie a number of tight knots to secure it in place. I tug to test; it's firm.

"Here you go." I drop the loose end to Max.

Immediately, it goes taut. Max grunts, breathes hard, huffs.

"Can I help you?"

A pained "No" rises out of the trapdoor opening.

I hold my breath as the harsh breathing continues. The rope wiggles from Max's efforts. The rod scrapes against the concrete. I wonder if it's as loud from the outside as it sounds to me. Maybe, hopefully, it's my anxiety magnifying the sound.

After what feels like hours but can only have been seconds, I see one hand, then the other, top the open edge. Then, with the rope still tight in his clutch, Max plants his hands on the floor and pushes himself up.

He drops onto the floor, a successful smile on his lips.

My relief is so great I almost throw my arms around him and give him a hug. Almost.

Max claps his hands once, twice, then stands and heads for the door.

I frown. "Hey! There's an injured girl down there, re-member?"

"Yes, Andie, I remember." His fake patience doesn't win him any points with me. But he goes on. "I'm going to check on the rope. I weigh a couple of pounds"—he waves down his large frame—"and it might have loosened some. I don't want Laura to fall again."

Swallow me, earth. He'd been thinking of Laura all along. "Sorry," I mumble sheepishly.

Once he tightens the knots again, he returns to the hole.

"Come here with me." He points to a spot a few steps to his left. "I want you to reach out to her once I pull her up high enough. The less she does with that leg, the better off she'll be."

Turning, he calls down instructions for Laura. The girl's voice reveals her fear, but she's brave and game to give Max's plan a try. I'm impressed.

And then we go to work. Less than five minutes later, Max pulls the teen to the edge of the hole, and I reach out to grasp her hands. I pull, help her out. Once she's out, Max unties the rope. He hurries over, and with painstaking gentleness, eases the injured girl to our side.

"Thank you," she says, tears pouring down her cheeks.

"Lean on me," Max says. Then, eyes serious, lips tight, jaw squared, he adds, "Don't thank me yet. We have a long way to go. Anything can happen."

A chill runs down my back.

11:00

My heart beats loud enough for Doña Rosario's goons to hear. Even though they're nowhere to be seen when we open the shed's door. It's early morning, and since the spread appears to be a working *hacienda*, I expect to see workers working. But the place looks deserted.

The isolation of the *hacienda*'s setting strikes me. We're trying to escape but there might not be any. We might wander—and wander and wander and wander—endlessly before we find any help.

When I look at Max, I see the same concern reflected in his tight jaw, his grim expression, his narrowed eyes. The guy's not stupid; he knows what we're up against. So does Laura.

"You shouldn't take me along," she says in a soft whisper when Max gathers her into his arms. "I'm only going to slow you down. Go for help. They've been feeding me. I'll be fine until you get back."

Yeah, right. Even she doesn't believe her words. Her voice

trembles and her liquid-chocolate eyes widen with fear. No way will we leave her to their not-so-tender mercies.

"We're going to need help with the language," Max says. "You're our translator. How could we leave you behind?"

I smile at him, grateful for his sensitivity. Not only is he not about to leave her behind, but he's also given her true purpose in our mission. No wonder I'm crazy about the guy.

Whoa! Where'd that come from? Crazy about Max. I know I care about him. Oh, let's be honest here: I'm getting used to the thought of loving him. But crazy about him? Head-over-heels, gaga, loony tunes?

I look at him, drinking in his strong frame, his determination, his decency, and I accept the truth. Okay. Fine. So I *am* crazy about the guy.

What am I going to do about it?

Especially right now, out here, and under our circumstances.

Again, the excess of ridiculousness in our situation hits me. Here, in the middle of Back-of-Beyond, Colombia, there's nothing I'm going to do about my feelings for Max. Other than pray we get out of this mess so we can maybe—just maybe—explore what direction God's going to take those feelings.

"You ladies ready?" Max asks.

I snort. "Never been so ready in my life."

"If you're sure I'm not going to be a problem," Laura whispers.

"Hey!" I say. "We need you just as much as you need us."

"Let's go," Max says.

We hurry off into that vast emptiness of flat grasslands.

The sun is starting to rise, and as it goes up, so does the quantity of sweat we produce. Poor Max. Not only is he hurrying to put as much distance between the *hacienda* and us as possible, but he's also carrying Laura. I have no room to whine, not even when the "dew" pours into my eyes, making them burn.

"Do you have any idea where we are?" I ask Laura after a while of traveling through a whole lot of nothing.

"Not really. I know we're in the eastern part of the country, where there are huge cattle ranches and lots of land for the animals, but I don't know any more than that."

"Any cities out here?"

"Not anything important."

I'd been afraid that would be her answer. All we can do is keep on keeping on until we find help. And water. Food would be good too.

After about two hours go by, I cast my zillionth look over my shoulder. "Wonder why they haven't come after us."

"Does it matter?" Max asks, his voice tired—understandably.

My heart goes out to him, but there's nothing I can do to help. "Not really, but I didn't expect to get this far."

"Doña Rosario spends a lot of time in Bogotá," Laura says. "When she's gone, I imagine her servants do what they want."

I roll my eyes. "When the cat's away . . ."

Max gives me a crooked grin. "Tsk, tsk, tsk. Those poor cats you just insulted."

We fall silent again, and I go back to praying. Then, as the fireball better known as the sun hits the midway point in the sky—and I'm positive I can't force my exhausted body

157

to take another step—I notice something far, far in front of us, just a bit closer to us than the horizon.

"Am I imagining things, or are those buildings up there?"

Max looks in the direction I point, and relief brightens his tired face. "Eureka! Water and someplace to sit."

"I can't thank you enough," Laura says, a tear rolling down her face.

"Don't thank me yet," Max answers. "Wait until we have you to a hospital, and a doctor puts your leg in a cast." He doesn't break the rhythm of his pace.

With our hopes renewed, we come up with enough strength to make our way to the smattering of buildings. But when we arrive, we look at each other in dismay. I have to unleash superhuman power to keep from groaning out loud.

I'd hoped for a town. Even a small village would've done. But no. What we've found is just seventeen hardscrabble structures clustered where a patchwork of agricultural fields meet. I don't see power lines. There'll be no phone service way out here.

But I have to recognize God's mercy in leading us here. "Hey, guys. Things are looking up," I say with a smile. "I'm sure there's water here."

Laura smiles. "I'd love a drink."

Max squares his shoulders; a major feat, since he's still holding the girl. "Well, let's get you one."

We approach the nearest house. To get there, we have to skirt a pigpen, where a half-dozen oinkers greet us with grunts and squeals. And guess what? They're dirty and stinky. The term *pigpen*? It's well coined.

Across the path from the pigs, a bunch of clucking chickens

are scratching the dirt in front of a small coop. Off to our right, I spot a small herd of cattle in one of the fields.

Still holding on to my positive vibe, I say, "I'm sure we can get help here. These people have to have a way to get their animals to market. I'm not picky. Whatever works to get us where we have to go."

Max grins. "You're right. We're here, and that's a road—not our idea of a freeway or a turnpike, but their version of interstate travel. A truck . . . a cart . . . a bike . . . who cares? All we need now is to figure out a way to get all the way over there—to Bogotá." He glances down at Laura. "Are you ready to earn your ride?"

Her brown eyes twinkle. "More than ready."

We approach the door to the farmhouse, and I knock. A tiny, white-haired lady opens up, suspicion on her wrinkled face. A barrage of rapid-fire Spanish hits us the minute she spots us.

Laura responds, then points to her swollen purpled leg. I wince, well aware how much it must be hurting. The woman's eyes widen, compassion softens her expression, she steps back, and finally gestures us inside. Before I step into the dark room, I pray for God's protection. Who knows what's lurking in the shadows of the tiny house.

Once my eyes adjust to the dim light indoors, I scan my surroundings. The interior is as stark and poor as the exterior. The only furnishings consist of an old sofa, probably the same vintage as our hostess, a sturdy table, four chairs around it, and two stools across from the sofa.

In the corner to the left of the sitting area, I notice a three-foot-tall basket piled high with blankets—this area probably doubles as guest room when the need arises. Behind the table, three shelves sag under the weight of bowls, plates, cups, and crockery of various sizes. Directly underneath, I see a well-used broom. Two doors lead off at each end of the back wall.

While everything is well used and old, it all is sparkling clean. I see no dirt anywhere; what I do see is an abundance of pride of ownership. This family might not have much, but they take care of what they have.

As my gaze takes another trip around the room, I notice the colorful picture of Jesus on the rear wall between the two doors. Our hostess is also proud of her faith.

It seems way clear we have nothing to fear from Anita, as Laura introduces the lady. She guides Max to the sofa, where she helps him make Laura as comfortable as possible. Within seconds, our hostess, chattering all along, trots out the right-hand door, then returns, holding out a flimsy wooden crate to prop up the girl's injured leg.

Laura thanks her, but Anita responds with an embarrassed smile and a shrug. She hurries back out the right doorway, and before we can wonder why she's disappeared, she returns, a glistening aluminum pitcher and three glasses in hand.

I guzzle down my portion and ask for more. So does Max, and Laura too. Anita returns to the kitchen for a refill. This time, when she comes back, she holds the pitcher in one hand, a plate of steaming *arepas* in the other.

Okay. I'll confess. I make a pig of myself. I had no idea how hungry I was until I smelled those delicious corn cakes. And it seems Anita has no end to her supply of *arepa*.

Once we're done, our hostess insists we all lie down to take *siestas*.

"She doesn't have to tell me twice," Max says, then yawns.

Which sets me off.

And then Laura.

But I have to admit, the nap in one of two small rooms off the left-hand side of the living area does me a world of good. By the time I wake up, there's no light coming in through the small window high on the wall—we'd arrived early in the afternoon, with the sun only a hair over the middle of the sky. And while I can't sleep anymore, at least not right now, I notice Laura still dozing on the other single bed in the room.

I step out into the hall and head toward the front of the house, following the murmur of voices, those of a man and a woman. The woman is Anita, but the male voice is one I don't recognize. The little hairs on the back of my neck rise to attention. Could this be one of Doña Rosario's henchmen?

Henchmen? Oooh! Love that word. Never thought I'd have reason to use it, but—well, you never know what life will bring. That's why I call on God to guide me.

In the living area, a young Colombian sits at the table, an empty plate before him. When I walk in, he glances over, smiles, but then returns to his meal. I breathe again. He's okay. He looks so much like our hostess I'm pretty sure he must be her son.

"Hi," I say. "Thank you. *Buena siesta. Gracias.*"

My pathetic stab at Spanish goes a long way. Before long, I too am sitting at the table, a plate full of food in front of me. I dig in, and discover what true Latin food tastes like. Forget chain restaurants with cute little Chihuahua mascots. If you want the real deal, you'll have to cross south of the border, many borders, to Anita's kitchen way out here in the middle of nowhere.

When I'm—as we say in the South—full as a tick, I scoot my chair back and just breathe. Um-yum. *"Muy bueno."*

"So your Spanish has made a comeback," Max says as he rises from a nest of blankets on the sofa, his voice rough with sleep. "But I agree with you. Anita's food is good enough to make me speak a language I don't know."

"Foul! You're telling me you got away without having to take a foreign language in college?"

"Don't you dare give me grief about my football years. I'll remind you, I went to school on an *academic* scholarship, not an athletic one."

Just to tease him, I sniff. "So you say. But who knows? Maybe you thought it was an academic scholarship, while all the while it was your muscles they wanted."

He shakes his head. "Give it up, Andi-ana Jones. I didn't imagine my 4.0 in high school or my 4.0 in college."

My eyes goggle. "You got a clean-sweep 4.0?" When he nods, I realize something else. "Then that means . . . oh no. I don't think I can stand this. Your summa cum laude trumps my magna cum laude. *Aaaarrrgh!*"

He blows on his nails and buffs them against his filthy shirt.

"Well, that"—I point at his hand—"just shows how little you really do know. You swiped your nails on the dirtiest piece of clothing I've ever seen. They're probably black with dirt now. From our jail's floor, if you'll remember."

"Which brings us right back to why we're here." He sighs. "I'm not sure how we're going to communicate with Anita and Enrique over there, but we have to get them to understand how urgent it is for us to get to the capital, and soon."

"We'll just have to go back to bed, rest up for the trip, and wait until Laura wakes up. She's really going to earn that piggyback ride you gave her."

"She's sweet. I can't imagine the pain she's in, and she's never once said a word about it."

"She's a great kid. I wish we could get word to her father. He must be frantic."

Max winces. "She must have been kidnapped right after we left the mine site. Rodolfo must be going out of his mind with worry." He runs a hand through his blond hair, leaving some of it standing on end, some tumbled over his forehead. "I know I'd be tearing up the country end to end if she was my daughter and she'd just gone missing."

"What makes you think he isn't?"

"True. We have no way to know what he's been doing since we left the mine."

As we both fall silent remembering the emerald vendor, I realize how intently Anita and Enrique have been following our conversation. I know they can't understand a word we've said, but their eyes have ping-ponged back and forth between Max and me the whole time. Then, as the silence lengthens, Anita skitters to the ancient stove out back and heaps more food on another plate.

A stream of chatter ripples from her when she returns. She points to Max, the table, and finally the food.

He grins. "My turn—again."

"No need to boast," I counter. "I'll get my fair share of her good cooking. Not that we're going to stay long, but I suspect you'll sleep more than I will. You're the one who carried Laura all that way."

"And you figure you'll sneak a snack while I'm sawing logs."

"You snooze, you lose."

"We'll see."

From the back bedroom, I hear Laura call my name. Before I can make it to her side, Max has sped past and left me in his dust—not literally, you understand. As poor as Anita and Enrique are, that's just how clean they keep their home.

Moments later, Max carries Laura into the kitchen. "She's hungry."

"Lucky you," I tell the girl, holding out a chair for her. "Anita's food is a treat. I'm just too full from the heaps she fed me while you were sleeping. Otherwise, I'd probably keep on pigging out."

Laura wrinkles her nose. "Pigging out?"

I laugh. "You speak such great English it's hard to remember sometimes that you're not American. 'Pigging out' means I'd make a pig of myself eating too much."

"Ah . . . I see." She takes a mouthful of her dinner. "But it works another way too. Anita's pork is delicious. It's their own pigs, the ones they raise to sell. She is a very good cook, you know. This roast is wonderful."

At the mention of Anita and Enrique's livestock, Max and I swap looks.

"We have to ask how they get their animals to market," he says to Laura. "Can you do that?"

While Max and I watch—I guess it's our turn to ping-pong our gazes between the three of them—a whole lot of chatter, smiles, and hand waving happens. Then Laura turns back to us, uncertainty on her face.

Uh-oh. Doesn't look good. Even though I'd tried to catch a random word here or there, I'd failed. My returning Spanish isn't returning that much. Then again, I suspect more was said than I would have wished. "So what's the scoop?"

She looks lost. "Scoop?"

I shake my head and give her a crooked grin. "Me and my slang. What I mean is, what did they tell you?"

A tiny line etches in between her eyebrows. "I don't know if it will help us. They say they take their products to a tiny little town, San José de Belén, on their cart. Enrique pulls it along behind his bicycle."

I hold back a groan and turn to Max. "You never told me you had prophetic tendencies. Maybe you shouldn't have mentioned carts or bicycles when we got here."

Max arches a brow. "So now it's my fault, just because I was looking for a silver lining in our thunderstorm."

I chuckle. "If the hat fits, then use it as sunscreen, surfer boy."

Just as I say those words, I realize what I've done. Never in the year-plus since we met have I let Max know how I think of him. Until now. Chalk it up to stress, the foreignness of it all, the possible necessity of riding a cart out of our mess. Who knows why my flap-trap let it out? The deal is, it did.

Max's jaw drops. Total "Huh?" blares from his eyes. He blinks. Sticks a finger in an ear and shakes it. "Say what?"

I hoot—not ready to go where he wants me to go. "Have we been rubbing off on you or what? That 'say what' means you've become an honorary southerner, Max, my man."

He gives me another befuddled look. "Last time I checked, Missouri's considered south. I lived and worked there for five years before Miss Mona hired me. 'Say what's' pretty common in Missouri, as far as I can tell. What's weird is that whole surfer boy thing. What are you talking about?"

My cheeks burn hotter than a jalapeño in your taco filling, but I try to bluff my way out of my blunder. "Oh, nothing. Just something that popped out."

He crosses his arms. "Uh-huh. And I'm one of those infamous flying pigs."

Try *habañero* peppers—I hear say they're hotter'n jalapeños any day. After all, I've invoked the flying oinkers a time or two when thinking about Max. Which leads me to say, "Oink-oink."

"Not so funny." He stares—hard. "Trust me. You and I are going to have that long, long talk I've been wanting sooner rather than later. And you won't be able to run, like your smart mouth does."

I know, I know, I know. It takes all my strength to keep from wincing. Even if in my heart I'm wimping out, as I always do. "Let's get to business, then. What do you want to do?"

He shrugs. "I don't see that there's much to do. We load Laura into the cart, hitch it up to the bike, and I pedal her out of here."

"He—llooooh!" I wave. "Did you just forget me? I'm here too. How'm I going to get to . . . to that San Somebody or Other?"

The corners of his mouth twitch. "You might want to walk." His eyes twinkle.

My temper soars. "Why don't *I* bike *her* out while *you* walk?"

"Fine by me. But when you can't get the cart to move two inches, don't ask me why it's not working. It's called muscle mass, Andie. And I've got it. You don't."

I sag. "You've got a point. But you're not going to ride off into the sunset and leave me eating your dust, are you?"

He grows surprisingly serious. "I told you before, and I meant it. We're partners. Don't you ever—get it? *Ever*—forget it."

My heart does a flip. But then my gut does a flop. He's saying something without saying something. Know what I mean?

I take a deep breath. I nod.

Then I head to the bedroom. I drop to my knees by my bed and pray. "Lord Jesus . . . I need your courage. Why'd I turn out to be such a wimp? What's there to be afraid of? He's just a man like a million others. And he's never done anything deliberately deceitful, nor has he taken advantage of Miss Mona's kindness or generosity. Why do I let my past color how I see him? Help me follow your leading. Help me trust."

So if God's on my side, and he says in his Word that he gives us the desires of our heart, then why do I have to find myself in mess after mess after mess?

I have prayed for peace and calm. Many a time.

So yeah. You get the picture. The next morning I wind up trotting by the cart behind the bike on our way to San José. I do get stuck eating Max's dust—literally, if not figuratively. He might not have left me behind, but half of me starts to wish he had.

Let's face it. This is not the way a business trip should go. Especially since we trade our disgustingly dirty clothes for whatever the neighbors around Anita's house can offer. Trust me, wrong-size *campesino* clothing—peasant's garments—aren't much to write home about, but for Anita, Enrique, and their neighbors, they represent the best they have. And they helped us however they could. Gladly.

I've never felt so humbled by someone else's generosity. Or guilty. They pretty much gave us everything they had. Faith in God's provision? Oh yeah. They have that. And then some.

I can only hope to do as much, and I promise I will, as soon as I get back home.

Note to self: send clothes to Anita. Send money. Send furniture, food, and letters to the American embassy. The embassy needs to help these dear folks; they need to help them build a road from their tiny neighborhood to a decent market where they can sell their products, electricity to their homes—refrigerators would be nice—and a clinic in the region would do wonders for their health. Anything. Everything. Whatever. The kindness of these *campesinos* deserves a generous reward.

Still, here we are, on the road to that San José de Belén, wearing clothes that don't fit, me running like a puppy dog, Max pedaling for all he's worth, and Laura biting her bottom lip to keep from crying out at the pain in her leg. Not great. But it's the only way out of our dilemma.

Oh, so you figure things get better once we get to San José?

Think again.

When Laura explains our plight, we're helped up into the bed of yet another rattletrap truck. You'd think we'd have better luck this time, right? Lightning's not supposed to strike twice in the same spot. Well, let me tell you. It can. And does.

That's why now I'm bouncing around the bed of the truck, holding my nose, wanting to plug my ears.

Oh. You want to know why?

Because our means of transportation is trucking along more than just us and the guy behind the wheel. At our backs, where we're encouraged to lean, is the driver's load of a quartet of pens. Sure, the pens are filled. He's going to market. In Bogotá.

What's he taking to market? Besides us?

If you haven't figured it out yet, then I'm afraid you're a banana short of a bunch.

Uh-huh. We're on our way to Bogotá with a haul of sniffly, snuffly, grunty, grimy, beady-eyed, curly-tailed oinkers. Anyone who's been downwind from a pig farm knows the truth. Pig poop stinks. Reeks.

It even beats Eau de Dead Dog.

12⁰⁰

When we finally hit the outskirts of Bogotá, I draw in a piggy-scented breath of relief. We're closer to getting outta Dodge—so to speak. And right now, from where I'm sitting, we need the American medical system big-time. I'm afraid Laura's leg's going to need surgery. It looks like a compound fracture that's spent time growing back together without the bones being properly reset.

Not good.

I glance down at the sleeping girl whose head I'm pillowing against my thigh. My heart goes out to her, and I can't help admiring her courage again. I send up a prayer for her recovery. It breaks my heart to think greed and brutality might maim her for life.

We can't reach civilization soon enough for me.

"Getting closer," Max murmurs.

"Okay, Matthews. When did you become some kind of mind reader?"

He reaches over and smoothes my wispy bangs across my

forehead. "I haven't. You're just easy to read. At least, you are to me."

The way he says it and the look he gives me make my heart hopscotch over a beat. I stare into those blue, blue eyes for long seconds, unable to speak, unable to breathe, unwilling to remember where we are.

He wraps an arm around my shoulders and draws me close to his side. "Relax," he says. "We're probably close to the market now, and then it'll be all about calling the embassy for help."

I lean into him, careful not to bump the sleeping Laura. Once I'm cradled against his shoulder, he leans close to my ear. "What about the emeralds?"

I shudder. "I don't even want to think about them. Look at all the trouble they've caused."

"No, Andie. The emeralds haven't caused any trouble at all. It's Doña Rosario's greed that's made all the trouble."

"Oh, you're right." I sigh. "But it's trouble all the same. Know what I mean?"

"Yeah, I know what you mean. I've been at your side every step of the way. Remember?"

I glance up. The tenderness in his expression blows me away. Can it be real? Really real? *Oh, Lord Jesus. Don't let me get carried away on the wings of emotion. Help me see what you want me to see.*

"You have. And I'm glad."

He arches a brow. "So I'm not a babysitter anymore?"

I wink. "I didn't say that. You're still a babysitter, but I'm not fighting you anymore."

"I need that in writing, Ms. Adams."

I give him a mischievous grin. "No paper here."

"I'm still holding you to it."

You're holding me, period. I don't let this thought explode into words, even though it tries. Real hard.

Then he turns serious on me again. "What about the emeralds? Did you ditch them along the way?"

"Are you kidding? You think I'd dump the cause of all this?" I wave toward the pigs. They oink away. "After all we've gone through? And all we might still go through? No way am I leaving them behind."

"You still have them? You lost everything you had with you. How can you still have them? *Where* can you possibly have them?"

For about half a second I consider telling him. But then I think twice. "You're going to have to trust me on this. I do still have them. I just hid them. Did a great job too."

A frown lines his forehead. "Why won't you tell me?"

Can I make him understand my concern? "I don't want anyone else to have the information if they're asked. I don't even want you to have to lie if it comes to that. I've got them, they're safe, and I'll get them to Miss Mona." I stretch my neck to look over the wall of the truck bed. "As soon as we're out of Colombia."

He gives me a gentle shake. "I'm going to have to teach you about partnership, woman. It seems that lesson's escaped your much-touted education."

I go to disagree, but then have to back off. I can't argue his point. My track record's not so hot when it comes to trust, and trust is the bottom line for any partnership.

Ohmyohmyohmy. Max wants to teach me about partnerships.

Gulp.

Then, as I'm busy gulping, I realize I really do want a partnership with Max. And while the thought of getting hurt still makes me want to barf, a little kernel of excitement at the prospect—of partnership, not barfing—seems to be making itself at home in my heart.

As I contemplate the prospect of a real partnership with Max, I notice new sounds over the rattle and rumble of the truck. I stretch again, and realize we're making our way down a city street, buildings on either side, the sounds of normalcy—normal to city-girl moi—rising and falling in a welcome tide. The pigs' grunts don't even bother me now.

"Woo-hoo!" I pump a fist. "We're here."

I notice the sudden flash of disappointment in Max's face, and my heart does that hitching thing it's begun to do when he comes close, maybe too close.

Okay. So I might have wanted our conversation to continue down the path it had started, but come on. What girl wants to talk sweet nothings in the presence of pigs?

Not this one.

I want candlelight, roses, and yeah, I even want "Stranger in Paradise" playing in the background.

"Take my hand . . . I'm a stranger in paradise—"

"Shh!" I hiss. "No, no, no, no, no, no, *no*"—I shake my head—"not here."

He chuckles. "Okay, Andi-ana Jones. Not here."

But somewhere else hangs over us in the pig-stinky air.

What a promise.

What a guy.

What a way to fall in love.

173

The "market" turns out to be a distribution center–type warehouse, where trucks drop off their products for the center to send them on to processing plants. Fortunately for us, it's not too far from the Hotel de la Opera.

The minute Max and I scramble out of the truck bed, Laura drags herself to the edge, and Max cradles her in his arms again. We hoof it off toward the hotel.

Just imagine the impression we make when we walk into the luxe lobby. Uh-huh. The stench precedes us. It clears a path through the gathered guests. They give us a wide berth as I approach the front desk.

"You!" the young male clerk exclaims before I even open my mouth. "You're back. What do you want this time?"

Embarrassment crashes into need. "Ah . . . sorry. Umm . . . we need help." I wave toward Laura. "For her. She's hurt."

The desk clerk doesn't look convinced. I understand. We do look super-disreputable. I doubt I'd respond any differently in his position. But I can't just quit. "And we need to contact the American embassy. Please don't kick us out. We'll leave as soon as we get some help."

I guess the promise of our immediate departure goes a long way. He picks up the phone, dials, and within seconds passes me the receiver. I plead our case, and finally relax at the promise of an embassy car to get us help—American help.

The clerk takes the phone I hold out. "Thank you. We'll be gone as soon as the embassy car gets here. We'll go wait outside."

Evidently, the idea of our hanging out where hotel guests

can get a good gander—plus a sniff—at us doesn't appeal to him. "You don't have to do that," he says. "Let me show you to the office. I'm sure the young lady will be more comfortable there."

And while the office does offer more comfort and privacy, we don't stay there long enough for it to make a difference. The embassy limo arrives in less than twenty minutes. We ease Laura into the broad backseat, Max and I join her, and we're whisked off toward the international section of town, where the embassies are located.

As beautiful as the Hotel de la Opera is, I can't say I'm sorry to see the last of it. Maybe if I'd come back to the place under different circumstances, I would have left with better memories. As it is, between my close encounter with hotel trash and now my triumphant—*not*—return, I don't think I'll ever think of it with fondness.

Our time at the embassy goes by in a blur. I know I call Rodolfo Cruz, and his sob of relief when I tell him his daughter's safe is something I'll never forget.

"You were so right," I tell Max as I step away from Laura while she speaks with her father. "The man was going out of his mind with worry."

Max shrugs. "It's called love, Andie. Anytime someone we love is threatened, we suffer. A father's love has to be an amazing thing. I don't know it yet, but I sure hope God's got that in his plans for my future."

A ripple of emotion runs through me at the thought of Max with an infant in his arms. But then, the reality of Rodolfo's agony hits me with the stark contrast between the two possible extremes. "Aren't you afraid of the pain? I mean, you just said you understood how much he must have hurt."

"Sure. But imagine the joy you get from loving someone that much. And that's the only way to get loved back, too. I'd rather let myself love and trust God with the outcome at the other end."

I suck in a deep breath. He's hitting me where it counts, right in the area where I've been limping all along.

As I go on a mental scramble for a way to answer, Laura calls my name. "My father wants me to go with you. He thinks I'll be safer in America."

"How're we going to get you into the U.S.?" I ask. "You need a passport, documents, an airline ticket. How long do you think it will take you to get all that together?"

"It shouldn't take long at all. Papá's going to arrange everything. He'll tell the embassy attaché where he should go in our house in Bogotá to find my papers and the credit card he got me for school trips. He'll follow us to Kentucky as soon as he gets back from the mine and goes home to get his papers, maybe even tomorrow. I can leave on the next flight out."

Laura's composure strikes me again. She's got me beat. "Just how old are you?"

"I'm fourteen."

"Are you sure?" I ask before I realize what I'm saying.

Max's laughter explodes.

Laura giggles. "Of course I'm sure. I'm fourteen years old. You can ask my father. He'll tell you."

"I think, Andie, you can trust the girl." Max snickers again. "Teenagers are usually very up-to-the-minute about their age. It's not something they kid about."

"Yeah, well. That didn't come out quite like I wanted." And it hits me again how often that happens with me. Gotta

176

backtrack and say what I really should have said—if I'd taken the time to think it through. "What I really meant is how impressed I am. You act much older, much more mature than fourteen."

"Thanks."

"Your mother and father have done a great job with you."

Her smile turns wistful. Details click into place. I wince, since I realize what she's about to say before she says it. And my heart aches for her.

"My mother died a long time ago." Her soft voice trembles. "My father's the one who takes care of me."

I have to fight down the lump in my throat. "I'm so sorry about your mother. But your father's done great with you. I can't wait to tell him myself."

She looks away. "I hope you do tell him. I hope you can."

Max and I look at each other. I turn back to Laura. "What do you mean, you hope I can?"

She shakes her head, but doesn't face me. I want to prod, to push for an answer, but Max's hand on my arm holds me back.

"Give her time," he whispers.

"Okay." I shake my head. "But I can't get rid of a funny feeling . . ."

I don't get the chance to think any more about that funny feeling, even though I'm unable to ditch it along the way. My old friend Mr. Sloan walks in, wrinkles his nose, and sends us to clean up. I feel like a rascally two-year-old.

His wife stops by to check with me, since she's been drafted to play the part of personal shopper for Laura and me. Mr. Sloan himself goes after clothes for Max.

Once we're dressed in decent garments again, I make sure

Mr. Sloan understands my firm determination—although he might call it mule-headedness—to help Anita and Enrique and their neighbors. Laura gets her passport from the messenger, who'd gone to the Cruz household for it, and Max and I are given emergency ones to take the place of the ones my purse snatcher and Doña Rosario's crew took. We get whisked into the limo again, and then zipped off to the airport. On our way there, I turn to Mr. Sloan.

"How is your military guard?"

The embassy attaché shakes his head. "That was terrible. But he is recovering. The nicked bone will heal, but the worst part is the amount of blood loss caused by the bullet wound. He's in a cast these days, and will have to wear it for a good while."

"I felt awful, having to leave him there. After all, he did come to make sure I was okay." Then I remember my irritation at all the "babysitting" going on. "I wasn't so happy to have a shadow along with me"—I look at Max—"especially since this one doesn't seem to get too far from me, but I appreciate the guard's efforts on my behalf."

Mr. Sloan gives me a rueful smile. "I'll tell Wayne. He's been beating himself up, thinking up possible outcomes, each one worse than the last."

"He didn't have to use too much imagination to come up with kidnapping and a dirt cell. But I doubt he could've imagined the cart and the bike and the pigs."

"Pigs?" Mrs. Sloan asks.

We take turns telling our tale, and while we do, I notice how quiet Mr. Sloan gets. When we have his wife in stitches, and we wind up our tale with our disgraced return to the glam Hotel de la Opera, I fall silent too.

His distraction piques my curiosity; the little niggling feeling in the back of my mind catches my attention again.

"What aren't you telling us?" I realize how little time we have left with him, so I'm not willing to beat around the bush.

He stares out the window. Hmm . . .

"I don't know for sure," he says after a minute or two. "But there's always been whispers about the Lopez family—Doña Rosario's father's side. I don't know if it's fear or respect, but people around Colombia make a point to not cross them."

I scoff. "After I negotiated the emerald buy she wanted, and especially now that we've snuck out of her rotten little hole-in-the-ground and taken Laura with us? I'll say we've crossed her."

"Who would have known you'd come up against Rosario Lopez Carrasco? When I first met you, all I had to deal with was a stolen purse and passport. And the hotel's accusations of your mischief in their back alley—as they put it."

With my head back against the leather upholstery, I close my eyes and sigh. "I know, I know. Those were the good old days. She's one scary lady."

Max makes a choked sound. "Lady? You're giving her a lot more credit than I would. She's a thug. Never thought I'd see the day I'd call a woman of her age that, but there you have it."

"Thug?" Laura asks.

"Crook, criminal, bad guy—gal, woman . . . whatever!" I shrug. "She's bad news, that's for sure. And I can't put enough space between us fast enough for my liking."

The limo rolls to a stop. Mr. Sloan glances out the window. "It looks like you're getting your wish, Andrea. We're at the airport. Your flight should leave in about an hour and a half."

A pinprick of light goes on at the end of the tunnel my trip has become. "Louisville, here we come!"

❖

The long flight? It went by in a blink. At least, that's how it felt. I did doze off, but I didn't sleep through the whole thing. I spent more time praying than I did sleeping. And I thanked God for his mercy and protection over and over again.

Our row had three seats, and Max and I agreed to put Laura between the two of us in the emergency-exit row seats we chose for their extra leg room. I took the window, while he took the aisle.

When we land on American soil, I have to fight my impatience. We can't very well haul Laura through the mass of lemmings fighting to leap out over the cliff—oh, wait. They're just getting off the plane.

When they're finally gone, an attendant waves to us. "The wheelchair is waiting for you."

An airport employee helps Max with Laura, then guides us out into the concourse, where we're met by one of those airport golf-cart thingies for travelers who need help.

Oh yeah. We need help, all right. More than I can list.

We chug down the concourse, people staring at us. At the luggage area, the cart dumps us . . . er, well, not really, but we're helped off, and we take a seat to wait for our rescuers.

Not for long.

"Sugarplum!"

"Andie, dear!"

I look at the two women rushing our way, and to my horror, I choke on emotion. That same emotion blinds me with tears. By the time I run into their wide-open arms, all three of us are crying, sobbing, a mess.

But, oh! What a wonderful mess. This one I like.

Finally, once I'm able to dredge up enough composure to speak again, I pull away from my Daunting Duo. "I'm never doing this again. You hear?"

"I hear, I hear," Aunt Weeby says, still holding on to me.

"I hear," Miss Mona echoes, but with less oomph. "What is it you won't do again? Cry?"

Now them's fighting words. I pull away, plant my fists on my hips, and glare. "Don't you do that to me, Miss Mona. You know I love you, and I love working for you, but you know perfectly well what I mean. I won't be chasing off after gems to all the weird corners of the world anymore."

"Andie—"

"Nope. No arguments allowed." I shake a finger at her. "Not again. You want gems to sell on-screen? Well, then, you make sure we get super-duper, big-time vendor traffic at the S.T.U.D. I'm not facing foreign loonies again. Not on their turf, I'm not."

"Oh, dear . . ."

"My goodness . . ."

"Ladies," Max says, humor in his voice. "I think it's time to get Laura to the hospital."

I ignore him and march off, leaving him to follow with Laura. Not to mention, the two elderly women who should bring up the rear. Somewhere in the line of vehicles at the curb I'm sure I'll find the studio's limo.

But no matter how hard I have to fight them, I'm determined not to give. I'm home now. And I'm so thankful the Lord's brought me back, alive and well. Now I just have to pray, day after day, that he'll agree with me and see fit to let me do my thing on-screen.

No more close encounters of the international intrigue kind.

Please.

13⁰⁰

The orthopedic specialists decide to operate on Laura's leg right away. So this morning I'm meeting Max at the hospital. During the course of our adventure—ahem—we've grown close to the girl and don't want her to face surgery alone. If I were in her place, I'd hate to be in a foreign hospital, facing a surgeon and his knife all on my own. Rodolfo's flight isn't due into Louisville until later on today, and the doctors feel it's best for them to perform the surgery right away, and he'd agreed when the diagnosis was reported to him the night before.

When I arrive in Laura's room, I find Miss Mona, Aunt Weeby, and Max gathered around her bed. "You guys are early birds."

Aunt Weeby gives me a hug. "You'd better not be calling this sweet child a worm, sugarplum."

"Not even because I found her underground." I shake my head, wonder about my aunt's view of things, then reach to hug Laura. "All I meant is you guys are up early today."

"The ladies called to ask me for a ride," Max added. "I couldn't turn them down, could I?"

I hug Miss Mona and chuckle. "Oh boy! You're setting yourself up for trouble if that's your reasoning. Who knows what these two will ask you next?"

"I'll deal." He opens his arms wide. "Don't I get a hug too?"

The Daunting Duo's sighs in stereo echo against the walls. Their excitement crackles in the air. Max's eyes dance with mischief.

What's a girl to do with a crew like this?

Hug the guy, that's what.

Then he kisses my head.

Now it's my gasp that resonates around the room. I look up, and see Max fight to keep a laugh from busting out. The rat. He knows exactly what he does to me. I'm in trouble now—

Oh, what am I thinking? I've been in trouble when it comes to this man from the minute I laid eyes on him the day of our first show together. I might even have been in trouble when Miss Mona went undercover and behind my back to scour the country for a cohost for my show. Not that I'd wanted one.

Don't know that I want one even now.

But Max? Hmm . . . maybe he's a bonus.

Then again, when I think about it, Miss Mona might not have been out there hunting cohosts after all. She might have been auditioning romantic interests for me, since she and Aunt Weeby were getting antsy, and I wasn't showing any likelihood of pairing up. Scary, scary thought. But a way too likely possibility.

Good grief. Just look at the rapturous expressions on Aunt Weeby's and Miss Mona's faces. Those two have known all along what they were up to. And I'm beginning to suspect Max has been a too-willing victim.

What does that really mean?

". . . Earth to Andie!" the rat says.

I'm saved from my embarrassment by the arrival of a nurse and an orderly who will be taking Laura down to the OR. Her eyes widen and she tenses visibly. I lean over the steel railing on the bed, give a squeeze to her shoulder, then whisper, "I'll be praying for you."

She gives me a look full of gratitude. "You've all been so nice to me. And you don't even know me."

I blush. "Oh, you know. It's that 'whatever you do for the least of these my brothers, you do it for me' thing."

"Then I'm glad you did it for me."

She's wheeled out, and we all follow, watching her go. Once the whisper of the closing elevator door fades, we turn to each other. "What next?"

Miss Mona squares her shoulders. "I think we should go down to the waiting room outside the operating room, like the surgeon told us to do. That way we'll be closer to her. For when he comes out after he's done, you understand." She pushes the elevator button.

"That poor little thing . . . " Aunt Weeby says. "When'd you say her daddy was coming, Mona?"

"He should be here this evening."

If nothing goes wrong. If Doña Rosario doesn't get to him. Worse yet: if she doesn't set her goons to do her dirty work for her. If, if, if. Too many ifs to deal with. My funny feeling keeps getting funnier by the second.

185

As we step into the elevator, Max turns to me. "Now that we're out of Colombia, Andie, how about you tell me what you did with the emeralds?"

"Then or now?"

He looks exasperated. "Start out with 'then.' We'll go on from there."

I shrug. "The lining of my walking shoes was easy to lift up, then stick back down. They started life out with a super-duper extra-special gel cushion in each heel. I think you'll agree there was no contest between the cushions and the emeralds."

His eyebrows crash into his hairline. "You mean you were *walking* on a fortune the whole time?"

"What else would you have had me do? At least I knew where the stones were. And Doña Rosario didn't find them when she strip-searched me, did she?"

The Daunting Duo looks aghast. Aunt Weeby goes pale. Miss Mona goes green around the gills, then turns and takes two shaky steps to the window, her back toward us.

"Hey!" I say before they comment. "I'm okay, you guys. The strip search didn't hurt anything more than my pride."

While Aunt Weeby looks unconvinced and Miss Mona's back stiffens even more, neither one comments. I'm not dumb enough to think the subject's dead. I'll be hearing more about it at some later time. Let's see how long I can put off that hearing.

Max looks down at my sandaled feet. "Those don't look to me like comfortable walking shoes where you can hide things. What'd you do with the ones with the stones?"

"Miss Mona has them. I turned them over last night."

He steps to our boss's side. "Please tell me you didn't funnel them into your high heels."

She turns, takes a deep, uneven breath, and taps the toe of her pump against the floor. "Pshaw! Of course I didn't, Max. They're in the studio's vault. Where else would you have me put them?"

He shakes his head. "You women are going to make me nuts."

Welcome to my world. Now he knows how I felt when I first learned Miss Mona had the vault access built into the far corner of the ladies' room at the studio.

The elevator dings open, and we walk out into the hall. While hospitals are rarely quiet places, there's an uncomfortable hush down here. I shudder. Pain, strain, life, death. It's all too real.

Without waiting for the other three, I head to the waiting room. There, I choose an overstuffed chair by the broad window. A glance at the fan of magazines on the table wedged between my chair and the next one to my right only registers a kaleidoscope of color, so I choose at random, then drop it on my lap once I sit. I'm not sure I can focus enough to read, but at least the shiny pages will give me something to do with my hands while I wait.

Max takes the chair to my left. "Hmm . . . I didn't know you had a burning interest in fly-fishing, Andi-ana Jones."

I look down, and get the picture. I meet his gaze. "What can I say? I'm concerned. You know I couldn't care less about fly-fishing."

"But you care about Laura."

"Just like you."

He takes my hand in his. "Let's pray."

Hours later, after the surgeon has given us the good news about Laura's leg and Rodolfo Cruz has arrived, we split up and go our separate ways. Rodolfo heads to his daughter's room, anxious to see her for himself. Miss Mona calls Davina, the studio's chauffeur, and she and Aunt Weeby go on home. Max and I opt for dinner at the hospital's cafeteria.

"Would you look at that?" he says as we walk up to one of the various food stations.

"At what?"

He indicates the cafeteria. "It looks more like a restaurant than a hospital dining room."

"Back when Aunt Weeby was in here about a year ago, I read something about the hospital bringing in a fancy chef to upgrade their chow."

At the stir-fry area, he takes a plate and points at the chicken breast strips for the gentleman behind the counter to dish out. "This is much better than I thought we'd get. At least it's real food."

The sizzle and scent of chicken and soy sauce makes my mouth water. "You're in the south, boy!" I chuckle. The pasta station calls my name, and I know I've found my meal. "We know how to eat around here."

He gives me a mock frown. "You'd better quit with that southern chauvinist deal. I've been a transplanted southerner for a long time now. I'm sure some of it has seeped in over the years."

"You're a sponge of the extra-large variety, huh?"

"Something like that."

The next hour passes by along those lines. Max enjoys his

stir-fry and I my linguine with clams. Once we're done with that part, we scarf down wide wedges of lemon meringue pie with steaming cups of coffee. By the time I'm about to pop, Max stands.

"I'm ready to go check on Laura before I head back home. I still need to spend a couple of hours catching up on some reading. There's a gem identification seminar coming up at the GIA in a couple of weeks."

I still can't believe he's really going through with the Gemological Institute of America's Graduate Gemologist training. Who'd a thunk the surfer boy would go that far? "How's that going?"

He grabs both of our trays and we head toward the conveyor belt along one wall. "Let's just say I have even more respect for anyone who's gotten to Graduate Gemologist. It's no cakewalk to earn that title."

This Graduate Gemologist—now Master Gemologist, I'll have you know—lets herself smirk. "Toldja."

He drops the used tableware on the rolling black rubber contraption, then with an exaggerated flourish, he gives me a little mock bow. "I genuflect at the feet of your greater wisdom, oh Poo-Bah of gemstone erudition."

Laughing, I swat at his shoulder. "Come on. I think the exhaustion from our trip really fried what brain cells you had left. Let's go see Laura so you can catch a few z's before we have to meet in front of a camera tomorrow."

As we slip into the elevator, it occurs to me that Max and I haven't had one single argument since very early in my trip to Colombia. In fact, we made a pretty good team down there, and now we're even having fun together. I glance his way, catch his gaze, and offer him a tentative smile.

He wraps his arm around my shoulders.

I lean into his side.

Then, just as I'm really getting the hang of enjoying the closeness without nerves or fear raising their familiar heads, the elevator door yawns and spits us out on Laura's floor. Max keeps his arm in place. He doesn't let me step away.

This is getting serious.

Lo and behold, I'm not shaking at the knees.

Miracles do still happen. *Thank you, Lord.*

In a haze of romantic contentment, I aim for Laura's room. We find the door slightly ajar. We hear muffled sounds from inside.

"Do you think we'll be interrupting one of the nurses?" I ask.

He knocks, then opens the door. "Only one way to know."

Neither of us is prepared for what we find. A man in dark clothes and a black knit cap pulled down low over his bearded face is struggling with Rodolfo, who is no match for the obviously younger and stronger attacker. Max rushes the two men and joins the fray.

"Help!" I yell. I turn to head back into the hall, but my shirt is snagged from behind, and I stumble past the fighting men. "Oh, help us, please!"

A particularly heavy thud tells me one of the three has landed a good punch. I hope it's Max. But then Rodolfo stumbles backward. I reach out to catch him. I miss. His head strikes the metal foot of the bed.

He grunts. Crumples to the ground.

No! No, no, no, no, no. This can't be happening.

"Rodolfo!" I cry. He doesn't respond.

Since I can't just barge through Max and the attacker, I

skirt by them, dodge flying fists, and rush to the emerald vendor's side. As I lean down, I catch a glimpse of Laura. What I see sends a chill down my spine. She's pale, white as chalk, and her chest . . . I'm not sure she's breathing.

Behind me, another fist lands a hit.

Another groan tells its tale.

"Max!" I call out. "Are you okay?"

"Silencio!" the brute in black hisses.

Silence? That beast wants me to be silent? Well, I'll show him. I scream. Again, again, and again.

My throat burns from yelling. Max and the goon pummel away. Rodolfo's too still. Laura . . . well, Laura doesn't look good at all. I'm torn. Do I help her? Rodolfo? Claw the monster off Max?

With dismay bordering on despair, I realize there's little I can do alone. I have to get help. Inch by inch, I edge toward the head of the bed, the call-button gizmo my goal. I have to buzz the nurses' station.

In another second, I'm there. I push the red button. Again. Twice. Three times.

I give another holler for good measure.

"Yes?"

The disembodied voice is more welcome than a life jacket during a seagoing hurricane. "Send security! There's a . . . a—oh, just send us help before someone gets killed."

With a last vicious jab at Max's gut, the masked man lets out what can only be a pungent expletive in Spanish. He turns and runs from the room.

My knees give way.

I sag against the bed rail.

A nurse runs in, followed by an armed and uniformed

guard. I've never been so happy to see one of Chief Clark's men. And I'm no fan of his PD.

The woman's frown would curdle milk. "What's going on here—"

Her eyes widen and she yanks the call button from my hand. When it crackles to life, she doesn't wait for a response. She rattles off a series of numbers—code for the situation, I'm sure. She signs off with the universally urgent "STAT!"

Everything happens on speed-dial. More uniforms arrive, nurses' uniforms as well as law enforcement ones. A gurney is rolled in, two orderlies load Rodolfo on its narrow mattress, and whisk him off. Max gets a great deal of attention, especially his bruised and cracked knuckles.

In the end, I go with Laura as she's wheeled into an elevator and rushed to the Critical Care Unit. I can't forget that promise to pray.

It takes the doctors no time to figure out she's been poisoned. And while they need more tests to know for sure what exactly she was given, it's clear that whatever it was, it's affected her breathing.

"I suspect whatever it was went into the IV," a Dr. Chapman tells me.

I know less than nothing about medicine, but I've watched my fair share of TV shows. For once, those lost hours in front of the boob tube pay off. "That would make sense. Maybe her father walked in on the creep as he was in the act."

"We can only hope," the young physician says. "Even the slightest amount he might have failed to deliver will help her."

Oh, Lord Jesus . . . please. "Is there anything I can do?"

"For her?"

I nod.

He shakes his head. "We've dosed her with something to help her breathing, but it's up to her body now to withstand the poison, since we don't yet know if there's a better medication. Once we get the lab results back, we'll be able to do more."

"I promised her I would pray, and I can at least do that."

Just then, Aunt Weeby runs up to my side. "We're back, sugarplum. Max had us called, and we hurried over as soon as we could. And you know we can both of us pray up a storm, can't we, Mona? We're fearsome prayer warriors, if I do say so myself."

I fall into the Duo's joint hug, irrationally relieved by their arrival. There's nothing they can do. Their presence, though, eases my loneliness.

Time creeps by, each second longer than the last. The three of us stay outside the glass-walled room where Laura lies frozen, staring at the slight body in the bed, the sweet girl hooked up to tubes and lights and beeping machines.

A short while later, Max comes back. "Any word?"

I turn. "Oh, ouch! You poor thing." Red is turning to puce around one of those beautiful baby blues. "Is your eye going to be okay?"

"I'll live." He dips his head toward Laura. "How about her? And Rodolfo? Any change?"

"How much did they tell you?"

"That she was poisoned with something that affected her breathing and her heartbeat, and that Rodolfo's in surgery to drain blood from his brain."

"That's what we were told." I'd hoped for more info, but I suppose there's not much more to know until Laura's test results return and the neurosurgeons finish with Rodolfo. "How are your hands?"

"They're no big deal. Not compared to Rodolfo and Laura. They're both trying to hang on to life. We don't know if either one's going to pull through."

"Hush, Max!" the paper-pale Miss Mona chides. "Don't give the devil a toehold with thoughts like that."

He slips an arm around her and gives her a hug. "Then we'll just focus on prayer. For that, though, you need your rest. You didn't have to rush back. Andie and I are still here, and if I know anything about her, no one's going to get her to leave until she gets word on both our patients."

I glance at Laura and see no change. "How about we go down to the chapel? It's quiet there, and they've hung a nice, big old cross on the wall behind the altar. That'll help us look in the right direction."

As they join me, and we head down to pray, I get the strong feeling I'll be spending a good chunk of time there in the days to come. I'm going to be learning what it means to keep a vigil.

Does that mean I'm finally growing up?

Lord Jesus? Father God? I sure hope so.

As I walk into the quiet room, a bolt of memory zaps me. Something I'd heard but let slide by. How I could have done that, I'll never know. True, it had happened in the heat of the moment, at the most frightening stage.

The man who'd poisoned Laura, gravely injured Rodolfo, and given Max a doozy of a shiner had spoken Spanish. We're no longer in Colombia. Kentucky's not exactly the heart of Latino immigration.

Who is he? What is he doing here?

194

Is he after the gems?

Or is something more going on?

Only God knows the answers to these questions. I'm going to have to trust him. I'm going to have to put the pedal of my faith to the metal of this gig.

Trust. That sticky little part of faith.

I hope the Father doesn't find me lacking.

This time.

While neither Max nor I are able to get Aunt Weeby and Miss Mona to go home, Chief Clark can. And does. But then, once they're on their way, the Andie-grilling begins. Why is it I've been subjected to more fire since I came home a year ago than the average slab of ribs at a July barbecue?

By the time I've answered more questions than I would think a body could ever ask, I'm glaring at the chief. Something I seem to do with alarming regularity. "You done with me yet? 'Cause I sure feel well done."

He arches a brow. "It's like this, Miss Andie. I'm thinking I'll be done with you once I have the guy who's done this behind bars, and not before then. Since you and Mr. Max here are the only ones I can ask, then I'm going to do all the asking I have to do."

I roll my eyes. "I get it. But you have to figure I don't have much more to tell you after all this." No response from the man. "Once more, with feeling, then. Max and I walked into Laura's room and found the man beating on Mr. Cruz. Max went for the guy to help Mr. Cruz. The creep shoved

Mr. Cruz, who bashed his head on the corner of the bed. Of course, I went to see about him. The creep told me to shut up—in Spanish. I pushed the panic button, and then the guy left before the nurses arrived—after he'd thoroughly punished Max."

"How 'bout you describe him to me one more time?"

"What's to say? I already told you about his black pants, black T-shirt, black cap, and full black beard. There's not a whole lot I saw other than a blur of black."

The chief gave me a disgusted look. "Tell me about *him*. Was he short, tall, thin, fat? His eyes? Did you get a good look at 'em?"

I point at Max. "He got real close and personal with the guy. Why don't you ask him?"

Max glares. "I got *too* close and personal. I didn't get much of a chance to look at him. I think he was shorter than me—"

"It doesn't take much for that, Mr. Long Tall Drink of Water," I say. "The guy was shorter than Max, and he looked pretty muscular under the T-shirt. But I didn't even come close to seeing his eyes."

"Dark," Max says. "They were so dark, they looked black."

"So neither one of you can tell me much." Chief Clark scratches his chin while he mulls over what we've said. "Doesn't it hit you strange-like that that man hushed you in Spanish?"

I sigh. "Of course. It's been itching my mind pretty much since it all happened. What do you think?"

He crosses his arms. "Seems to me, Miss Andie, I just asked you that, didn't I?"

"Tell you what." I stand, grab my purse, and turn to go. "You get the guy, lock him up, and then we can both ask him what's up with that. Right now, I'm worried stupid about Laura, and I'm in desperate need of coffee." I turn to Max. "You with me?"

He fights a grin. "Chief, I think Andie's right. We don't have anything more to tell you. You'll just have to wait for the results of the toxicology tests, just like everyone else. Maybe once you know what the man gave Laura you'll have more to go on. And we can hope the fingerprint guys can match up the ones you lifted."

My law enforcement nemesis sighs. "I suppose you might could be right, but nothing says I have to like the circumstances. Remember, I have me a little girl and her daddy, pretty near to dead." He skewers me with his piercing stare. "From where I'm sitting, it looks the same all over again. Here Miss Andie goes out of town to some foreign place, and next thing you know—"

"Don't you dare!" I stomp to the elevator at the end of the hall. The men's footsteps follow close behind. "I had nothing to do with this creep. Or any of Creepella's other goons."

As I blurt, I realize the can of worms I've opened.

"Creepella?" the cop asks. "Who're you calling Creepella?"

Max and I look at each other. "Oh, just a nasty woman we met in Colombia. No one you need to worry about, I'm sure." But even as I say it, it doesn't ring right.

Clearly, it doesn't to the chief either. "A nasty woman in Colombia, you say." He rubs an index finger along the length of his nose, skepticism smeared all over his face. "Let's see if I've got this right. A Colombian girl's poisoned in my suburban Louisville hospital. Her Colombian daddy lands in critical with a cracked-open head fighting off the guy who poisoned her. And you and Mr. Max spend some time fighting off the man what caused all the other ills. And that's the man who shushed you in Spanish."

I refuse to look at him.

His eyes keep boring into me, regardless. "You're wanting me to think that nasty woman in Colombia isn't connected? I think, Miss Andie"—his easygoing voice gets just a hair tighter—"you and I need to have us another little chat. But I agree. We do need to get some sleep before we can do any more chatting." He slaps his notebook shut. "I'll be seeing you in the morning."

That's more threat than promise. "Gee," I mutter under my breath as he saunters off. "I can't wait."

Max takes my hand and gives it a healthy squeeze. "Watch your mouth, Andi-ana Jones. It's almost as hazardous to your health as the guy in the black ski hat."

"Yeah, okay. Fine. But why should the chief think we— I—know more about the nutcase who came to kill Laura than what we already told him? Does he really think we'd lie about it?"

"We were the last men standing, so to speak. We're the only witnesses. Who else is he going to hit up for info?"

"Oh, stop being so rational, willya?" I blow a frustrated gust of breath. "All I want is for Laura to recover. And her dad."

"Who are you kidding, Andrea Adams?" He shakes his head. "It's me, Max. I know you know you want to know what's really going on here."

His gaze goes deep. The guy has come to know me too well.

"Yeah, but—"

"Then let the chief do his best. He doesn't have too bad a record going in, you know."

As I step into the elevator, I slant him a look. "You were there. You know I've had to give him a nudge or two."

He tightens his grip on my fingers. "Not this time."

"Not this time. I'm out of the figuring-out-whodunnit business."

"And I'm going to make sure you stay out of it."

I head for the parking lot instead of the cafeteria, suddenly swamped with exhaustion no river of coffee's going to help. "I won't do Laura any good if I don't get some real sleep," I say when Max asks me where I'm going. "I'll see you first thing in the morning."

"I'll be here." He looks as though he wants to say something more, but then he shrugs.

"G'night, Max."

"Good night, Andie."

As I head for the car, I can't shake the sense of something missing, something left unsaid. Something important.

I cast a look over my shoulder. Max hasn't budged. He's still under the awning right by the hospital door, his gaze glued to me, a hard-to-figure expression on his face.

Oh yeah. There's a whole lot left unsaid. And I don't think it has much to do with either Laura or Rodolfo Cruz.

It won't be just Chief Clark I'll be having a tête-à-tête with soon. And with every day that goes by, I'm less and less chicken about it.

About him.

Could Chief Clark be right?

Could *I* be right?

The idea has taken permanent residence ever since the

moment I woke up, and now, on my way to the hospital to meet Aunt Weeby, Miss Mona, and Max, I'm in the same place in my head. I know Doña Rosario wanted those emeralds, not just any emeralds, the spectacular ones Miss Mona bought. She still does, I'm sure. And I also know Rodolfo Cruz didn't do business with her—not that I'm sure she wanted to actually *do* business in the first place. I got the feeling she wanted the emeralds just because, payment optional. After all, she did say she didn't like leftovers. And I did buy Rodolfo's absolute best.

Besides that, you and I and the fly on the wall know Rodolfo's attacker spoke Spanish.

Is that enough to go ahead and connect the dots? Did Doña Rosario send a man to . . . to what? Kill the Cruzes? To scare them? To shake the emeralds out of them? All of the above, and then some?

If that's the case, is she going to send him after me too? I'm not sure she believed the results of her search. I got the sense she *knew*, not just thought, I had the stones all along.

A shudder shakes me. Can't say I want another face-off with Creepella. Or her creep.

As far as Chief Clark goes . . . well, I don't want him to grill me again, but I guess I don't get a choice there. I want the man who did this caught and behind bars. So I'll deal.

I pull into the hospital parking lot, lock up the car, take a big breath, and head upstairs. Aunt Weeby and Miss Mona are already in the Intensive Care Unit waiting room, excitement on their faces.

"Guess what!" my aunt squeals as she hugs me.

Since I'm smarter than the average fence post, and we are where we are, and since they both look livelier than a

201

string of Christmas tree lights . . . you get my drift. "Laura's doing better."

Instead of congratulating me, they both look disappointed. "How'd you guess?" Aunt Weeby says.

I roll my eyes and laugh. "It doesn't take a genius, you two. We've all been worried silly about her. But that's great news, no matter what. Now, how about Rodolfo?"

Aunt Weeby's cheer melts away. "He's not doing so hot, sugarplum. No change, and he was in pretty sorry shape last night, you know."

"I'm sorry. I was hoping for better news about him too. Poor Laura. It's great that she's better, but I'd hate for her to be worrying over her daddy. That won't help her one bit."

"It sure won't," Max says as he walks in. "Good morning, ladies. I stopped by the nurse's station and learned they're moving Laura back to her regular room. She regained consciousness during the night and her breathing's fine now, even though she'll have to keep doing breathing exercises for a few days. We'll have to make sure she does them. Then, too, her heart doesn't seem to have been damaged."

Miss Mona offers her cheek for his kiss. "Looks like you used all those sweet-talking charms of yours to get the nurses to tell you what they wouldn't tell us, son."

Max frowns. "I thought when I walked in I heard Andie say Laura was better. They talked to you."

I give him a crooked grin. "I did say that, but that's all I could get the nurses to tell me. Nothing about moving her back to her regular room, breathing exercises, or about her heart being okay."

"Maybe they had nothing to say when you asked. Maybe

they were waiting for test results or doctor's orders or some-thing."

"Five minutes before you walked in? Don't think so."

Miss Mona and Aunt Weeby tease him about his effect on women, while I bite my bottom lip. Nobody needs to tell me about it. I'm living proof of his abilities. What's worse, he knows how he affects women . . . certainly this woman.

When the orderly wheels out Laura's bed, we all gather around to escort her back to her regular room. While we're all thrilled she's doing so well, our concern for her father becomes a sixth entity in that room. Then a seventh shows up.

Of course, it's Chief Clark, back to drum me with even more questions. He leads me to the waiting room, and then wastes no time firing away. "Mind telling me who that Creepella woman you were talking 'bout might be, Miss Andie?"

I wince. "You're really serious, aren't you? You think she's involved. Even though she's back in Colombia. It wasn't just my hyperactive imagination going to town on me, then."

The chief leans against the wall, crosses his arms, shrugs and makes a face. "Dunno about her being back in Colombia. Last I checked, you've had plenty of crazy folks come chas-ing after you and those fancy foreign stones you sell. And I only have one way to find out what's what. I gotta focus on doing plain, old-fashioned police work. So how 'bout it, Miss Andie? You going to tell me about that woman?"

Max walks up as I consider my options—none I can see. "Can I join you?" he asks.

The chief shrugs. "You might could help, even." He looks my way again. "So, Miss Andie. How 'bout it?"

I tell the chief everything I can remember about our

encounters with Doña Rosario. I describe her as best I can, with Max adding a detail or two as I go along. We even do what we can to come up with decent descriptions of her men.

When there's nothing more to tell, we all stay quiet. I can see the wheels cranking in Chief Clark's head—not really, but I can tell he's dissecting everything I've told him, filing bits and pieces together with whatever data he's received from Colombian authorities.

How do I know he's been in contact with Colombian authorities?

Easy. I've been down this road before. And I'm getting mighty sick of it. At least, by the grace of God, no one's dead this time.

Rodolfo's image forms behind my eyelids.

No one's dead this time—yet.

I pray it stays that way. *Please, Lord?*

"Dunno if I can agree with something you said before, Miss Andie," the chief says. "Or maybe you didn't rightly say it, but you sure were doubting the possibility. I'm pretty near sure that Rosie-woman is behind all this. Just as you know she was behind you being kidnapped and all."

I draw a deep sigh. "And all because of a bunch of rocks."

"Hmm . . ." Max says. "Am I hearing things? Is that the one and only Andi-ana Jones calling gemstones rocks? The woman I once saw run into a burning house to save her rock collection? The same woman who, just to see where rubies come from, went burrowing underground into a mine that wound up caving?"

"Guess it's called growing up, Max." I slant him a glance, a wink, and a grin. "Can you deal?"

204

He leans back into his armchair and crosses his arms. "Oh, Andie, Andie, Andie. I can deal. I absolutely can deal."

A shimmy of excitement runs through me. I meet his gaze, and find myself caught in the intensity there. Am I deluding myself or do I see a responding excitement, anticipation, caring and warmth and—

Don't get ahead of yourself, Andie. That's the quickest way to that broken heart.

With every bit of strength inside me, I tear my gaze away and focus on Chief Clark again. I have all the time in the world for Max. "What do you know about this whole nightmare?"

"Well, Miss Andie, I can't be saying much right now. It's an ongoing investigation. But if I need to know something more, why, you can be sure I'll be asking you."

I roll my eyes. "No kidding."

His easygoing façade takes a dive, and a totally serious law enforcement officer stands before me. "No, Miss Andie. I'm not kidding. I'd think you know me well enough by now. I don't kid when the law's been broken in my jurisdiction. I said it last night, and I'll be saying it again. There's more to this than just them stones. There has to be. I'll be finding out what before too long."

Anyone with something to hide who makes the mistake of thinking Chief Clark's slow drawl and walk match the pace of his thoughts won't make that mistake for long. If they do, they'll soon be guests at his lockup.

I nod.

He turns and heads toward the hall. "And if you haven't been telling me all I need to know, why then, I'll be finding that out too. And why."

"Bu—but I don't have anything else to say . . ." I let my wail fade, since he's gone. "All righty, then. Now what?"

That's when I realize Miss Mona and Aunt Weeby had walked in at some point, but hadn't said a word. Never known that to happen before. I face them, and am stunned by the anxiety in their faces.

Oh no. No, no, no, no, no. This is hazardous to mankind. Womankind. My kind.

Whenever these two have what they perceive as a problem, they don't quit until they "solve" it. The solution? Well, it usually means trouble. Of the sinking-ship kind.

I'm not up for a cruisin', if you get my drift.

"Um . . ." I look around. "Don't think there's much we can do around here. The hospital won't be too happy if we hang around and stress Laura out. At least Max and I have a show to prepare. What are you two up to today?"

Aunt Weeby gives a vague wave. "I don't suppose it matters much anymore, sugarplum. Things have gotten themselves all tied up in a fine kerfuffle since we made us any plans."

This is scary stuff. Especially since Miss Mona's letting my aunt do all the talking. The Duo at loose ends.

Think, Andie, think! "I don't see where that should stop you from doing whatever you had planned. I mean, there's nothing any of us can do for Rodolfo—other than pray, and we don't need to be here to do that. And Laura?" I shrug. "She's on the mend. The nurses'll probably tell you the best thing for her is sleep, and lots of it."

Aunt Weeby's eyes grow wide. "Are you trying to tell me you're wanting us to leave that poor child all alone in this hospital again? I spent the most unsettled night, worrying myself sick about her. If you'll remember, that guy slipped her that something when we weren't here."

Water's up around my chin, folks. "But, Aunt Weeby, you and Miss Mona need your sleep."

A triumphant smile brightens her face. "Why, of course we do, sugarplum. And we're going to get it." She points to the massive tote bag leaning against her feet. "That's why Mona and I went shopping this morning. We bought us some real cute jammies. We're ready for duty, taking turns napping on the waiting room couches until we can take little Miss Laura home with us."

I can see them now. Their idea of cute jammies leaves a lot to be desired. And their staking a claim on the waiting room is nothing but trouble waiting to happen. "But—"

"Mona's got the sweetest set of pots and jars of yummy toiletries in her bag," Aunt Weeby adds, oblivious to my dinky shot at objecting. "We're all set to move in with Laura until we can move her in with us."

The hospital's not ready for the Daunting Duo. This is a disaster. I have to come up with something; I gotta pry these two lovable nuts out of here one way or another. First, though, I have to buy myself some time. Maybe Max will do his white-knight impression.

Maybe not. Take a look at his brand-new, wild-eyed panic.

He's come to know them pretty well, and looks about as freaked out as I am. It's not hard to get to know my aunt and her pal. They're nuts. But sweet. And I really don't want them tossed out on their ears. Nor do I want Chief Clark hauled out here to drag them to the pokey and book them for loitering or as squatters or practicing medicine without licenses.

How's that, you say? My aunt has a disgusting habit of bringing out her bottle of Great-Great-Grandmother Willetta's cod liver oil. Aunt Weeby's sure it cures all that ails you.

Gotta move, gotta groove. And fast. "What *were* you two planning for today? I'm still curious."

Aunt Weeby shakes her head. "It seems so long ago now . . ." She sighs. "We haven't hit our favorite flea market in ages. You know the one. It's out by Buck Creek Road, about thirty miles away, and I was wanting to go hunt us up some chamber pots."

My eyes goggle. "Have you been to see a doctor about this problem?"

She gives a dismissive wave. "Oh, no, no, sugarplum. I'm not plagued with no continence or nothing like that. Chamber pots just make the sweetest planting pots. You know, the ones with red trim for geraniums, the blue ones for pansies or purple petunias."

"But you don't even have a house right now. Well, you do, but it's got to be patched back together since the fire."

"It's not for my house, Andrea. It's for Mona's garden we're hunting."

Yeah, right. Chamber pots on the grounds of Miss Mona's zillion-dollar mansion. Are they nuts?

Oh yeah. They are.

Me? I'm skeptical. "And you're trying to tell me you two were going to head to a flea market with only potties in mind?"

Aunt Weeby has the decency to blush. "Oh, you know . . . every once in a while we trip on some splendid doodad or two."

Uh-huh. And I'm a fireplug on Main Street. What does she plan to do with her doodad or two while the house is being done? They're not coming into my little cottage. No way, no how. It's already stuffed to the rafters with Miss Mona's french-fried frou-frou and gilt.

Why do these two always come up with impossible situations? I mean, on the one hand, they want to crash the hospital. On the other, they want to go junking. The Duo in jail versus the Duo in junk heaven.

Yech. There's really no choice. "I think you should go junking—er . . . flea marketing. The break will do you wonders." And when they're back, lugging someone else's trash, I'll have to find some way to deal with the stuff. "Everyone can always do with a bit of R & R."

For a moment, a spark brightens her eyes. But then she squashes it. "No, sugarplum. A body's gotta do what a body's gotta do. And our duty's with that little girl. Why, her daddy's in worse shape than a tired ol' boxing ring punching bag."

And how would she know what a tired old boxing ring punching bag looks like? But I don't dare ask. She might just tell me. Something—experience—tells me I'm better off not knowing.

"Okay, Aunt Weeby. Here's the deal. You tell me. When you were here for your surgery a year ago, would you have wanted someone hovering over you when you were trying to sleep?"

Miss Mona snorts. "She wouldn't even let me visit more'n a half hour at a time."

Aunt Weeby glares at her best friend. "But this is different. Laura's a child."

I'm not going there, okay? Nothing about pots and kettles is coming from my mouth.

Instead, I say, "She still needs to sleep. Tell you what. Why don't you two go jun—*flea marketing*, and see what kind of trash—*treasure* you can dig up for Laura?"

I hope and pray the girl will someday forgive me. It might take years.

As lame as my suggestion seems, not just to me but to the about-to-bust-a-gut Max too, it catches hold of my aunt's imagination. "You might be onto something there, sugar-plum. If we do a real bang-up job getting her something, maybe we'll have us a new partner for our adventures once she's outta here."

Max claps a hand over his mouth. Above his fingers, his blue eyes do a mischievous jig. He knows just as well as I do how hard we're going to have to work to get Laura out of the mess I've just put her in.

For the moment, though . . . "Okay. It's a done deal. Off you go to hunt the elusive Treasusaurus Laurus. I'll see you both later. For a late dinner after our show. How's that sound?"

Miss Mona shrugs.

Aunt Weeby says, "Eh. So-so. I guess we might could go."

Although things are looking up, I'm not about to declare victory until they're on their way to their junk haven. I wave. "See ya!"

The Duo stands, gathers their toxic-colored totes and, bickering good-naturedly, head down the hall toward the bank of elevators.

I collapse against the back of my chair. "Phew! I was afraid they'd never leave."

Next to me, Max squirms.

Then he shifts.

Finally, he wriggles, taps a foot, drums his fingers on the armrest. When he starts to hum a monotone drone, I reach the end of my rope. "Come on, come on. Spill it, already."

He leans forward to brace his elbows on his knees, clasp his hands, and prop his chin on the laced fingers. "Something's wrong. Miss Mona didn't say more than two words the whole time since I got here."

Now that he mentions it, she had been uncharacteristically quiet. But I'm not ready to go borrowing trouble. I'll worry about her silence some other time, later. "She's not really as much of a chatterbox as Aunt Weeby. Let's go see Laura, then head to the studio. We're due on-screen in a couple of hours, and we haven't even chosen the merchandise for the show."

He stands, worry in the tight lines of his face. "You go ahead. I'll be waiting for you in my dressing room. Tell Laura I'm glad she's doing better."

"You're not coming to say goodbye?"

He shrugs. "It's best if you handle it in true girly-girl fashion."

Huh? "Okey-dokey."

I'm not buying it. He's up to something. And he wants me out of it, whatever it is.

Fine. Let him be that way. But I'll find out what he's up to. And like our show, it's gonna happen sooner rather than later. I'll make sure of it.

15.00

I spend the day trying to catch up with Mr. Magnificent.

He spends the day dodging me.

Except there's the minor matter of a show we have to do—together. It's what cohosts do. By the time the cameras zoom in on us, I'm wound up tighter'n one of the girdles our channel sells by the truckload. The two-hour show feels comfy-cozy, like a session with my favorite—*not*—dentist.

Finally, as the last notes of the theme song fade into the now-dark studio, I whirl on my partner, jab a finger at the middle of his broad chest. "And you have the gall to bug me about partnership? Huh? How about it, *pardner*? Spill the beans, already."

He shrugs. "Let that poor bee out of that bonnet, Andie. I just know something's bugging Miss Mona, and they're not back yet. I won't relax until they're home again."

My nerves set up a rhythmic rattle. I don't want to consider the awful possibilities, even though unease is playing my song. "How do you know they're not back yet? You've spent the last two hours on-screen with me. You don't know who's come in or out of the building."

"Hannah's got the perfect view of the hallway. I asked her to give me a heads-up during the show once she saw them."

I look at our favorite camerawoman, who's covering her equipment. She shakes her head. My stomach lurches. We've just done the last live show of the day. It's nine thirty now. Unless they're home, then Max is right. Something's wrong. Very wrong.

I scoot my chair back and march off toward my dressing room and cell phone. "I'm calling them. They probably went right home. Maybe there's a message on my voice mail telling us where to meet them for that late dinner we talked about before they left."

The echo of Max's footsteps follows me. I race to my purse, pull out my phone—no message.

Then I speed-dial my aunt. It goes straight through to her voice mail. Unless she's making a call, the phone's been turned off. Not at all something Aunt Weeby has a habit of doing.

"Well?" Max says.

I shake my head. A queasy wooziness starts in my gut. A chill runs through me. "Maybe they . . . maybe—"

Someone raps on my door. "Come in."

Chief Clark walks in. The queasy wooziness goes right down the sour road to nausea. His frown doesn't give me the warm fuzzies, know what I mean?

"Are they hurt?" I ask.

"Hurt?" He looks back out in the hall, around the room. "Who?"

"Aunt Weeby and Miss Mona. They're the reason you're here, right?"

He sighs. "Sure are, Miss Andie, but not on account of them being hurt or anything like that. Leastways, I'm hoping not."

"Then why are you here?"

He drags off his official hat, scratches his head, then claps the worn-to-a-shiny-edge-on-the-brim thing back on. He rubs his chin, shifts his weight from foot to foot.

What is it with these men and their fidgeting when they're trying to avoid giving a straight answer? I'm fresh out of patience this time. "Please tell me. You don't usually come around just to hang and chill."

The chief clears his throat. "Do you know any reason Miss Mona would be getting dozens of phone calls from Colombia? Real short ones, hang-ups, and not from that Rodolfo guy in the hospital, either. Dozens, Miss Andie. Dozens in the last coupla weeks."

No wonder she was so quiet in the waiting room this morning. She probably hadn't said a thing to the chief about those calls. Then he came out with his warning about not telling him everything. I suspect that's when she began to put the pieces together.

There's way more here than meets the eye, all right.

Houston? We have a problem.

◆

By midnight, Max and I are in my living room, staring at each other, he on my sofa and me in my chaise, our fear, worry, and love for the Duo mingled and heavy in the air.

"It's all my fault!" I finally grind out. "If only I hadn't sent them off on a stupid junking trip—"

"Stop it," he says, his voice quiet and far calmer than anything I could come up with under the circumstances. "There's no way you could've known something was going to happen. And we don't even know if anything *has* happened to them. For all you know, they're holed up in some motel, getting ready to hit the flea market again tomorrow."

I shake my head. "Don't even try, okay? You don't believe a word you said, so you can't begin to convince me. You know something's happened just as well as I do. You know they would've called."

He sighs. "Yeah, but you can't blame a guy for trying to ease your mind."

"Thanks. I just can't stand the thought of them winding up hurt."

"Neither can I. But we have to trust. They love the Lord, and he's in control. We aren't."

I burst up and start to pace—again. "But that's the whole point. God didn't send them off into trouble, I did. And there's got to be something I can do to help them out of the mess they might be in. Because *I* sent them."

"God might not have sent them off into trouble, but you didn't either. Out of love for Laura, and for the two of them, you figured they'd be better off having a good time rather than making trouble at the hospital. Where's the blame in that?"

What, did he suddenly take a turn down Dumb Alley? "Don't you get it? I *sent* them. They'd be here, and fine, if I'd let them stay in the waiting room."

He points at his über-purple swollen eye. "Did you forget

the guy I fought? He was there, in the hospital, and neither Laura nor her dad wound up okay." Max reaches out, then wraps his hand around mine. I stop pacing to meet his gaze.

"Do you trust God?" he asks. "Do you believe he can and will work this out to his will and purpose?"

His words suck all the energy out of my nerves, my anxiety, my strength. I pull out of his grasp, stumble a couple of steps past him to drop into the chaise again, too aware of my weakness. "Oh, Max, what a mess I am. I'm scared to pieces to let things happen just because. And scared's not a very faith-filled way to feel. I have to find the strength to trust, to believe God's mercy will win out in the end."

Max stands, crosses the distance between us, and drops to his knees at my side. He curves a finger under my chin to make me meet his gaze. "And you think you're the only Christian who has to deal with that? That's where we all live at one point or another. Ease up on yourself."

I bite my bottom lip.

He tugs it free with his thumb. "Remember in the book of Mark, when the father brings the son with the evil spirit to the Lord? The father has a great need, and he asks Jesus to heal the boy, *if* he can. Jesus answers, understanding where we all live. He says everything's possible for the one who believes."

With a nod, I murmur, "'Lord, I believe; help my unbelief!'"

"And what did Jesus do?"

"He cast out the evil spirit . . . and that strengthened the believers' faith." I sigh. "Growing up is hard, sometimes too hard."

"You ready for the alternative, Andi-ana Jones?"

I chuckle without humor. "Not really. I have a lot of growing to do yet. And I've been doing more like a dog chasing its tail."

The doorbell rings. I leap to answer.

And then my stomach plummets again. Why does it have to be the chief?

He strolls in but doesn't remove his hat. "I have me a smidgeon more info you might like."

My eyebrows fly up. No "Hello," no "How are you?" No nothing. And no phone call to tell me whatever he wants to tell me? Doesn't look good. I brace myself. "Don't know why you're waiting to tell us."

He finally doffs his hat. "Well, it's like this." The hat makes a complete revolution in his hands. "I had me a time trying to track down them phone calls, but I got some help from a Mr. Sloan at our embassy in Bo . . . Bo-go . . . whatever. The capital of Colombia."

"We know Mr. Sloan."

The hat keeps on turning. "He went to the telephone company and had them track that phone number."

"And?"

"And I also reckoned Miss Laura might know something about it. She does live down there." He slaps the hat against his thigh, then pulls the notepad out of his pocket, flips to a particular page. He stares at the writing there, as if it were about to reveal everything he wants to know. "The girl's sharp, all right. She recognized the area code—or whatever they call it down there—right away. She says it comes from the ranching regions in the east—"

"Doña Rosario!"

He nods. "Uh-huh. That's what I said, and I said it before we knew anything 'bout ranch-house phone numbers or any old thing like that. Which we just got confirmed by Mr. Sloan right now, Mr. Sloan, who'd just heard from his man at the phone company. But I'd be willing to wager just about anything, Miss Andie, that you don't know nothing about what I'm gonna tell you next."

All this circling around is making me more than dizzy. And the fact I could barely choke down a bite or two of fast food a couple of hours ago instead of a decent dinner doesn't help. "Please, Chief. I can't take the suspense. I'm going crazy with worry about my aunt and Miss Mona." I give him a crooked grin. "Besides, I'm lousy at Twenty Questions."

"I toldja that there Rosie woman had to have more invested in this than just them stones. Looks like she has a chunk of her past and more'n likely a piece of her heart—or maybe it's more like her pride—in the deal."

I grind my teeth to keep from yelling, lace my hands together to keep from reaching out and shaking him. "What's the connection? Please. You're killing me here."

"Well, Miss Andie, it's like this. Seems that Rosie woman was once married to little Miss Laura's daddy. The divorce didn't go too well, and she's not real happy at his success. She's not happy 'bout not cashing in on any of it these days. You know."

That clunking sound you just heard? That was my stomach diving down to my toes. "Oh. My. Goodness."

Max grinds his teeth behind me.

"Something like that," the chief says. "But I got more for you. That Rosie woman comes from some old, rich family who got tangled up with that coca smuggling business. Looks to me like her big brother wound up in trouble not so long ago. His smuggling plane got shot down by the tough president's anti-drug folks. No plane, no smuggling—"

"No smuggling, no big bucks." I'm not likely to forget the opulence of that unlikely ranch in the middle of the back of beyond. "She needs to replace the income to keep herself in the lifestyle to which she has become accustomed. And run-of-the-mill emeralds won't bring her the kind of money she likes."

Chief Clark's brows draw together. "I think you're saying what I'm thinking, but you sure do have a tangled-up way of putting things."

I whirl, plunk my fists on my hips, and beam a glare at Max—a preventive glare. "Don't you dare laugh! Or make some snarky comment, either. This isn't the time." When he makes the universal zip-the-lip move across his mouth, I turn back to the chief, ignoring the twitching at the corners of Max's mouth. "She lost her direct hookup to the profits from the emeralds when she signed on the dotted line and went her way, so she figures she's entitled to a little sum'n-sum'n here."

"It's worse'n that, Miss Andie. She wants the money from them extra-special emeralds you got to buy a new plane for the family business. Seems even the regular expensive green trinkets don't bring in the kind of gravy she's wanting."

Talk about dizzy. "This is big. Big-time big. Like those big-boy, king-of-the-universe emeralds I bought for Miss Mona. Any one of them would make a nice dent in the invoice for the average corporate jet. No wonder . . ."

Max eases me into my chaise. "And, as usual, you're stuck smack in the middle of things."

I roll my eyes. "It's a gift."

Memories of the trip to Colombia whirl through my head. Creepella d'Eville . . . close encounters of the trash kind . . . dunkin' dungeons . . . flying pigs—well, they weren't really flying, but you get the picture.

Nothing makes much sense, other than the clear evidence of greed in a woman's life. It's hard for me to understand how one can sell out like that for the sake of a crystal chandelier or a pair of Stuart Weitzman pumps. Or Christian Louboutin high heels, which is what Doña Rosario was actually wearing at dinner that night. Yes, there is a difference. And yes, *yes*, I know the difference.

Look at Miss Mona. She's got a bundle of money too, but it's not as if she lavishes the big bucks on herself. Sure, she bought a McMansion with it, but at the same time she gives well more than her tithe to further the cause of Christ through missions and schools and all kinds of other seriously good ministries. Not to mention all the jobs she's created with the studio.

The difference between the two women couldn't be greater.

So . . .

"Why would Doña Rosario call Miss Mona? What would link the two of them? I mean, I know Miss Mona wouldn't have anything to do with someone so unlike her."

The chief barks out a humorless laugh. "Seems to me, Miss Andie, that's the job I have to be getting back to. I have the poisoned girl, the daddy in a coma, Mr. Max all beat up, and two missing ladies. It all adds up to a bushel of trouble, and no answers in hand."

When neither one of us has anything further to offer, he

claps the hat back on. "I'll be going now. If you happen to think up anything important, am I gonna be able to trust you to call and tell me? Not run off like some dog with a juicy bone and keep it all to yourself?"

I tip my nose up into the air. "I always call you when I find out anything. You just don't listen to me all the time."

"I'll have you know, miss, I've always listened." He tugs down the brim of his hat over his eyes. "I might not always do things the way you're wanting me to, but I do take my calling to serve real serious."

There might just be more than a teensy-weensy bit of truth in that. "Ah . . . well, I guess I did know that."

"And don't you be forgetting it. I'll be seeing you in the morning sometime. But if you think of anything—any little ol' thing, you hear?—you just go right ahead and call me. I'll let the missus know you might could do that. She won't mind. She's mighty partial to your Aunt Weeby. They been friends for years, like your daddy and I."

The burning behind my eyes threatens to turn to out-and-out waterworks. "Thank you. I appreciate your concern. And your wife's."

A hint of red splashes across his cheekbones. He shrugs, then turns. "I'll be letting myself out, Miss Andie. You don't need to bother showing me the door."

Once he's gone and the soft sound of the closing door melts into the night's hush, I realize the tears that had earlier threatened now pour down my cheeks. I swipe the back of my right hand across both eyes in a useless attempt to stem the flow. As I blink and blink, I realize Max has again come to my side. He kneels and looks at me, worry in his gaze. "Are you okay?"

"Not right now, but I will be." I take a deep breath and force a smile. "I have enough faith to believe that."

"Then come on. Let's get you something to drink and at least a paper towel to dry your face."

I follow him to the kitchen, where he leads me to one of the bistro chairs, then searches through my cupboards until he finds a glass. He shoots me a grin over his shoulder. "Nothing like making myself at home."

"No big deal. You've been great today." Not to mention the other times in our acquaintance when I've needed him and he's been there for me.

Earth to Andie! He's one of the good guys, the really good guys.

Yeah. Okay, okay. I did figure that out. True, it took me longer than it should have, but I do know it now.

A paper towel and the glass of water appear before me. I dry my cheeks, and only then realize how thirsty I am. I haven't had anything to drink since we drove through the Golden Arches around ten o'clock and I tried—but failed—to force down a pre-fab burger and an iced tea.

I drain the glass, plunk it down on the table. "You know what I have to do, don't you?"

His eyebrows fly up and he holds out a hand, palm flat out at me. "You're not going to make me guess what's going on inside that redhead's head of yours. I'm just a guy, a regular guy. Mind-reading you is way beyond me."

"Fun-ny." I stand. "But, yeah, you do know. Think about it. I have to figure out what's going on here. And I have to start at the beginning."

"I'm shaking in my shoes, having to ask you where you

think the beginning might be. But I guess I don't have a choice. Where exactly do you plan to start?"

"I suppose you could say the real beginning from my side of this mess was Rodolfo's visit to the studio. But since he's out of commission still, we can't go there. Sure, I went to Colombia after that, but from what the chief just told us, Miss Mona started getting the calls right around the time he came by, well before I left. That's where I have to start. I have to figure out why Doña Rosario would've been calling Miss Mona."

"I'm not sure it's that important. She probably thought Miss Mona would travel to the mines to pick out the stones herself. Doña Rosario was probably keeping track of Miss Mona's actions, trying to see when she was in the office, and when she finally left for Bogotá."

"Well, it's either that or I get busy tracking down drug scum."

He shakes his head. Wiggles a finger in his ear. "Come again?"

"Come on, Max. Don't pretend you're dense. You couldn't have missed how rotten, slimy, creepy, and disgusting her henchmen are. I'm sure they're involved with the brother's dirty drug dealings. So I have to follow the drug scum trail."

"Now you've really gone off the deep end. We have nothing on the guy who showed up at the hospital. How do you plan to track him down, or anyone from Colombia, for that matter? There's millions and millions of them out there."

"Do I have to figure it all out by myself? What? Are you just the pretty face here?"

To my horror, a smug, very male smile beams out from every inch of the guy. "The pretty face, huh?"

My cheeks go from zero to sizzle in no time flat. "Oh, you know what I mean. I'm asking you to come up with an idea. Help me out."

"I seem to remember you promising you were going to leave this mess to Chief Clark and his men."

"They haven't done anything. What do you want me to do?" I waggle all ten fingers at him. "Sit on my hands?"

"Now that you mention it, I'd like you to get some sleep. You're going to need it."

"Oh, sure. Like I'm going to fall asleep in the next century."

"Maybe not that soon"—he winks—"but a short time after that."

I huff out a breath. "I know what you mean, but honestly, Max, you couldn't possibly expect me to sleep. I'm so worried, and there's not a single, solitary thing I can do tonight."

His arm drops over my shoulders, a warm, solid support. I lean into him. "Come on," he says. "At least you can lie down for a while on your couch. I'll hang around until you fall asleep—hey! You never know. It could happen."

"And the sun could start revolving around the earth, but I'm not going to hold my breath."

I don't balk, but rather let him lead me to the living room. He settles me on the couch, and to my amazement, he shakes out the soft chenille throw to tuck it around me. As I gape, he grins, then drops a soft kiss on my forehead.

"Relax. That's all you have to do. Just relax."

Yeah, right. Like I'm about to relax when the man I've fallen in love with starts treating me like the most precious of treasures. How ridiculous can my life get? My aunt's missing, my boss is too, and he goes down the wonder of wonders road.

But I can't tell him any of this, and I try to ease into a more comfortable position on the couch. He turns down the overhead light and drops onto the chaise. He stretches out his long legs, crosses his arms, and closes his eyes.

"Trust him, Andie," he says. "He loves them as much as you."

Another tear rolls down my cheek. *I believe; Lord, help my unbelief.*

◆

Hours later, just as a hint of light appears at the horizon, I find myself kneeling on the window bench at the front bay window, staring out at the sleeping world. Tears have been flowing down my cheeks for the last forty minutes as I try to think, try to pray, and accomplish nothing.

Max, of course, fell asleep the minute he crashed.

I wish I could have done the same.

A sob breaks in my throat. "Oh, Lord Jesus . . . have mercy, protect them . . ."

That's as close as I've been able to come to a decent prayer, but I know God knows my heart. I'm sure he knows what I'm feeling, and how much I love those two kooks. I press my forehead against the cool glass and then feel a warm palm gently land in the middle of my back.

"Scoot over and share," he whispers.

I ease closer to the window. He fills the greater part of the seat, then wraps his arms around my waist, clasping his hands over my belly button. With gentle pressure, he draws me near, my back against his chest, our legs extended on the cushion, parallel to each other. I let down my defenses enough to relax a bit, and lean back. It's amazing how much I've come to trust this man.

"You know you don't have to fight every battle by yourself, right?"

I nod. "The Lord's always with me."

"And . . . ?"

"And he'll never leave me nor forsake me."

"And . . . ?"

I turn my head to meet his gaze. "And what? What's on your mind?"

"That you're no longer alone, Andie. You've got me. You have to let me in. Please join forces with me. We've made a pretty decent team before. We need to do the same this time. It's the only way we'll succeed."

"But I can't drag you into danger again. It's bad enough I sent them out to . . . to . . . whatever. I could never live with myself if anything happened to you because of me—"

"How do you know any of this is happening because of you? Have you given any thought to God here? For real?"

"Of course I have. I don't know what you're getting at."

His hand comes up and cups my jaw, his long fingers warm against my cheek. Welcome warmth seeps through me. My heart beats harder and faster. The light in his eyes rivals the brightest star, the fullest moon, the hottest sun.

"Andie, I love you. Don't shut me out anymore. I believe God brought me here to put us together. Are you going to keep on fighting him? That's what you're doing when you fight me."

I love you . . . I love you . . . I love you . . .

His voice turns to an intimate whisper. "I can't say I know your prayers. They're inside you, for you and God to know.

But what if I'm the answer to those prayers? I know you enough to know you're not the kind of woman who wants to spend the rest of her life alone."

I sit up a fraction. Huh? I blink. Did I just hear what I think I heard? Did I really hear him say he's the answer to my prayers?

Max? Answer to my prayers?

Nuh-uh. No way. He's just a good-looking stud Miss Mona brought to the S.T.U.D.

Right?

Maybe. Maybe not.

"Boy, you've got a swelled head—"

Then he kisses me.

Long and hard.

On the lips.

Oh my . . .

16 00

"*Dum-de-dummm . . . dum-de-dum-de-dum-dum-de-dummm . . .*"

Those sweet familiar notes sweep through my head as I drown in the tenderness of Max's kiss. Warmth, comfort, love, and passion—yes, mind-boggling passion—fill me, sweep me away to a world I've never visited before. I really am a stranger in the paradise of romance.

"*All lost in a wonderland . . .*"

Max sings the words against my lips, his touch breath-light and more moving than I could have imagined. Oh my. "Am I dreaming?"

He slides a hand through my short-short hair, then presses me closer to his chest again. "Neither one of us is dreaming. I won't kid you and say it's going to be easy, because nothing with you has ever been easy, but I do promise you it'll never be boring."

The emotion in my heart expands, spreads, fills every inch of me. I don't want to presume anything, but this sounds like the real deal to me. Of course, it's happening at the weirdest time, but, hey! This is me here, after all. You know how things go for me.

Why should falling in love be any different?

It's happened, though, and I guess that's what counts.

"Could you cut a guy a break for once?" Max asks.

I crash down out of my rosy-romance haze. "What do you mean?"

"It might be a good idea if you told me how you feel about me. I stuck my neck out, told you I love you, and all you've said is that I have a swelled head. Am I barking up the wrong tree with you?"

I shake my head, slowly at first, and then with more oomph. "Nope. You're not barking up the wrong tree. But I am trying to really believe this is happening, that I'm not imagining things . . . imagining you."

He grins—a smug grin, if you ask me. "That kiss didn't feel like much of an imagination thing to me. Here, let's try it again, and see if I can convince you."

Before I can answer, he swoops down. This kiss is the stuff of fireworks, John Phillip Sousa marches, and breath-stealing passion.

Max . . . Max . . . Max . . .

When he moves away just a fraction, I blink. "Wow!" I blush when I realize how close to a croak the word sounds. Time to clear the throat. "I don't have anywhere near that much imagination, Max. I might have to start pinching myself just to make sure I haven't dreamed it, but, yeah. It sure felt real."

"That's a start." He gives me a lopsided smile. "I've been trying to catch your attention for a while now. You haven't made it easy."

"Once burned, twice shy—it's a cliché, but totally true."

"Tell you what. I don't want to hear about the idiot who burned you, but I'm glad he was that stupid. He left you free for me to find."

"I'm glad you found me."

"Or that God crashed us together."

I curl into his chest, warm and solid and broad. I breathe in the faintest hint of his woodsy aftershave, and nod a response to his goofy comment. I wish I could surrender to the moment, to the awesomeness of falling in love, to the enormous gift God's given us, but I can't stop thinking of Aunt Weeby and Miss Mona.

Just the thought of the Duo makes me groan. "You know we're in trouble, don't you?"

"What do you mean?"

"Just think what Aunt Weeby and Miss Mona are going to say when they figure out . . . well, when they realize we're . . . umm . . ."

"In love?"

"Yes . . ."

The rumble of his laugh reverberates against my ear. "They're going to take credit for it, of course. I can just hear them too."

"Wish I really could hear them."

"Me too."

We fall silent for a while again. The rise and fall of Max's breathing under my cheek soothes my frazzled nerves. Just as I'm about to—finally—doze off, though, he sighs.

"I'd just as soon stay like this than do anything else, but I really need a shower, a shave, and clean clothes. Something tells me we're going to have to deal with more meetings with the chief, and I know you're going to cook up more of those ideas of yours for us."

"I don't have any ideas right now." I reluctantly rise. "But you're right. I need a shower too. And I have to prepare myself for what I'm sure's going to be another tough day."

He stretches, reaches almost to the ceiling, and then heads for the front door. "I'll see you later. At the studio?"

"Sounds good."

"Just remember"—he turns to face me again—"I love you. You're not alone anymore."

The warmth in my chest spreads and turns to a blush on my cheeks. I give him a tentative smile. "I . . . I love you too."

Then, without another word or kiss or hug, he leaves, closing the door quietly behind him.

I stand and stare, stunned by the night's events. My emotions have been riding a rollercoaster, and I'm breathless from the adrenaline rush.

"Lord, did you really send Max?"

My deep breath does little to settle nerves—what am I talking about? To settle *me*.

Could Max really be the answer to some of my prayers?

Scenes from the past year click through my thoughts. Little by little they drop to form a mosaic picture of Max. His patience with me, his caring for Aunt Weeby and Miss Mona, his willingness to learn, his determination to protect me . . .

Rats.

"It sure does look like you did, Lord. So what's next?"

Because of the S.T.U.D.'s rotating schedule of shows, ours today is slotted from ten to noon. By the time we're done,

I know what I'm doing next. If Max wants to join me—you know, in that partnership he keeps bringing up—I'll be more than happy to have him. If, on the other hand, he's going to be a wet blanket and get in my way, then he's going to have to be happy sitting at home, twiddling his thumbs, and waiting for me to find the Duo.

When the studio lights go off, I turn in my swivel chair, ready to do battle. His grin catches me by surprise.

"Whatever you're up to," he says, "I'm in. That look on your face means trouble, and I know you too well by now to let you go barging blindly into danger."

"Oh, right. By that line of logic, you're going to join me so we can *both* go barging blindly into danger."

"No, I'm coming so I can be the voice of reason."

I bite my tongue—hard—so as to not spout off something I might regret. I swallow. Two deep, heartfelt gulps of air later, I square my shoulders. "Okay, then. You'll be happy to know I'm only going to Miss Mona's office. If I don't find anything of any value there, then we'll hit her house."

"Do you have a key to get in?"

"No. But she keeps an extra one under the most revolting plastic dog . . . umm . . . *dropping* out in the backyard."

Max howls. "That's so Miss Mona."

"Worse. Where do you think she got it?"

He shakes his head in helpless humor.

"Aunt Weeby gave it to her for her birthday a few years back."

His chuckles die off. "We're going to find them. We have to. There's no other choice."

A sob hitches its way up my throat. "I just hope we're in time. Let's go hit her office."

"Let me stop in my dressing room first. I don't want to go off Duo-hunting in a suit."

Even though I'm impatient to get on with it, his words make me take a step back. "You've got a point. I'll meet you at Miss Mona's office in ten."

By the time I get there, he's inside, hands in his jeans pockets, turning slowly, staring at the bookcases, the file cabinets, the enormous desk with its multiple drawers. "Where do we start?"

I look around, and the sheer volume of stuff in the office threatens to overwhelm me. But I can't let that kind of roadblock get to me. Miss Mona and Aunt Weeby come first.

"Tell you what. Since you're taller than I am, how about you go through those bookshelves? I'll hit the desk. And then maybe we can do the file cabinets together."

"Sounds like a plan." At the set of shelves closest to the door, he stops and turns. "Mind telling me what we're looking for?"

"Hmm . . . I'm not sure. If I knew, I'd tell you. Since I don't, you're just going to have to wing it. The best I can do is tell you we're looking for something that doesn't quite . . . oh, I don't know. Fit, maybe?"

"Oh man, am I in trouble here. That actually made sense."

A rush of daring overtakes me. "See what love can do to a man?"

He laughs and heads for the nearest bookshelf. "That's a subject for later, Andie. And we'll have that talk too, the one about later. I promise."

Blushing, I slide behind the desk and sit in the massive leather desk chair. I may talk a mean streak, but I don't have a clue what I'm looking for. Something that doesn't fit? Good grief.

The top center drawer seems like a good place to start.

But aside from a beautiful collection of true fountain pens and their accompanying rainbow of ink bottles, there's nothing there. So it's on to the right-side stack of drawers for me. And then I hit my first snag. It's locked. I don't have that key. Or a fake dog plop under which to find it.

But I do have Max.

Who does the deed with his magic metal gizmos, and within minutes, I'm rifling through contracts, employment records, banking statements, all kinds of information I don't feel right looking at. "I can't believe I've become such a sleaze, going through her stuff like this."

"You want to join me over here and leave the desk for Chief Clark?"

"Not on your life. I don't know how long it'll be before he gets here. I don't want to wait any longer than I have to."

After I've plowed through the right side and find nothing unusual or interesting—about the emeralds, Colombia, or Creepella—I hit the left-side stack. With the same frustrating results.

"How's it going?" I ask Max once I'm done.

"Aside from dueling massive collections of books—gemology and historical romance novels—I haven't found anything too—"

I wait. Count to ten. "Well? Too what?"

"Hmm . . . this might be something."

I fly to his side. "What did you find?"

He pats a group of tall, slim, leather-bound books with gold writing on the spines. "There's something about these books . . . something about them rings a bell with me, but I can't quite put my finger on it. Did you know she keeps all her school yearbooks here in the office?"

"Oh, those. Yeah. You know Miss Mona. She's very loving, and sentimental to the max—no pun intended. Every so often she hauls them out and tells me stories from when she was in school. She went to some snooty boarding place."

"I'll bet those stories are pretty funny."

"Trust me. They are."

"But they'll have to wait. We have to find her and Aunt Weeby first."

I glance at him with gratitude. And love. He takes the few steps over to my side, then reaches out a hand to pull me to him. I close my eyes and breathe in the distinctive scent of his aftershave. But behind my eyelids a rapid-fire cascade of images clicks down, and I gasp, straighten upright, and bang my head against his chin.

"Ow!" I cry.

"Oooof!" He winces. "What'd you do that for?"

I rub the top of my head and answer him absently, my thoughts totally into the mental pictures still vivid in my wacky mind. "Hey, I'm Calamity Andie sometimes, didn't you know?"

But in the back of my mind, a sense of been-there-done-that grows, strengthens, until I get to that aha! moment. "Oh! Oh-oh-oh-oh! Max, the books. There *is* something hinky about those books."

He continues to rub his chin, but walks back to the bookshelf and points at the yearbooks. "These books? They look pretty normal to me. Old, but typical."

"No! I mean, yeah. They're normal but I just remembered

something, something important. Think, *think*. And look at them. Where have you seen those books before?"

He gives me one of those you-really-lost-it-this-time looks.

"No. Seriously. Look at the books. Don't just touch them."

"I'm looking, I'm *staring* at them, but I'm not seeing the same thing you are—obviously."

I stomp over. "Okay, okay. Stay with me here. These are Miss Mona's school yearbooks. But I saw another set just like them recently, very recently. And you did too."

"I did? Where?"

"In Colombia, of course. At—"

"Doña Rosario's office!" He rubs his hand over his forehead and shakes his head. "I remember now. Can't believe I forgot. How could I? She stood there, running a finger over the books. I guess that honking emerald must've distracted me so much I didn't pay much attention to what she was doing."

"It boggles my mind." I walk over to the books. "You know what this means, don't you?"

He takes a deep breath. "I know what you're getting at, but I'm having a hard time digesting it. It's . . . it's unbelievable."

"It's the stuff of heartburn, for sure. But didn't you at least wonder how she came to speak English so well?"

"To be honest, I was so caught up in the danger of the situation, and worrying about getting you out of there in one piece, that I didn't think about much of anything beyond that."

"That's where I was too. But we should've noticed." I look at the yearbooks again. "To think they must have gone to

236

school together . . . but that still doesn't answer all the questions. Or does it?"

"She must have known Rodolfo was coming to offer the stones to her old schoolmate."

"And that's why she kept checking on Miss Mona." My finger runs over the gold lettering. *Riverview Preparatory Academy.* "There's more to this, Max. I'm sure of it."

"I think it's pretty straightforward. I would imagine a major emerald vendor would be well known in Colombia, and if someone wanted emeralds, then they would keep an eye on him. When he headed here, she somehow managed to track his movements, and realized he was coming to sell stones to an old school friend. I think it's easy to add two and two."

"We're still missing the somehow of your equation. How'd she find out Rodolfo was coming to see Miss Mona?"

"We'll find out, and soon." He squares his jaw. "This isn't over. It won't be until we find them—and Doña Rosario."

I snag the last one of the yearbooks, hug it close, and spin on my heel. "Let's go."

"Whoa, Andie. Go where?"

"To find them."

"Yes, but where? Where do you want to look?"

I slump. "You're right. I'm not sure what to do next."

He comes to my side and takes my hands. "Much as I know you're not going to want to do it, we do have to call Chief Clark."

"Yeah, but you know he's going to tell us to let him 'take care' of things. And I can't. I *can't* just sit and let that crazy woman hurt Miss Mona or Aunt Weeby."

"Calling the chief isn't just sitting there. It's helping. Even if it's not in true Andi-ana Jones fashion."

I roll my eyes. "All right, all right. I'll call the man. Maybe I'll get an idea while talking to him."

But our conversation gives me nothing, no ideas, no hunches, no nothing. It doesn't even help when the chief commends me for my observations, because he follows that up with another warning to stay out of trouble and leave the detecting to him.

"I'll leave the detecting to you, but tell me this. How did an old schoolmate from a foreign country track down Miss Mona? And how did she know Rodolfo Cruz was coming to sell her the gems? Don't you think if we could figure all that out we'd be able to find them?"

A moment's silence gives me no satisfaction either. We all have more questions than answers. And a nasty feeling has started to crawl around in the pit of my gut. Something tells me the longer we take to get those answers, the greater the danger the Duo faces.

"I'll get those answers, Miss Andie. It's my job, and I do know what I'm doing."

He doesn't give me a chance to comment, since he hangs up on me. Which is probably just as well. I do have a history of blurting out the worst possible thing at the worst possible time.

"How?" I ask Max as I whirl around to face him. "How did Doña Rosario track Miss Mona down?" And then, something really hideous hits me. "Oh, no. You don't think . . ." I stumble and land against the office door. "Could she have been working with Rodolfo? Could they have some weird kind of racket going?"

"They could," Max answers. "But I'm not sure it would make sense. If they were working together, why wouldn't she just have gotten the stones from him?"

"Maybe it's one of those 'no honor among thieves' deals. Maybe he'd promised the stones to her, but then reneged. Or maybe it's just more greed. You know, they want the stones *and* Miss Mona's bucks."

"Could be." He doesn't sound convinced. "But this isn't doing the Duo any good. Let's go get something to eat. I think better on a full stomach."

"How you can think of eating at a time like this, I'll never know."

"That's why you're the girl and I'm the guy."

Who can argue with logic like that?

At the cozy seafood restaurant, I chew what looks like a shrimp but tastes like sawdust. I know I'm not scintillating company right now, and Max is being a good sport about it, but I can't get Aunt Weeby and Miss Mona out of my mind. And I can't convince myself I'm hungry.

I spear another shrimp with my fork, bring it up to my mouth, and have a brainstorm. The fork clatters down to my plate. The shrimp takes wing and flies straight at Max.

"Of course!" I cry. "Stupid, stupid, stupid! How could I miss it?"

Max daubs at the cocktail sauce on his light blue shirt with his napkin. "Care to let me in on the secret? I'd love to know why you're calling yourself stupid."

And probably why I catapulted food at him. I cringe. "Sorry about the mess. But it's just so obvious now. Doña Rosario tracked Miss Mona down through the school. It's the one connection between them. We just have to call the school,

239

and I'm sure we'll find out she called to get Miss Mona's phone number recently."

"And . . . ?"

I frown. "What do you mean, and?"

"Sure, Andie. Once you confirm she did call to get Miss Mona's phone, what then? What difference will it make to know for sure she got the number from the school?"

Before I can answer, my cell phone rings. While I generally hate phones in public places like restaurants—I really don't want to hear all about Aunt Fanny's bunions, blow by blow—as long as the Duo's missing, my phone's not going silent.

"Hello?"

"It's Chief Clark, Miss Andie. I just got me some information you oughta know. Mr. Sloan from the embassy in Colombia just gave me a ring. It seems that there Rosie woman's taken herself a trip. She's in America right now."

In the middle of his pause, I gulp. Loudly.

He goes on. "I want to make sure you understand. This is dangerous, Miss Andie. Sooner or later that woman and her partner'll come outta their hidey-hole and strike again. You and Mr. Max are the two most likely targets."

The lonely shrimp I ate does a tap dance in my belly. "I see . . ."

"No, miss, I'm not so sure you do. Her brother's killed at least a dozen men by now. I doubt that family's gonna get squeamish about killing again. And again and again. You and Mr. Max need to stay outta trouble, now, you hear?"

"I hear," I whisper.

He hangs up.

I do too.

Max says, "Well?"

I shudder, feeling colder than the bed of ice my shrimp's remaining buddies are nestled on. "Well, Max, sometimes you kiss a cat and get a mouthful of fleas for your trouble."

His jaw drops. His eyes widen. He shakes his head. "Cats . . . fleas?"

"Doña Rosario's no longer in Colombia. Looks like she took me at my word when I told her back at the hacienda that I didn't have the stones. She probably assumed I had them sent to Miss Mona. Wanna bet Doña Rosario's in Kentucky? Right where we'll find Miss Mona and Aunt Weeby?"

"I don't bet."

"Neither do I. Especially not against a sure thing."

17<u>00</u>

I wait with a massive case of poorly hidden impatience for Max to finish his surf 'n'turf. So sue me. I want to get going to find Miss Mona and Aunt Weeby. I don't really want to watch the love of my life stuff himself with food when I can't even stand the thought of eating while they're out there. No way.

With every second that crawls by, I fidget more. I squirm in my chair. I tap my fingers, the toe of my shoe; I tug on the way-too-short scrap of hair at the nape of my neck—losing your hair in a house fire really stinks, literally. Finally, when Max decides to forgo dessert and asks for the check, I grab my purse, sling it over my shoulder, and head out.

"I'll meet you in the parking lot," I say. "I'm making a pit stop while you pay."

Once outside, Max turns to me. "Where are you going in such a hurry? It seems to me we have no idea what to do . . . or, maybe more important, what not to do."

"What do you mean? We have to hit the Internet, find the school's website, and get their phone number. I want to

242

know what the school knows about Doña Rosario. They may be the quickest way for us to track her down. Maybe she said something that would give us some idea what she was planning. Or maybe she said something that might lead us to their location. I just know in my heart that when we find her, we'll find Aunt Weeby and Miss Mona too."

"Can't argue with that last part."

He holds out a hand.

I take hold.

He goes on. "My laptop's in the car. Want to hit one of those coffee shops with wi-fi? There's one about three blocks away—that's closer than the studio. Plus I could use a cup of java."

While I do roll my eyes—I mean, the guy just ate a cow and a mutant giant lobster's tail, washed down with an ocean of iced tea—I do recognize an opportunity when I see one. "Fine. But make it the closest one."

He taps his forehead in an irreverent salute. "Aye, aye, Cap'n!"

I wince. "Sorry. I don't really mean to sound so bossy. I just have this weird kind of bubbling inside. I'm afraid to let even one more second go by. If we waste time, something awful could happen to them."

The grin he sends me is the picture of wry. "I'm with you. I want to find them too. Good thing that coffee shop's so close. Let's go hop onto the info superhighway."

By the time we're seated on two stools on stilts at the tall bistro table, Max with his ginormous cardboard vat of caffeine and me with the 'puter, I'm about to jump out of my skin with impatience and urgency.

I boot up the computer, then have to force myself to wait

until I can start clicking away. Finally! Riverview Preparatory Academy . . . Riverview . . .

After a frustrating twenty minutes, I push the laptop away. "I can't find anything other than a reference to a former governor's wife who went there many moons ago."

"What does it say about the school?"

"Nothing. That's the whole point. It's just a mention of where the governor's wife graduated in a bio of the governor."

"And there's no other mention of the school on Google?"

I shake my head. "That probably means it shut down years ago."

I glare at the innocent if disappointing machine. "I was afraid you'd say that."

"Maybe we need to go back to the studio and check the yearbooks a little closer. Maybe there's something there we can use to track her down."

"Good idea, but we don't have to go anywhere farther than your car. I grabbed one of the books before we left."

He grins. "Good work!"

"Now that you brought it up, I don't remember checking the address, headmistress's name, or anything like that back at the studio. I just looked at the books, and they jogged my memory of Doña Rosario's library. Then I got that call from the chief." I nod slowly. "We have to find that school—or someone there who can track down Creepella."

We hurry out to Max's SUV. I grab the yearbook from the vehicle's backseat, and search like mad for the information we need.

Seconds later, I stab the appropriate page. "Look at that. It's in Simpsonville."

Max stares at me, then holds out his hand palm up and folds his fingers toward his palm a time or two. "You're going to have to give me more than that. I don't see what's so interesting about a Simpsonville address. I assume it's close."

I huff out a gust of breath. "Of course it's close—about a half hour drive from Louisville. More important, it's about five miles from that flea market Aunt Weeby and Miss Mona love so much."

"Do you have a picture of the ladies with you?"

"Always do. Right in my wallet."

As we head out to the hall, he says, "I know the PD's been out to the flea market, asking everyone if they saw Miss Mona or Aunt Weeby, but it won't hurt if we do it too. The officers might have missed someone who stepped out when they went by."

I give him a thankful smile.

"Hey, I'm pretty crazy about them too."

"Let's go find them."

Back into Max's SUV, ignoring the chief's warning, which pops into my thoughts a time or ten. Max pulls out of the parking lot and into traffic. As he zips through town, then out to the road toward Simpsonville, I decide I'll get further if I focus on praying. I mean, I have all these crazy questions worming around my head. And through the chief's warning. Not to mention the memory of my disastrous encounters with the chief in the past year.

Let's face it. Is there any way we're going to find what the police didn't? Is there any chance the Duo left a trail? Did they even make it to the flea market in the first place? The police didn't learn anything there.

I don't voice my questions for fear that Max will simply

make a U-turn and head back to town. Even though the drive to the flea market is a short one—and in my occasionally logical mind I acknowledge that—the time in that rolling tin can of Max's feels like a full eternity.

So I pray.

"Hang in there," he says after a while. "I'm going as fast as I dare. Don't want a ticket—it would slow us down."

My only answer is a cross between a murmur and a grunt. I close my eyes and reach out to my heavenly Father again.

"Hey," Max says a short while later. "We just passed a sign for the market. The turnoff's in about a mile."

Thank you, Jesus.

I barely wait for him to stop the SUV before I throw open my door and hop out. Picture of the Duo in hand, I rush toward the nearest one of the five long, skinny, warehouse-like buildings that make up the indoor part of the flea market. While it's not as busy today as it could be, the booths aren't exactly a vast wasteland either. I dodge and dart between customers so as to hit up a number of vendors.

I go booth by booth, but before long my enthusiasm droops. Before Max catches up to me, I've hit a lace, costume, and porcelain-dolls-for-grown-up-women booth, a gems and jewelry shop, an Amish furniture store—don't they and their buggies live in Pennsylvania?—a cubby decorated with an endless collection of CDs by total unknowns, a platoon of vacuum cleaners in marching formation, and of all things, a salvage grocer (yes, he says he sells salvaged groceries—yikes!). None of the vendors has seen either of the ladies.

"What's up?" Max asks.

Tears well up in my eyes. "Nothing. No one's seen them."

246

He wraps his arms around me. "We're going to find them. God is merciful, Andie. Have faith."

"Yes, I know he's merciful, and sure, I have faith. But what if . . . what if he wants them with him? I know they'd be happy, but I don't want to miss them that much. Not yet. I only came back home a year ago. Sure, it's selfish, but I want more time with them."

Max holds me tight as I sob. I don't even care that shoppers give us a wide berth, gawking at us. When my anxiety— and waterworks—is spent, I look up at him through melted mascara-glopped lashes. "Sorry about that."

I dig through my purse for a tissue to clean my raccoon eyes. It also gives me something to do while I get myself together again. "Sorry," I repeat.

When I toss the tissue in a trash can, Max slips his hand around the back of my neck and rubs. "Don't apologize. I can relate. I'm frustrated and worried too. Remember, I love them, and I've had even less time with them than you."

"It's so easy to forget how short a time I've known you."

"Go ahead and forget it. I'm going to make up for that by sticking around for the long haul."

My smile wobbles, but at least it's a smile. I drop my cheek back on his chest and stare at the booth with the freaky dolls. Then an idea starts to take shape. But that booth owner isn't the one to help me; I already talked with her and her dolls.

I stare up and down the aisle until I spot someone who might help. She's older than Noah's Ark, has a warm, sweet smile, and a cheerful comment for everyone who walks past her. I send up a quick prayer.

"Come on!" I grab Max's hand and drag him along.

"Where are you taking me?"

"You'll see." Once I reach my quarry, I give her my best smile and scan her junk—er . . . wares.

"Well, aren't you the sweetest couple?" she asks as she straightens four blue-and-white plates before moving a cut-glass bowl to an empty spot next to a copper teakettle.

My impatience threatens again, but I bite it back. "Thanks. You have some beautiful things." It's true—some are beautiful, just not all. "Have you been selling here long?"

"Since before we had these snazzy buildings put up and our rent hiked up." She waves. "Even before flea markets became fashionable."

"You've seen a lot of local history, then."

A woman walks up to the booth, picks up a small, funny-shaped blue and white pitcher, and studies it intently. The booth owner's attention zigzags between her customer and me. "It ain't happened around these parts if I ain't seen it, hon."

Behind me, Max murmurs, "Aha . . ."

"Then you're probably from around the area."

"'Course. I was born here." She turns to the woman who'd asked about the pitcher's price. "That'll be twenty-two fifty. It's a genuine, Occupied Japan, Blue Willow gravy boat and ladle, without even the tiniest chip on it."

They haggle some, and after the spirited back-and-forth, agree on a price of eighteen bucks.

The buyer hands her a twenty, and the booth-keeper fumbles in her apron pocket for change. When the customer's gone, her gravy boat clutched to her bosom in absolute joy, my new friend turns back to me.

"Sorry, hon. I do need to make a living."

I take the hint. "How much is that bowl?"

She points to the amber cut-glass piece she'd rearranged as we walked up. "This one?"

"Um-hmm."

"Fifteen, for you."

Before I can get into my wallet, Max hands her a twenty.

As the saleswoman gets the change, I fight to curb my again-stampeding impatience. She gives him his five, wraps my new "treasure"—you know I'll never hear the end of this from Aunt Weeby and Miss Mona, don't you?—while I gnash my teeth.

"So you grew up here in Simpsonville?" I finally ask.

"Not in Simpsonville proper, but out a ways. We did always go to church in town, though."

"Did you ever hear of Riverview Preparatory Academy?"

"Oh sure," she says, her tone dismissive. "That was that school where rich folks too busy to grow their own kids sent their girls. Us townies always felt so sorry for them."

Hmm . . . "Can you tell me how to get to the school? I'm having trouble finding a listing or an address for it."

"That's 'cause it closed down back in the early seventies. Not too many free spirits wanted to go to a fussy, dressy, and awful pricey girls' school back then."

Rats! "Did any of the students stay around this area? How about the teachers?"

She shrugs. "I couldn't tell you."

Think, think! Nothing brilliant comes to mind. So I thrust out the picture of the Duo. "I'm looking for my aunt and her friend. Have you seen them?"

"Mona and Weeby?" she asks. "'Course I seen them. They bought a real nice brass spittoon from me yesterday. It's not often I come up with spittoons. Or chamber pots. Didn't have none of them, though."

So they're Mona and Weeby to her. Chummy, don't you think? "You seem to know them. Had you met them before?"

A couple walks up and points at the crystal candelabra the vendor has sitting front and center on the antique chest of drawers at the back of her booth. She brings the beautiful piece forward, they ooh and aah, and money changes hands.

My impatience soars. I tap my toe, cross my arms, stare at glass tchotchkes.

The saleswoman smiles at me. "Mona and Weeby are two of my best customers. Regulars, you know?" She turns and grabs a sheet of newspaper to wrap the candelabra for the ecstatic new owners.

"I'm sure I've seen a bunch of things they've bought from you. But you know, something you said rang a bell for me. Is there a chance you and Miss Mona might have met while you were girls? She went to the Riverview Preparatory Academy, you know."

"You don't say?" She shakes her head. "Couldn't tell you if I saw her or not. Might have. But us townies didn't get any chances to even say boo to them girls. They were kept behind the fence all the time."

"A fence!"

"Looked more like a jail than anything else to me."

Poor Miss Mona. She certainly had gone the opposite way. She was warm, kind, generous, and didn't have a snooty bone in her body. "I can't imagine going to a school like that."

"Well, you don't have to do much imagining. You can go look at the place if you want. It's been sitting empty for years now, and what's left of the fence is a mess. But it ain't far from here. If you want to go see it."

Wow! A break. Umm . . . maybe.

What kind? Beats me, but in the absence of other clues, hints, ideas, or anything that might help us, visiting the school feels like doing something. "Sure. Can you give us directions?"

Max takes over—I'm not exactly gifted in the sense-of-direction category—and before long, we're headed back out the way we'd come in.

He aims his remote lock widget at his car. "Is there any reason we're going out to some dilapidated old school?"

"Do you have any better ideas?"

"Nope. And that's driving me crazy. But is this idea any better?"

"Now you know where I'm coming from."

"I knew all along, but I hoped you might have had another brainstorm back there. One that gave you a hint what to do."

"I should be so lucky. I don't have any ideas, good or bad. I'm just curious."

"Do you think they might have taken a side trip out there?"

"Could be. You know them. They're nothing if not spontaneous." I recline my seat, hoping to ease my worsening headache. "I'm sure Miss Mona's taken Aunt Weeby out there a dozen times . . . or more."

He slants me a look. "Don't fall asleep. We'll be there in minutes."

I close my eyes, and immediately the image of the Duo materializes, laughing, bickering, mothering me over the years even when I didn't need mothering. In spite of all her money, Miss Mona is in most ways a carbon copy of Aunt Weeby—nothing at all like Doña Rosario.

How could two women who grew up at the same boarding school turn out so different? It boggles the mind.

As if in slow-motion, Creepella's image slithers over theirs, hard, harsh, and dressed to ki—

No!

Not even as a cliché will I say that. I fist my hands to push myself up. The seat recliner button works again, and I stare out the window, not registering much more than tall trees and green shrubs. A few minutes later, Max flicks on the left turn signal. Through a thicket of brush on my side, I see a large stone and concrete marker sign. As Max guides the car up the rutted drive, I make out an R and a handful of other, less distinct letters. Evidence of swanky times long ago.

The trees on either side have grown wild, creating a thick, lush canopy overhead. The shade gives me the creeps. It's a tad gloomy for moi. And when we pull into the clearing, the grand estate takes me back to my teen years when I devoured gothic novels by the bushel load.

A shiver runs through me.

"It must have been nicer back then," Max says.

I study the Georgian brick building—can't really call it a house, since it's closer in size to Queen Lizzie's digs at Buckingham than it is to my little cottage—and sadness fills me. It should be stunningly beautiful, but years of neglect have left it to die.

And yet . . . the more I stare, the stranger everything seems. The windows on the first floor gleam in the sunlight, and the black paint on the front door and first-floor window shutters is shiny and fresh. Way different from the peeling upstairs shutters.

The fence the woman at the flea market had described lies in neat piles at the edge of the clearing to my left. I can't tell if all the pieces are there, but it's a decent-sized stack.

"Someone's been working out here," I say.

"I noticed."

When I take another close look at the building, I spot tire tracks leading around the side yard toward the rear. My heart starts pounding. The weeds are crushed. Those tracks are recent. "Did you notice those?"

Max nods. "It's time to call the chief."

"No way. You know he's going to tell us to get out of here and leave everything to him." Max goes to object, but I hold out my hand to stop him. "By now, whoever made those tracks is either gone or well aware we're here. Do you want to risk them hurting the Duo while Chief Clark and his guys get around to getting here?"

"Okay. They're probably ready for us to make a move, so watch yourself. You don't want to give them any more reason to act."

Fear steals my next breath. "I'll be careful," I say when I can function again. "It's just that I can't sit and wait any more than I can turn around and leave."

He gives me one of his here-we-go-again sighs, but doesn't argue any further. Instead, he kills the engine. "Let's be quiet, then. That small element of surprise might be all the protection we have."

It might make a difference. Then again, it might not. Another look at the abandoned school sends a shiver right through me. I sigh. I can't take the chance.

I glance at Max and spot the glint in his eye. He's got me. We might not want to go this alone, after all. "Fine. How about *you* call the chief?"

"I'll call him. But he might not get too worked up about our finding a ruin someone's starting to restore. It could take some convincing."

"Maybe, but it is the school both Miss Mona and Doña Rosario went to. It's within spitting distance from the Duo's fave flea market. And they did go junking but never came home."

He shrugs and flips open his phone.

"Exactly." As Max waits for the chief to answer, I nod toward the crushed grass. "Trust me. That wasn't Big Foot."

"Wait for me—Hello, Chief Clark."

I let them talk. I don't interrupt even when I think I can tell the story better, and again find my patience challenged. While he gives directions to the school, I walk toward the tire tracks. Behind me, Max spits out a hurried goodbye, and two seconds later, grabs my hand.

"Together," he says, his whisper serious.

I nod, but keep on walking. Then we reach the corner of the old school building. What I see knocks my world off kilter. Behind the house, its trunk yawning open, all four doors gaping wide, is Miss Mona's brand-new Jaguar. Worse yet, at the far end of the clearing sits a brand-new, platinum-colored . . . good grief. It's a Bentley.

My stomach lurches. I feel sick.

My worst fears have come true.

The madwoman got to the Duo before we could.

18 00

I take a step toward the cars, but Max claps a hand on my shoulder. "Easy," he whispers. "You don't know who's here—or where they might be hiding."

Everything inside me shrieks "Who cares?" but I don't say it. That would really freak Max right into his most protective posture. And I have to find the Duo. So I settle for nodding.

We make our way to the Jag, careful not to mess up any prints or the tire tracks. Who knows what Chief Clark is going to need to build his case?

Spread out over the Jag's backseat are the spoils of the Daunting Duo's shopping expedition. There's the brass spittoon, a large, solid contraption that has obviously seen its share of use. Next to it, four chamber pots, three trimmed in red and the other in blue, all of them wearing dings, dangs, and chips, evidence of long years of service. Four newspaper-wrapped lumps suggest additions to Aunt Weeby's English transferware collection, and on the floor, leaning against the seat, there's a weird metal contraption I'm not sure I can identify. It's cylindrical, about three feet tall, and consists of metal bars held in their circular positions by round iron constraints at the top, middle, and bottom.

Doesn't matter much to me what its original purpose might have been. "Look," I tell Max. "A weapon."

Yeah, yeah. He gives me one of those you're-nuts looks, but so what? He's going to want something to bash a head or two. Me? I'm taking the spittoon. It looks sturdy enough for some head-bashing of my own.

Then, making the least amount of sound, we approach the former school building. Only when we're a few feet away do we hear voices inside; those thick brick walls muffle a whole lot of sound. A glance in each of the eight first-floor windows of the main section of the structure reveals nothing. But as we go around the corner, the voices grow louder. Max gestures for me to follow.

We make the turn around the corner and hug the contours of the long wing. As we approach the last window, the voices are getting much louder. The nice, shiny, unbroken and new window is open, and the argument inside, in Spanish, spurts out, breaking the peace in the clearing with venom and rage. Too bad we can't understand a word being said. We're at a real disadvantage.

"Can you see inside?" I ask.

Max shakes his head. "The window's just a bit too high. The property slopes down from the front of the house."

"Tell you what. Let me climb on your shoulders. I'll be careful, and we might get an idea what's going on."

He frowns. "I can't let you do that. It's too dangerous—"

"It's more dangerous to let time go by for Miss Mona and

Aunt Weeby. Who knows what's up with them? Come on. Don't be such a drag."

Max mulls over my suggestion, but doesn't seem too moved by my argument.

"Quit wasting time. Get down on your knees, and let's get this show on the road."

While he looks ready to argue again, he does squat and help me scramble up. Once I'm settled, and let me tell you, it's not the most comforting and secure place to sit, he stands slowly and approaches the window. I lean one hand on his head for balance, and in the other, I clutch my spittoon.

I pray. Oh, yes, indeed. I turn to the Lord for mercy, for protection, for wisdom and courage. I figure I'd better cover all the needs that come to mind since this is such a loony-tunes effort on our part, I probably will want every one of them met before I'm done.

The closer Max gets to that open window, the harder my heart pounds. My breath grows shallow and my hands turn into blocks of ice.

Did I ever mention once upon a time I used to be scared of everything? Well, I did. When I was a little girl, even shadows gave me the willies. Now here I am, approaching a bunch of drug smugglers and murderers, and I'm doing it in a way that gives them all the advantages.

Smart—*not*.

A truism that's reinforced when I get my first look into the room. Creepella and her buddy are standing toe to toe, rage in their faces, arms waving wildly as they each try to make a point. The man has a gun in one hand. One of those wildly waving hands.

Against the far right wall sits a couch, Aunt Weeby propped in one corner, Miss Mona in the other. Both ladies sport silver duct tape bracelets and muzzles and matching fear-filled eyes.

"They're there," I whisper.

"Shh!"

I snort. "Those two couldn't hear an elephant stampede, they're arguing so loud. So what do you want to do next?"

"Is the Duo there?"

"Yep. On an old couch, tied up, and their mouths taped shut."

"Weapons?"

"I see one—the man's armed."

"Then we have to distract him. Maybe we can get him to come outside. Whatever we do, we want that gun as far from the Duo as possible."

"You got it. What's the plan?"

"Plan? What plan? I'm winging it here."

I was afraid he'd say that. An itch starts up right between my brows, and I scrub the back of the hand with the spittoon against the offending patch of skin—I'm not letting go of that fistful of blond hair; it's my one and only anchor. While scratching, a wacky idea occurs to me.

"I know what we can do. You still have the weapon you picked up from the Duo's junk haul, right?"

He raises the metal thing so I can see it. "Have umbrella stand, will travel."

"It's an umbrella stand?"

"Yeah. What'd you think it was?"

"I didn't. I had no idea that's what an umbrella stand looks like." An especially shrill shriek spews out the window. I wince. "They're getting more steamed by the minute in there. I don't want that gun to go off by mistake."

"How about telling me what you want to do with the um-brella stand, then?"

"Oh! That's right. Let me down."

"Now you tell me."

But he does squat ever so slowly. Once I'm back on terra firma I feel much better—but I don't tell him—and wave my spittoon. "Here's our soldier's helmet."

You know, it's a little disconcerting when every time you tell something to the man you love he looks at you as though you've grown eight heads to go along with the original one God gave you. But I gotta cope.

"Look. We want to distract the gunman, and neither you nor I want to get plugged doing it, so the best thing to do is wave the stand with the helmet on it, and hope it looks enough like a human to draw him and Creepella out of the school."

Max smacks his forehead. "You know I'm in trouble when your goofy ideas start sounding good."

"You got a better one?"

He shakes his head.

"Well, then, don't diss this one until you've tried it."

We plop the spittoon on the top of the stand, Max creeps close to the window again, and raises our "soldier" to the center of the opening. And . . .

Nothing. The arguing continues.

"Shake, rattle, and roll," I tell him. "We have to catch their attention, and they're too much into their fight right now. Give it a good whirl."

Which he does. The racket of brass against iron is impos-sible to miss. What's also impossible to miss is the *zing* and *pop* of the bullet that responds. It nails the "soldier" right in the noggin. The spittoon flies off. I go after it.

The gunman appears in the window, weapon trained on Max's disappearing figure. I snag the spittoon and take off after my love.

And while I don't think my idea was a brilliant one, I never did think it all the way through. You see, I figured the goon would run to the nearest door, which is nowhere to be seen on this side of the house, and we would have enough time to get in, release the Duo, and make our getaway.

Lousy plan. *We* have to get inside the place to help.

And I never expected the goon to do a reverse pike with 3.5 twists and a somersault-for-extra-points-type of dive out the window. He then bounds back up and takes off after Max, sparing only a glare for me. It's only then that I realize he's dropped something . . . his gun.

Okay. Now it gets tough. My beloved Duo is in Creepella's clutches. The love of my heart is hoofing it away from a killer. And that's when I stumble on the boon of a lifetime—a gun. Loaded too. Figures.

However, there's one teensy-tiny problem. I'm scared stiff of guns. What if the thing goes off?

"Oh, for crying out loud, Andrea Autumn Adams!" I shake myself. "Get over yourself. Pick up the dumb thing and go after the goon before he does serious damage to Max."

Fighting back wave upon wave of revulsion, I grab the gun in my free hand, gag at the warmth from Creepella's pal still in the metal grip, and hold the ugly thing as far from my body as possible. Then I run.

As I pelt around the corner and run out to the front, I come to a screeching halt. Max and the goon are locked in a vicious embrace, fists flying, blows landing, grunts bursting. They pummel away.

"Stop!" I yell.

Of course, they do no such thing. Then things get worse. Creepella comes to the school's front door. She erupts into a barrage of furious Spanish, punctuated with hand gestures, none of which I understand.

Whoops. Correction: I do understand two words. *Más duro*—harder.

A weird thudding comes from inside the house, rhythmic and steady. And then, to my horror, the Duo appears behind Creepella, their duct tape accessories still in place. Before I can do anything, they look at each other, nod, and hurl themselves at Creepella. The three seniors tumble down the five front steps in a tangle of limbs.

What to do, what to do?

Do I check on the Duo? They are elderly, after all. Or do I go help Max, who's getting beaten and is beating his fists to a pulp?

I glance at the three women. Aunt Weeby's rolling over. Miss Mona's fighting to sit. Creepella's flat out and motionless on a bed of weeds. Then I look at the men, still tangled in a fight to the finish.

No contest. I gotta help Max.

So I run to the men . . . and stop. I look at my hands. Spittoon . . . gun. Gun . . . spittoon.

Again, no contest.

I drop the gun, raise my spittoon-armed hand, and bring the heavy brass bucket down on the crook's head. The sound isn't quite as crisp as that of an orchestra's cymbal, but it does ring out like a bell.

The man stops, fist in midair, then glances over his shoulder, a somewhat dazed look on his face. Max takes advantage of his opponent's distraction and whams him in the gut.

A tortured "Ooof!" bursts from the man's mouth. For good measure, I wield my musical masher against his head again, and Max delivers the final blow to the underside of the man's chin. He crumples like the payload from an overspun roll of toilet paper.

In the background, Chief Clark's sirens sound a welcome serenade. Too bad he didn't arrive five minutes earlier. I could've used the help.

But at least he's here now. His men run to help Miss Mona and Aunt Weeby and to clap cuffs on Creepella's wrists. Another couple of cops hurry to the rousing creep on the ground.

Max stumbles to my side, hand held out. *"Take my hand, I'm a stranger in Paradise . . . "*

As he sings the first few lines of the song, I take hold, and then collapse into his arms. I finish the verse. *". . . a stranger no more."*

Then he kisses me.

Long and hard.

On the lips.

Oh my . . .

"Woo-hoo! Didja hear that, Mona? There's wedding bells and babies in our future."

"Hallelujah, let's go shopping!"

Epilogue

Five days after the schoolyard brawl, we're all sitting in Miss Mona's gorgeous living room. Miss Mona and Aunt Weeby are enthroned in matching wing chairs, Laura is tucked in under a quilt on a chaise, and Max and I are shoulder to shoulder on the sofa, our hands clasped, fingers woven together.

I let a lot of the chatter go over my head. What girl wouldn't? I mean, really. With the most spectacular mandarin-orange spessartite garnet, surrounded by a crown of diamonds, sitting snug on my left-hand ring finger, I'm a happily engaged woman. It's especially exciting to see that symbol of the promises Max and I have made when his stronger fingers are laced with mine.

"Earth to Andie!" my fiancé—get that? I have a fiancé—says, humor in his voice. "Miss Mona wants to know when you scheduled Laura's next appointment with the orthopedic surgeon."

"It's a week from tomorrow. Next Thursday." I look at my boss. "I'd really appreciate it if you have the producers schedule our show around the appointment. I want to go with her."

Aunt Weeby sniffs. "I'll have you know, we'll be taking care of our girl. Mona and I are her legal guardians now, while Rodolfo recovers, and when he goes back to Colombia—and don't you go forgetting it." She turns to Laura. "We're gonna be having us such a big ol' barrel of fun, sweetie-pie!"

I groan.

Aunt Weeby sniffs again. "You have a job to do, Andie, what with all your fighting and making up with Max on-screen. And a wedding to plan."

Miss Mona frowns. "But not without us, she's not planning that wedding. She can't. In the first place, she wouldn't even be heading up that aisle if it hadn't been for us."

I shake my head. Oh boy. "Laura, honey, are you sure you know what you're getting into with these two?"

From the twinkle in the teen's eyes, I think she's looking forward to the impending madness. "They need me to keep them out of trouble," she says.

"Uh-oh," Max murmurs into my ear.

I sigh. "My feelings exactly."

Who can stop a tide? And let's face it, my aunt and her best friend are a whole tidal wave unto themselves. "Let's make sure your father really wants to leave you here when he goes back to Colombia. I still think the pain meds scrambled his brains enough to get him to agree to that lunacy."

A brilliant smile lights up Laura's face. "He'd wanted to send me to America to finish school, and then to attend college. Now Miss Mona and Aunt Weeby have offered me a home—"

"A family!" Aunt Weeby cries. "We're an all-girl family—"

"Ahem." My fiancé arches a brow.

Aunt Weeby sends a glance ceiling-ward and shakes her head. "All-girl plus Max. That's what we are, sweetie-pie. And don't you go forgetting that, you hear?"

"I hear." It's great to see Laura's cheeks wear a rosy tint, look normal. "But you know," the teen adds, "I don't want to go back to Colombia. At least, not right now. All this . . ."

I shudder. The girl doesn't need to say much more. "It's been awful, hasn't it?"

Everyone murmurs agreement. Then I remember something. "Did you know Doña Rosario was once married to your father?"

Laura shakes her head. "I knew my mother was his second wife, and that she was many years younger, but he never talked about his first wife. I knew it had been bad, but not how bad."

"It must have been pretty bad," Miss Mona says. "Rosario was always a bit snooty in school, but I got along with her well enough. I can't believe she went criminal over the years."

"People change," I say. "Maybe years behind bars will make her think and change again."

Miss Mona shrugs. "We can pray." She takes a deep breath. "I suppose this is as good a time as any to tell you about Livvy's and my newest project."

Uh-oh. "There's more?"

She smiles. "This is good. Your auntie and I have been fixing up the school on the quiet—didn't really want to make waves before we were ready—and thinking up what to do with the place. It's too big for a home, but I think it'll make a perfect place for teens who might be wanting to turn their lives around. Kind of a training center and counseling center all in one."

I nod. "Taking it back to what it once was, but with a twist."

Miss Mona smiles. "The twist of helping girls who don't want to end up like Rosario, betraying her husband and a former friend, and breaking all kinds and flavors of laws."

Aunt Weeby tilts her nose up. "Humph! I don't cotton to no crooks, thieves, divorces, or nothing like that, really. The Good Lord does say marriage is 'until death do us part' and I listen to 'im, but I guess I can't blame Rodolfo too bad for dumping her way back when."

Miss Mona shrugs. "Rosario started stealing stones from him to sell on the black market. What kind of wife does that?"

My aunt does a classic finger waggle. "A rotten, greedy one's what I say. Not the kind Andie's gonna make our boy, Max, here."

He squeezes my hand.

I squeeze back.

"I know!" Miss Mona bursts out of her chair. "I have the perfect idea. Why don't we have us a wedding on-screen? We'll have our customers join us, and it'll be such fun. They love you and Max, you know."

"NO!" I cry. "How can you even suggest that? It's my wedding. I want a small group of friends and family. Not something with ratings and sales and phone calls and what-not." What a nightmare that would be. *Quick, quick! Think of something better to catch their imaginations.* "Maybe we can time it for Mom and Dad's next furlough—"

"Speaking of that brother of mine," Aunt Weeby says with a canary-feathered grin. "You'd better have cleared your calendar for tonight like I toldja."

I pop up to my feet. "Do you mean . . . they're coming?"
She nods and beams.

"Why didn't you tell me? Why didn't *they* tell me?"

"We all of us wanted to surprise you."

"Well, I'm surprised, all right."

"Oh, and there's more to come," Miss Mona chirps in. "This one's big, a whopper, I tell you."

Something about the glint in her eyes gives me a shaky feeling in the gut. I sit back down, clutching Max's hand for strength. "So break it to me gently."

She reaches for an envelope on the round side table between her chair and Aunt Weeby's. "We have an invitation here, for you, Max, and the channel." She waves the invitation.

I wait, frozen with dread. This is Miss Mona, you know.

She goes on. "I can hardly believe it. We've been invited to go see the tanzanite mines in Tanzania!"

Max and I jerk our heads toward each other. We spin back to Miss Mona.

"Nooooo!" we both yell.

"Why, yes, my dears," our boss says, ignoring our objection. "Of course, it's true. And so splendidly marvelous! Just think about it. We're going to Tanzania. Start packing your bags."

I collapse against the couch. "Why, Lord? Why are you letting this happen again?"

But he doesn't answer. Not right away.

With a sigh, I settle back to wait. And to see what the Father's got in store.

Tanzania?

Ginny Aiken, a former newspaper reporter, lives in Pennsylvania with her engineer husband and the youngest of their four sons—the oldest is married, the next is in grad school, and the third's headed there too. Born in Havana, Cuba, and raised in Valencia and Caracas, Venezuela, Ginny discovered books at an early age. She wrote her first novel at age fifteen while she trained with the Ballets de Caracas, later to be known as the Venezuelan National Ballet. She burned that tome when she turned a "mature" sixteen. An eclectic list of jobs—including stints as reporter, paralegal, choreographer, language teacher, retail salesperson, wife, mother of four boys, and herder of their numerous and assorted friends, including soccer teams and the 135 members of first the Crossmen and then the Bluecoats Drum and Bugle Corps—brought her back to books in search of her sanity. She is now the author of thirty published works, but she hasn't caught up with that elusive sanity yet.

Stunning jewels, endless shopping, exotic travel—
what woman could resist?

"Ginny Aiken's gift: masterful storytelling, witty dialogue, and characters you will never forget."

—Lori Copeland, author of *Simple Gifts*